THE GHOST LOVERS

THE GHOST LOVERS

A Novel

David Orsini

Quaternity™

THE GHOST LOVERS

Other Books by David Orsini

Bitterness / Seven Stories

The Subtleties of Seduction

The Woman Who Loved Too Well

CONTENTS

1	Five Executions	9
2	Uncertainties	55
3	Turmoil	97
4	Combat	133
5	Summoning Ghosts	181
6	Other Wily Meetings	211
7	The Ghost Lovers	237
8	Hunter	285
9	Hunted	319

"Before you do battle with your enemy,"
his father warned him,
"be certain that you have conquered yourself."

Chapter One

Five Executions

War-hardened and bitter, Marc Roussillon watched while Gaston and Fabien tortured and then questioned once more the first of the two men who had been accused of collaborating with the Nazis. All around him, candlelight was dispersing the dark energies of the crypt vault to which he had been summoned to participate in the interrogation and, if necessary, to witness the killings. Cavernous and austere, rooms in the distance glimmered upon his quick notice and then hurried beyond his clarified perceiving. They, too, held within granite enclosures the rotted bones of the long dead. Here, though, spools of bleak space also defined elliptically an imagery of living men who were carrying knives and handguns. That space encompassed even more clearly the well-honed muscularity of Benoît Lacombe, a young, brown-haired man whose naked and bleeding body lay bound by chains on a long table that had been purloined from the surgery of a hospital nearby.

On the long table next to him lay the equally rugged body of

Raoul Lefebvre. His athletic handsomeness—usually intensified by his dark-red hair, blue eyes, aquiline nose, and full sensual lips and by the flawless proportions of his body—appeared disarranged as well as diminished by the fresh blood trickling down his chin onto his broad chest and by the purple welts and bruises that had overtaken the surfaces and contours of his form. Marc noticed how his eyes, half-shut because of the blows that had been directed at them, revealed nonetheless an incisive awareness and a defiant glare. Quickened by his presence, the eyes were studying him cautiously. They had been studying him ever since he entered the cavernous space of this vault. The mind behind those eyes was trying to interpret the reason for his being there. Had he come as friend or as executioner? Would he be the one to slit his throat or carve through his heart with a Fairbairn-Sykes knife? Was he the one who had been chosen to strangle him or to shoot him with a Browning handgun as proof that he himself was not a double agent?

Marc returned Raoul's squinting gaze with teeth-clenching detachment. He did not enjoy seeing this man who had been his friend lying there on a hospital table, naked and suffering.

The uses which the French Resistance was imposing upon the hospital tables might have, in a safe and more civilized era, appeared as incongruous and as subversive as the scenario that their freedom fighters were activating here in the Basilica of

Sacré-Coeur, at 35 Rue de Chevalier de la Barre in the district of Montmartre, within the northern part of Paris. But the summer of 1944 in Europe was neither safe nor civilized. The German Army, Navy, and Air Force were destroying everything that was safe and almost everything that was civilized.

Four months earlier, at the white stone altar that on the main floor of this building enhanced the precision and dignity of a religious ceremony occurring there, the Nazis had even killed a Jesuit priest, Father François Mercier. Fearless and honorable, this priest had preached against the Nazis and had called on the churchgoers listening to him to rescue the people of France, including its Jewish population, from the German invaders. On the same morning that they shot him, the Nazis closed the church. Their army might have made it their barracks. But the German High Command feared that, if their army used the church in that way, the allies were going to target the building and its grounds for bombing.

From time to time after that, Fabien and Gaston secretly used the crypt vaults of the church for their interrogation and torture of men and women suspected of having betrayed the French Resistance. Usually, seven or eight loyal cohorts watched the brute force and murderous impulses that the two men brought to their interrogations. Tonight, though, having summoned him away from London two days earlier, they had invited only Marc to be a witness.

He had made a risk-taking journey in a Whitley that was piloted by two comrades in the Free French Air Force. Flying at one point as low as fifteen hundred feet, the pilots enabled him to make a parachute jump over the greenery of an affluent man's vineyards in Aix-en-Provence. That drop was the nearest he could make to Paris without immediately drawing the Nazis to himself. It brought him to this risk-taking and anonymous friend of the Resistance who, besides offering temporary refuge, had secured for him the false identity and ration cards, the clothes, and the Mauser semi-automatic pistol he would need. From Aix, while wearing the uniform of a major in the German army and while driving his friend's Mercedes-Benz 540K Cabriolet B, he made a well-calculated, four-hundred-mile journey into Montmartre. Though he was stopped at several Nazi checkpoints, he still maintained a speedy passage. He was in a great hurry. He understood that danger had ensnared Raoul and Benoît and was even then sealing their fates. He was aware as well that, from the moment he had set foot on French soil, the same danger began closing in on him.

These were the thoughts that flared their blunt complications across his awareness. But only for a moment would he allow them to give him pause or to keep him from doing the thing that needed to be done. He had come here to learn the truth about

Benoît Lacombe, a man he had known for only three months. With an even greater urgency, he had come to discover whether Raoul Lefebvre, a man he had been happy to call his friend for two years now, ever since they were part of the same squadron in the Free French Air Force, was actually a traitor—a double agent working on behalf of the Nazis. That both he and Raoul had not only been flying bomber sorties across Germany, but also working as agents in French intelligence missions made their friendship seem extemporaneous and even inevitable.

Now that friendship was imperiled. The French Resistance believed that Raoul had been collaborating with the Vichy government and with the Nazis. Under his most recent code name Thibaut, he had—his accusers said—leagued himself with Benoît Lacombe (whose code name was Sylvain) to create a wireless telegraphy radio network that intercepted the messages of the allies. By means of this network, they had discovered for the Germans the troop movements of British, American, and Free French armies. Thousands of allied soldiers had died from aerial bombings as they made their way by train or on foot to battle stations in central and northern France.

This radio network had recently learned and passed forward to the Germans the names and locations of resistance fighters who had killed a Nazi commander and six other field-grade officers in Brittany. Moving quickly to avenge the killing, the

Nazis pursued, captured, and shot the four men who had been responsible for the deaths of the German officers. They also killed eighty-one Frenchmen who belonged to the same guerrilla forces in Brittany, fighting there against the Nazis from the mountainous areas of northwestern France.

That Raoul and Benoît were the traitors whose radio network had led the Germans to the Free French fighters in Brittany, both Gaston and Fabien were certain. They had proof. It was they—Gaston and Fabien—who had captured and tortured the three French officers (two captains and a lieutenant) that with Raoul and Benoît had planned and then participated in the massacre of the eighty-five men. It was they—Gaston and Fabien—who, while accompanied by six other freedom fighters, had surprised these three French traitors as they were taking their pleasures in a brothel on Rue des Francs-Bourgeois in the district of The Marais, which is situated in the southern part of Paris. There, inside an impressive brick-and-stone building that wore deep slate roofs and dormer windows over arcades, they had stormed into the three bedrooms where the French officers lay with their favorite prostitutes. At the point of their enemies' .303 caliber Bren guns, the French traitors had quickly dressed and followed their captors into the darkened enclosure of a long, sleek hearse. From the jagged and bombed avenues of The Marais, the hearse had made its way with careful dignity to the night-time streets of Montmartre and to the secrecy of the crypt vaults within the Sacré-Coeur basilica.

It had taken a week for Gaston and Fabien to break the spirit and the self-command of the lieutenant, whose name was Lucien Chardonne. Wily and athletic, he had been the equal of the battle-scarred and still-murderous captains. Like them, he had withstood hours upon hours of grueling interrogation. Like them, he had endured days and nights of endless-seeming torture.

Hearing of this lieutenant's ability to endure days and nights of torture, Marc was impressed. His own experience had taught him more than a little about prolonged suffering and about the adamant will that refuses to be defeated by suffering's stern and proprietary laws. Years of rugged athleticism had hardened and disciplined him. That training had shaped his tolerance for pain and his capacity for meeting unforgiving challenges without flinching. But his experiences hunting sea lions in Africa and red stag in Patagonia or kayaking across the white waters of Finland or boxing a middleweight opponent in a Paris gym had been only a part of his life. Those challenges had, of course, tested his courage as well as his physicality and his stamina.

But other essential influences had also shaped him. That his parents continued to risk their lives so that France and all of Europe might be free again had intensified his own determination to conquer the Nazis. His years as a Free French Air Force pilot flying combat missions with the RAF from air bases outside London had configured in even more radical ways his tough-minded responses to danger and to pain. Those combat missions and his equally hazardous assignments as a freedom fighter working in French intelligence units had further probed and defined his understanding of who he was in the world. He had learned well the folly of self-pity, of hesitation, and of guilt and recrimination. His realistic view of things had taught him to give no quarter to his specific enemies or to the adversarial world in general.

What he had learned was valuable and came with a heavy price. No longer could he believe in his uncompromised humanness. No longer did he feel that he had a soul or that a beneficent spirit prevailed over even the so-called civilized forms of existence. No longer, without an awareness of the liabilities involved, would he choose to express the softer aspects of his nature.

He imagined that the lieutenant whom Gaston and Fabien had tortured and then murdered had lived through experiences similar to his own. Educated and scientific, he too—before the war came—must have envisioned ways that his being in the world as a creative and original presence would influence the world for the better. As adventurous as he was well-traveled, this Lucien Chardonne probably came from a privileged background. He also may have learned how to question the idealized conceptions of the world that his elite schooling and his socially insulated background had granted him. That he felt closer to this Lucien Chardonne than to the two cretins who were reveling over their execution of him left Marc feeling uneasy and bitter.

An hour earlier, when Gaston and Fabien recounted for his benefit the seven days and nights of torture that they had inflicted upon their three prisoners, Marc found himself strangely displeased. He had never liked Gaston or Fabien. During these wretched years of war, he had met more than a few men like them. He knew their type. It was not their humble backgrounds that roused his antipathy. In peacetime, Gaston had repaired public roads and bridges. Fabien had been a lumberjack. Those were honorable trades. He could respect the two men for the hours of hard labor that they brought to their jobs. But he despised them for enjoying the war and for exulting in all the murders they committed under the guise of patriotism.

From time to time, they also murdered their own comrades in the Resistance. They would accuse them of treason and, after the grueling interrogation and torture, would kill them. Usually, they would allow a group of trusted cohorts to witness the killings. But, occasionally, they would kill in secret. That they failed to call to these secret interrogations the men and women in their unit who might speak on behalf of the accused roused his enmity and his distrust of them.

Nearly forty, Gaston was shorter than most men, though he was powerfully built. He carried his five-foot frame like a boxer. It was not only his broad shoulders, muscular arms, and large hands that made him appear sinister and threatening. His face—with its narrow squinting eyes, broken nose, and grimacing mouth—looked savage and, at times, not even human.

Fabien, not yet thirty, stood six foot, four inches. Everything about him appeared oversized. His brawny frame, hardened by years of cutting big trees from the forests in northern France, was a natural fit for physical challenge and formidable adventure. When war came, he hurried into it, though not as a Frenchman joining the Allied infantry, where despite his size he would have been rendered anonymous, merely one of the hundreds of thousands of soldiers testing their powers while in the midst of battle. Rather, he chose to join the Resistance. Working within the secrecy of a small group of freedom fighters, he could win the adulation of men whose raw courage he matched, but whose characters were far more honorable.

Marc had thought as much earlier than on this afternoon when Gaston and Fabien had recounted their capture and torture of the three French officers who, they said, had participated in the killing of eighty-five allies. Months before that, he had witnessed the deranged glee with which Fabien and Gaston killed their enemies during several night raids that, with their underground unit (the Lyon division of Force Française d'Interier), he had made against the Nazis. Recently, a new and more furious savagery was activating the punishment that these two Frenchmen inflicted upon their Nazi enemies and sometimes upon the comrades they branded as traitors. Their brutal treatment of the three French officers they had captured did not surprise him.

As sadistic as they were methodical, Gaston and Fabien had broken the arms and legs of their three prisoners with ropes, pulleys, and mallet. On the second and third days, they held their drowning faces in toilets. On the fourth and fifth days, while the cries and groans of the prisoners anchored themselves once more to new levels of relentless pain, they lashed the bare flesh of their backs with heavy whips and razors. On the sixth day, they hung their nakedness from heavy wooden beams that spanned the width of the ceiling within the crypt vaults that cast a funereal glimmer upon the bleeding and writhing bodies. On this sixth day they hung each man from his ankles and with bared wire sticks beat his penis and his testicles with a heavy rope. The pain ripping through his groin threw him out of consciousness.

Even then, after six days of torture, the French officers did not break.

But on the seventh day, after they gouged out his left eye and threatened to cut away his right eye, as well, the lieutenant— Lucien Chardonne—told them what they wanted to hear.

He was alone with them.

The two captains, who had not yet had their left eyes ripped out of their faces, were hanging from the wooden beams of adjoining vaults. Semi-conscious and pain-racked, they must have allowed their bodies to hang slack—momentarily freed from their tautened responses to the latest wire-floggings of their backs and chests and testicles and to the burning of their fractured arms and legs with hot candle wax.

(So Marc imagined, having been told only an hour ago the story of their capture, when he first returned to Paris from his drop-point in Aix. For four weeks before this time, as the leader of his London-based squadron, he had flown fifteen bombing missions over Munich, Berlin, Stuttgart, and Frankfurt.)

"Tell us now," Gaston urged the young, dark-haired lieutenant whose blue left eye he had ripped away with a V-42 stiletto. "Tell us the names of the double agents who have betrayed us."

Sinister and determined, Gaston had spewed the words

between his stained teeth. The graveled timbres of his quiet voice were anchored to the rough pleasure of having at last broken Lieutenant Chardonne, this ruined handsomeness whose one blue eye studied his persecutor matter-of-factly, without tears or even a momentary expectation of mercy. The bony socket where his left eye had been was clotted with blood and watery fluid that spilled down his face and came to rest upon his left shoulder. There, the viscous remnants of the eyeball that had been ripped out of his face melded with the smashed cornea, iris and pupil.

Bound to a high-backed chair, his head leaning into its smooth cedar wood, the lieutenant waited an instant before answering. In this hour, which his unflinching realism took to be the last in his brief life, Lucien Chardonne might have appeared subtly detached to men more insightful than his captors, as though he were standing outside or apart from himself. His time had come to die. But even in death he would outwit his savage enemies.

(Upon hearing the outcome of this incident, Marc imagined that the French lieutenant had reacted to Gaston and Fabien in a stoic and cunning manner.)

"Give me some water first," Chardonne said.

He was addressing Gaston, the man who had gouged out his left eye. In these few words, there was a modulated inflection that balanced command and negotiation.

That afternoon, Gaston chose to ignore the suggestion of a command. As the price for the information he and Fabien sought, the water seemed a fair exchange.

From a flask, Gaston poured water into a paper cup and watched while the lieutenant drank it. He drank slowly, because his parched throat and swollen lips could receive the water only if he sipped it gradually. When he was done, he stared at the cup as intently as he had observed the water. Even Gaston, whose savage nature was not given to interpreting the nuances or subtexts of other persons' characters or circumstances, understood the Nazi's one-eyed glance as a farewell notice of something that was finished and done with forever—the drinking of water or peering at its very image or perhaps the willingness to endure the excruciating pain of torture.

Once more now, held within a prolonged stillness, Chardonne observed his torturer. For an instant, Gaston thought that his prisoner was playing for time, reluctant even now to divulge the names of the French agents who had collaborated with the Nazis and had become catalysts in the deaths of so many allies. But he had no sooner pondered that thought, when the lieutenant began speaking rapidly the words that Gaston was waiting to hear.

"A Frenchman with the code name of Sylvain has been our

most important source of information," Chardonne began. "Because of him, we have been able to bomb your troop trains, identify and kill your secret agents, and target the resistance groups for our organized massacres."

Gaston wanted to know more.

"Who is the man who disguises himself with this code name?" he asked. The grating sounds of his words hung upon the air even as they pushed forward their harsh command. "Who is Sylvain?"

Again, Chardonne paused. The thin line of a smile crossed his still-parched lips. He appeared (so Gaston told Marc later) to enjoy watching his torturer's impatience.

Now, as if he were discarding information that he no longer found important and as he imparted his words in raspy understatement, he identified the first of the double agents.

"He is Benoît Lacombe."

Again the lieutenant paused. Again Gaston pushed him forward.

"Describe him."

Lucien Chardonne closed his one eye, possibly because he was summoning to his mind's eye the imagery that Benoît Lacombe inhabited. When he resumed speaking, he spoke with the assurance of a man who has called forth an accurate memory.

"He's fairly tall—maybe five-ten or five eleven. He has a wiry build, blue eyes, a perfectly straight nose, and brown hair. He is proficient in German, English, and French. He's an aviator, too, and a superb marksman."

Gaston pushed on, drawing from his captor the necessary answers.

"How do you know all these things?"

Sure of his way now, the lieutenant answered him quickly.

"I met Benoît twice. The first time was in Vichy, at a meeting of German operatives, spies, and officers. The second time was in Lucerne, when I was on a week's leave with my girlfriend. Benoît was there with his girlfriend, too, and in the same hotel."

Gaston pressed him further, his own guttural inflections binding themselves to a quickened emphasis.

"Who are these girlfriends?"

Chardonne's one-eye observed him with muted contempt.

"The women are beyond your reach," he said. "They are Swedes and have nothing to do with the war."

All this while, Fabien had stood apart from the two men, as if his business there required him to stand as a sentry at the entrance to the crypt and, from that distance, to critique the thoroughness of Gaston's interrogation of their prisoner. Now he stepped forward until he was standing next to Gaston. Like him and with the same calculated menace, he hovered about the lieutenant. The frown that creased his brow indicated that he was not completely satisfied. They needed more information from Chardonne.

"Who was the other agent?" he asked with blunt intensity. "What other Frenchman was working for you Nazis?"

Chardonne began coughing suddenly, his pale face soon flushed because of the seizure and because of the feverous heat of his body. He knew that he was dying. His two captors knew it, as well. Impelled by a pragmatic awareness that their prisoner might die before he revealed the name of the second double agent, Fabien grabbed the flask of water and held it before the lieutenant. Impatient yet self-controlled, he waited until Chardonne's seizure had stopped. Then he offered the flask to him.

Chardonne sipped the water slowly. Then, having drunk his meager fill, he handed the flask to his oppressor. His blue eye was rheumy now and curious. Even in this final hour of his life, he was measuring the effect of his words upon the Frenchmen who were killing him. (So, hearing of this episode several days afterward, did Marc imagine.)

Wily and elusive yet, Chardonne lingered within a calculated stillness that suggested a reluctance to divulge any other information. Instead, his solitary blue eye gazed, adamant and secretive, upon his captors.

His anger rising, Gaston drew closer to the depleted body of the lieutenant. Days earlier, he had noticed a silver crucifix hanging on a chain from Chardonne's neck. Neither he nor Fabien had bothered to tear it away from the young man's nakedness. Now he noticed the crucifix once more as it dangled about the upper part of the lieutenant's chest. The thought that Lucien Chardonne was a believer spurred Gaston forward to the new words that were meant to persuade his captive to reveal the identity of the second man who had been the catalyst in the deaths of so many people.

"Tell us his name," Gaston demanded. "Tell us for your own good. Before you die, make amends for all the killing you have done for your Nazis leaders. Cleanse yourself. Give us the name of the second agent."

For the next minute, made emphatic by the protracted tension, the lieutenant held himself inside an unnatural stillness. Then, because he was weary of the war and weary of life and weary of his executioners, he spoke the name for which Gaston and Fabien were killing him and his fellow officers.

"He is Raoul Lefebvre, and he uses the code name Thibaut."

Once again, as if they were reciting by rote the questions that would discover necessary answers, they pressed onward.

"Describe him," Fabien said. "Prove to us that you know

Raoul Lefebvre."

In this very instant, a spasm of coughing overtook Chardonne. A long and anguished moaning was his only answer, anchored as it was to his hollow breathing and his heaving chest. Blood trickled out of his mouth, as it had many times during these days of torture. Once again, and for the tenth time on this day, the young officer drew into himself, pain-racked and dazed. He no longer knew where he was.

Gaston and Fabien waited, their furious hatred of the French traitor harnessed to the need for temperate responses that might yield the rest of the information they sought.

They did not have to wait long.

As abruptly as it had taken hold of Chardonne, the seizure of coughing stopped. His one eye, bloodshot now and rheumy-blue, stared at them quizzically. He appeared to be coming back to his awareness of them. Harbored within this new stillness, he stared ahead of him and saw them as a blur of rough imagery—a startlement of simian forms closing in on him menacingly. Then, summoning in these last minutes his ingrained discipline and his acquired tolerance for pain, he spoke the words for which they were searching.

"Lefebvre is very tall—maybe six-four. He has dark red hair, light blue eyes, the vague outline of a scar across the left side of his nose, and full lips. He is a fine athlete, a first-rate scientist, and a well-tested aviator."

"How do you know?" Fabien asked. "How do you know what he looks like and what kind of man he is?"

"I saw him in Lucerne, on those same weekends when Benoît was there," the lieutenant said.

He was carefully measuring the effort he would have to make if he were to say the things his captors were waiting to hear. His words came more slowly now, bound by soft timbres and jagged breathing.

"We skied together. We skated and we went tobogganing. We were there with our girlfriends. We had a good time."

Though they implicated Raoul and Benoît with this French traitor, these words did not altogether satisfy Gaston and Fabien. They wanted to know more. They wanted (they later told Marc) to hear the more essential words that would identify Raoul and Benoît as traitors to the French Resistance.

But Lieutenant Chardonne did not yet say those words. His one eye closed and his ragged handsomeness winced with new jolts of pain.

Now Fabien took from his vest pocket a flask of brandy. He poured a few drops into a cup, which he placed within the lieutenant's grasp. Hate-filled and repellent, he watched him sip the liquor and then slowly revive.

In this way, Chardonne resumed his narrative about Raoul

and Benoît. His voice, weakened now yet unfaltering, stayed matter-of-fact and decisive.

"When we were in Switzerland, Lefebvre and Lacombe gave me information about Allied troop movements. They were very specific about locations and times. They also gave us the names of the four men who killed one of our commanders and three officers in his unit. Within twenty-four hours, the German Air Force bombed the trains that were carrying thousands of troops to the front. On that same day, a German infantry unit hurried into Brittany and massacred more than eighty of the mountain guerrillas who had killed the German officers."

The lieutenant paused once more. His one eye carefully observed the effect his words had upon his captors. To reaffirm the truth of those words and to give them further heft and impetus, he pushed himself to say more.

"Lefebvre and Lacombe belong to us," he said. "They are the double agents my German contacts sent to infiltrate your group."

Having said so, he lay back and waited for his captors to set his execution in motion. He had told them the things they wanted to hear. He had fed them half-truths and lies. Their torture of him was over. They would kill him swiftly.

(That was the way, Marc imagined, that this French lieutenant, this Lucien Chardonne, had responded in the last moments of his life.)

But Fabien did not yet take hold of his Bren light machine gun. Nor did Gaston grab with his laborer's hands the Colt Government Model 1911 A1 revolver that stayed perched inside the holster harnessed to his left shoulder. Instead, they glanced at each other uncomfortably. They were not absolutely certain that the lieutenant had given them accurate information.

Impatient with the delay, the lieutenant spoke with steely emphasis. He might have been giving them a military order.

"Do it," he said. "Do it right now."

Without pausing further to plumb the truth of Lucien Chardonne, Fabien took out his Bren gun and shot him through his heart. The body sank into itself and then collapsed. But the lieutenant's one blue eye stayed open, staring in glazed detachment upon his murderer.

Quickly thereafter, Fabien shot the two captains who were hanging from the ceiling, semi-conscious and dying. Their bodies buckled, spewing forth blood and intestines.

Then, because he wanted to claim his own part in the killings, Gaston fired his Enfield into the dead bodies of the lieutenant and the two captains.

"We did the Nazis a favor," Gaston told Marc a week afterward.

Clearly, he relished telling about these executions. His

gleaming brown eyes, yellowed teeth, and crooked smiling mouth gave him the look of an ogre that one usually meets in a nightmare or in a Gothic tale. He was a creature from whom life had expunged all the essential emblems of humanness.

Fabien, the chief perpetrator of these crimes, appeared even more monstrous. His grinning contempt of the men he had just killed and the dark shadow enfolding his hulking posture made him appear spectral and menacing. Brusque and predominant, he wanted full credit for the killings. He hurried to echo Gaston's remark that the execution of their own officers would please the Nazis.

"They'll be as pleased as hell," he said. "Those three guys were Jewish."

"How do you know?" Marc asked him coldly.

"We have our ways of finding out things," he said. "They were Jews all right—the three of them."

"I thought we were fighting this war to help the Jews," Marc said.

"That's not why I'm in the war," Fabien said. "It's not why Gaston's in it."

He eyed Marc suspiciously.

Formidable and self-assured, Marc responded with his own penetrating gaze of him.

For a moment, it appeared that they would clash—with their

fists perhaps or with the guns they were carrying.

Aware of the tension between them, Gaston intervened.

"You're in occupied territory now," Gaston said. "It's not safe to let people know you're a Jew-lover."

"I'll take my chances," Marc said.

These two disgusted him.

From the moment he heard the story, the grim imagery of the three French officers whom Gaston and Fabien had tortured and maimed a week earlier stayed with him. Even now, an hour after hearing it, that imagery coiled about the scene unfolding itself before him. The Spartan imagery of the three French officers whom Gaston and Fabien had executed rose before his seeing as if those lost, captive men were apparitions meant to meld with the here-and-now reality of the two other Frenchmen who were accused of betraying the Resistance.

But he knew these two Frenchmen. Raoul and Benoît had fought bravely on behalf of a free France. For two years, they had put their lives on the line for their country and for their comrades. They were not those unhappy French officers who may have been executed not because they had remained friendly with some Germans, but because they had discovered the identities of the real traitors in their midst. Raoul and Benoît were war-hardened Frenchmen who had won the trust of their commanders and of all the other freedom fighters who belonged to their combat units. Their loyalty to the cause of freedom was a proven thing. The charges that Gaston and Fabien had brought against the two men required an altogether different language for interpreting them. The charge of having transmitted radio messages to the Nazis did warrant both torture and execution. Yet the clues or codes that might validate this new perception of Raoul and Benoît seemed forced and insufficient. Thus far, to his mind at least, the evidence against them anchored itself to coincidence and, probably, to fabrication.

Other men and some women in the Resistance also received and transmitted radio messages involving the allies. They intercepted German military information, as well. Sometimes, they used the same radio transmitters and the same temporary identity codes that Raoul and Benoît had used. They used the names of Thibaut and Sylvain during those weeks when Raoul and Benoît were away, flying combat missions from their air base outside London. Any one of those persons could be the double agent who had told the Nazis about the allies' planned troop movements in central and northern France. Anyone from that same group of resistance fighters might have revealed the names of the four Frenchmen who had killed seven German officers in Brittany.

He pointed out as much within the first hour that he arrived within the shadowy confines of these crypt vaults. He said at that time that he could vouch for Raoul's loyalty and his integrity. In combat missions over Germany and in espionage assignments here in France, they had often risked their lives together. There was nothing about Raoul that could rouse his suspicion or alter his trust of him. Nor would he accuse Benoît of betraying the Resistance. He did not know enough about him. What he knew was all in Benoît's favor. That conviction (derived from Benoît's unflinching courage in combat and his crafty work in French intelligence, which had saved the lives of thousands of freedom fighters as well as French Jews), he also pointed out to Gaston and Fabien.

Now he reminded these two sadists of the unsafe path they were treading.

"You're going too far with this," he said, while he peered at the naked and bleeding bodies of Raoul and Benoît, chained as they were on the long hospital table that was being used as a vehicle for their torture.

He paused deliberately, taking once more the measure of Gaston and Fabien—these two rancid Frenchmen who liked to torture and kill men, even if they were innocent. He stared at them directly, grim-faced yet self-controlled.

"You're treating them as if they were Nazis," he said. "These men are not Nazis or even Nazi-lovers. They have risked their lives again and again for France and for our allies."

With hulking stance and angry words, Fabien defended his and Gaston's ongoing torture of the two prisoners.

"The bastards are traitors," he said. "They deserve to die."

Still Marc stayed in control. His voice was level and matter-of-fact.

"You don't have enough proof," he told them. "A double agent *has* infiltrated our group. But he could be any one in our network who has been assigned to our radio communications."

Gaston stepped forward now, his bantam-weight muscularity a blunt threat before the formidable six-foot- two, dark-haired younger man who was observing him with his own wily awareness.

"You're either with us or against us in this thing," Gaston said.

Marc noticed how carefully this belligerent man's big right hand stayed near the Colt revolver that was perched within a shoulder holster.

His own rugged hand was already in contact with the Mauser handgun that kept its place in the pocket of his raincoat.

"I thought we were all in this together," he said.

Then, as if he meant it as a coda to their brief exchange of words or as well-reasoned counsel or as an understated condemnation of their torturing these two men, he spoke other words, as firm and as reliable as all the words (few though they were) that he had thus far directed to Fabien and Gaston.

"It is not a good thing to kill our own men unless we have sufficient evidence."

His voice both contemptuous and impatient, Fabien rejected this too-careful regard of men suspected of being traitors.

"We have more than enough evidence," he said. "We have the confession of Lieutenant Chardonne."

"You have the words of a man who was willing to say anything, as long as you stopped torturing him," Marc said. "You have the words of a man who may have met Raoul and Benoit before the war or who may have been told about them by the double agent that you are looking for."

"A dying man doesn't lie," Gaston mumbled. "I'll take the words of a dying man as truth any day, even if he is a Jew."

To this remark, which he regarded as obtuse and offensive, Marc gave no reply. Instead, he compelled these two sadists once more to confront their unjust actions.

"You're not giving these men a fair interrogation," he said. "Where are the others who could tell you that these men are innocent? Where are Antoine, Didier, and Julien? Where are Yves, Henri, and Emile? Where are all the other men in my squadron?"

"They are busy with more important assignments," Fabien mumbled. "Anyway, their being here isn't necessary. We don't need them to find excuses for saving their friends."

He saw that, even without sufficient proof of wrongdoing, these torturers were going to declare Raoul and Benoît guilty. He doubted that Lieutenant Chardonne had mentioned Raoul and Benoît in his confession. Now he understood why Gaston and Fabien had summoned him to this scene. They wanted to implicate him in the execution of Raoul and of Benoît. His countrymen would regard his being here as a form of consent to the murders. To many, his being here would be tantamount to an active participation in the killings. But, should he protest the killings, Fabien and Gaston were ready (he was convinced) to treat him as an enemy. His being a Roussillon did not intimidate them. Even national heroes might stumble. Even tough-minded combat pilots might involve themselves with players from the wrong side. Perhaps, if he were to protest the deaths of his friends too vehemently or attempt to rescue them, Gaston and Fabien would kill him and lay the blame on the Nazis or even on Raoul and Benoît.

That he was Jewish as well as French may have been the strongest reason why they had drawn him to this place of execution. They had killed the lieutenant and the two captains not because they were traitors, but because they were Jewish. Cynical and savage, they might be planning to kill him, too, here in this burial place of old, rotted bones and of the stinking flesh of the recent dead.

No, he did not like Gaston or Fabien. But he would let them play out their version of this scene. He would give them enough rope to hang themselves. He would play out his own scene, as well. He had questions to ask Raoul and Benoît. He had answers to seek that could overturn the charges against them. He had strategies to devise to keep Fabien and Gaston from killing them before he could discover the clues that would save his two comrades.

His instinct told him to rescue his friends immediately. But Gaston had taken his Colt revolver out, ready to kill him if he made the wrong move or if any intruder hurried into the crypt vaults. So he waited, accepting the moment with bitter patience and with a belief that the rigorous punishment about to be inflicted upon Raoul and Benoît would dispel, after all, whatever doubts his realistic sense of things was compelling him to consider.

Pensive and conflicted, he drew nearer to the long hospital tables that held the bruised body of Raoul, his friend of long standing, and the more damaged body of his new friend Benoît. Their captors had not yet broken their arms and their legs. Nor had they held their drowning faces in toilets or lashed the bare flesh of their backs with heavy whips and razors.

But, before he arrived inside the crypt vaults, when the first hours of the interrogation did not yield the necessary words that Gaston and Fabien wanted to hear, they stripped Raoul and Benoît naked and hung them from the heavy wooden beams that spanned the width of the ceiling. They hung each of their captives from his wrists, with heavy weights tied to his legs. Not even the firm shoulders and strong biceps of these athletic men could subdue the agonizing pain that made each of them imagine that his arms were being pulled from their sockets.

Their bodies writhed with the pain that rode in jagged waves through their arms, necks and chests and through their groins and legs. Their quickened breaths heaved upon the air long spates of nearly-suppressed moaning and guttural cries. And, all this while, Fabien and Gaston went on questioning them, encircling their trussed-up athletic bodies as if they belonged to hardened traitors locked in a medieval dungeon.

"Tell us the truth," Gaston said every time that he hurled his accusations at Raoul or at Benoît. In those moments, the snarling energy of his clipped, low-pitched words struck with billowing intensities the bleak, candle-lit atmosphere of this crypt vault. "Tell us that the two of you led the Nazis to our people in Brittany."

Trapped as they were in this first cycle of torture, both Raoul and Benoît continued to protest their innocence. So Fabien and Gaston had explained to Marc, as they drew him into their interrogation of the two suspects.

Now they were going to begin the second and more intense cycle of torture.

They had bound in thick chains the naked bodies of the two men on the long hospital tables. Once they began this new method of torture, they were going to press the chains deep into the flesh of each man as though they were making a tourniquet. Perhaps the jagged cuts or the purple welts that strew their traceries across their young bodies or the red blood spurting out of their arms and chests and legs would break the spirit of their prisoners. Perhaps the welts and bruises and the searing pain and the spurting blood would hurry the two men into an anguished confession of their guilt.

There was no way that Marc could reach for his handgun. Grim-faced and tight-lipped, he watched Gaston begin pressing the chains into Raoul's arms and legs. He watched, too, while Fabien held his Bren gun steady and, as though he were prepared to confront an enemy, pointed it toward him, from the shadowy surround of the entrance where he now stood.

The pressings of the chains within Raoul's naked flesh did their work swiftly. Welts and bruises (purple, green, and blue) were already making inroads upon his arms, legs, and groin. Blood, deep-red and profuse, kept spurting in small fountains from his rugged body. The grueling punishment tore from his throat a low moaning and then a wild, jagged howling.

With no show of emotion, Marc watched the pain-twisted face of his friend and listened to his anguished howling cries fall away to a thin and tattered groan.

Now, methodical and abrupt, Gaston brought this latest round of torture to a stop. He was ready to heave upon his prisoner a rat-a-tat momentum of snarling questions.

But Marc interrupted him.

"I'll question him," he said as he moved closer to the table on which Raoul lay. "I know him well. If he does not tell me the truth, I'll know that, too."

To this assertion of his own leadership here in this gruesome place, both Fabien and Gaston frowned their displeasure. Once again, Gaston's right hand moved toward the holstered gun held upon his left shoulder. In the same instant, Fabien moved forward with his Bren gun raised ambiguously. Their beady eyes, dark-gray and belligerent, targeted him for more incisive inquiry. Then, pausing inside each other's glance, they held themselves still. Cautiously, they watched as he approached his wounded friend.

With matter-of-fact inflections and an unsmiling manner, he began questioning Raoul. He had chosen to maintain a military manner. Yet the language of his steadfast gaze signaled his friend that he would be on his side if he were innocent of the crimes of which Fabien and Gaston were accusing him.

"Did you know Lucien Chardonne?" he asked.

Raoul's answer surprised him. So, also, did his friend's uneasy glance, anchored as it was to uncertainty and sorrow.

"Yes, I knew him," he said. "We went to school together in Paris and in Heidelberg. Before the war, we were the best of friends."

"What about after the war? Were you still friends?"

"We were," Raoul explained. His deep voice seemed far away and gravelly, and his words sounded pensive. "Our friendship had nothing to do with politics. How many friendships do?"

"Did you meet Lucien Chardonne in Lucerne?"

"Yes," he quickly answered. "We did meet, but only by chance. We were there with our girlfriends. We skied and skated and went tobogganing. We ate the best food and danced at a nightclub. We had a good time and forgot all about the war."

Now Marc asked the most important question of all.

"Is what your accusers are saying true?" he asked. "Did you ever pass information about the war to Lucien Chardonne?"

"Never," Raoul answered without a pause. "Nor would Lucien have any reason to confess that I did so."

Raoul grew excited now. He was angry that anyone would

believe that Lucien had lied about him.

Marc probed further.

"You can tell me, you know. Tell me if you made a mistake," he said. "Tell me if you did anything wrong."

Raoul returned his friend's steady gaze. He was exhausted and pain-racked from the cycles of torture he had thus far endured. His wrists (Marc noticed) were swollen and may have been broken, wrenched when he was hanging from the ceiling with heavy weights tied to his legs. His senses were still disarranged and reeling from the punishments inflicted upon him. It took him a minute or two before he found the words that might ease Marc's doubts.

"I am innocent of all their accusations," he whispered. "I have done no wrong. And neither has Benoît."

"Do you know who has done wrong?" Marc asked.

Raoul fell silent. His eyes turned from Marc to observe Gaston hulking nearby and, in the distance, Fabien with his Bren gun pointed in the direction where Marc stood by him.

Hesitant still and non-committal before the menacing presence of his torturers, he chose his words carefully.

"I can't say," he said. "I need to find more clues before I can say for certain."

Marc guessed that his friend did know or suspect at least the identity of the traitor in their Resistance unit. But, in the presence of Fabien and Gaston, he did not want to say the name. They were his torturers. He had rightly guessed that they were in league with the traitor.

Suddenly Fabien and Gaston were surrounding him.

"Your friend Raoul needs the chains again," Gaston said. "Your questions won't accomplish anything."

Wily and determined, Marc quickly devised the scenario he must follow, if he was to save his two friends and save himself.

"You're right," he answered Gaston. "Torture is the only way we'll get the truth out of these two."

Gaston eyed him cautiously. He was pleased that he had convinced him of the guilt that the two prisoners were concealing.

"You are thinking smart," he told him.

An ugly grin took hold of his face momentarily. He was (Marc could see) enjoying the prospect of torturing his prisoner once again, before he killed him. The grin told Marc that Gaston was already contemplating the moment when he and Fabien would turn upon him. The traitor for whom they were working must have ordered them to murder him as well as Raoul and Benoît. Not only was he a Jew. He was also the friend of the two prisoners who would go in search of the traitor and find the reason why he had ordered the murders. Raoul and Benoît must have uncovered a trail that would eventually lead them to the double agent infiltrating their Resistance unit.

Without giving any sign of his hatred and contempt of Gaston and Fabien or his awareness that they were his enemies, Marc willed himself to enter these next moments with an efficient and convincing show of collaboration.

He addressed his new conciliatory words to Gaston first of all.

"You can go on with your torture of Raoul," he said. "You should be able to break him within the next hour."

Gaston grinned again, accepting as a compliment the words that suggested he knew how to play the game of torture. With swift and well-practiced aptitudes, he turned his attention away from Marc and resumed his twisting of the chains that bound Raoul.

Now Marc approached Fabien, who was standing at the entrance to the crypt, having once again returned to his post as a sentry.

"Show me how to work the chains," he said. "I'll handle the torture of Benoît, and you can go back to your post."

To this suggestion, entwined as it was within a militant assertion, Fabien did not at first respond. He stood, adamant and proprietary, by his post. All the while, he was studying him carefully. Then, accepting as authentic this gesture of collaboration that would prove Marc was on their side, he hurried to the table where Benoît was bound in chains. Already, upon the adjoining table, the body of Raoul was writhing with new gradations of torture. His shattered breathing and anguished groans broke away from his body, only to strike feebly against this eerie labyrinth of the dead.

As they approached the table, Benoît stared at both Marc and Fabien. A rigid stillness overtook his young and rugged body. A questioning frown distorted slightly his sandy-blond handsomeness. Though his blue, penetrating eyes held at first both men within his quickened assessment of the scene, his inquiring gaze came to rest upon the ambivalent sight of Marc. Surprised and despairing at the same time, he turned his gaze away from both men. Enchained and apparently betrayed and abandoned by his new comrade, he prepared himself for the torture that was going to kill him.

Marc could feel Benoît's despair. But there was nothing that he could at this time do to allay it.

Instead, he waited for Fabien to give him directions about the proper way to invoke this torture with chains. To demonstrate how to work the chains that cut into the arms and legs and chests of the prisoner, Fabien would have to place his Bren gun on a nearby medieval stone bench that had been built so that mourners could take a seat there and pray when they visited the crypts inside which their dead were enclosed.

At first, Fabien did not separate himself from the machine gun. He simply led Marc to the bound form of Benoît and described the specific twisting configurations that would bring the most pain to the prisoner.

"You need to make a tourniquet of the chains," he said. "Press them deep into the flesh. That should get him talking."

Marc played dumb. Leaning over Benoît, he fumbled with the chains without creating the tight pressure that would bruise and wrench the flesh of Benoit's body.

"No, no," Fabien protested. "You're not doing it right."

Then, placing his machine gun on the mourners' bench, he proceeded to demonstrate the hold upon the chains that would turn them into a cutting weapon.

In an instant, Marc had his pistol in his hand and was pointing it at these two savages who were so eager to torture and kill the innocent.

Startled, both Fabien and Gaston stopped in their tracks.

"Move and I'll shoot you," he said.

Fabien as well as Gaston stood motionless at the hospital tables, on which their prisoners lay within the stillness of their own surprise. The torturers waited for Marc to make the next move.

Now Marc became the interrogator.

"For whom are you working?" he asked. "How much did he

pay you to kill these men?"

Gaston was the first to protest.

"You're talking crazy," he said. "Nobody paid us anything."

Fabien joined in, blunt and resentful.

"We're doing what we've been trained to do."

Marc hurried forward with new accusatory questions.

"When did you decide to work for a traitor?" he asked. "What specific day convinced you that the Germans were the winning team that you needed to join?"

To these questions, neither Fabien nor Gaston offered any answers.

Marc had not expected that his questions would yield honest answers or, in fact, any answers at all. If there had been time and if the five or six freedom fighters who had earned his trust had accompanied him here to the crypt vaults, they would have tortured Fabien and Gaston until the two savages revealed the identity of the double agent who had infiltrated their group. But there was no time, and he had come here alone. Besides, Gaston and Fabien were too dangerous to hand over to an organization that might protect them.

He would have to kill them quickly. He was surprised that the thought of killing two unarmed men in cold blood gave him pause.

Just at that moment, Gaston made things easier for him.

From his place at the table where he had been torturing Raoul, he made a wild move to draw his Colt handgun from his holster. No sooner had he taken hold of it, than Marc fired a bullet into his chest.

The impact from the bullet threw Gaston back against the table. He grimaced and watched his blood spattering across his soiled vest.

"Bastard," he cried out in a voice suddenly gone thin and tattered. "Lousy bastard. You'll get your bullet from the Germans. They'll bury you and your kind."

Marc fired his handgun again. This time the bullet entered Gaston's forehead. Blood and tissue and hair exploded out of the back of his head and out of his mouth. His left eyeball popped out of its socket and his nose collapsed, as more blood spattered his vest and shot out of his ears. The body crumpled into itself. For an instant, it leaned back into the long hospital table and then dropped, as if it were sinking in slow motion, upon the stone floor that was already soiled by the blood of all the men he had brought to this place for execution.

In this same moment, Fabien rushed to the bench in which he had placed his machine gun. With a swift, lunging movement, he took hold of the gun and, facing his adversary, fired. The bullet flew past Marc, missing him by a wide margin.

Fabien did not have a chance to fire again.

With split-second accuracy, Marc shot him once and then again and again. The first bullet ripped through his face, scattering the tissue and flesh and bone of his cheeks and nose in a swirl of blood. The second bullet entered his left eye and tore through the back of his head. The third bullet smashed into his heart.

For a fleet second, Fabien's body was lifted after the impact of each bullet. Then it reeled and buckled and fell backward onto the mourners' bench.

With military precision, Marc now hurried into the actions that would bring Raoul, Benoît, and him away from this place of execution. As swift as he was adept, he freed them from their chains and helped them to dress in the laborers' clothes that had served as part of their disguise when they entered Montmartre. Battered by the hours of torture, they had difficulty lifting their arms to receive the sleeves of their shirts and jackets. It was even more difficult for them to place their legs within their trousers.

Marc encouraged them.

"We're almost finished with this thing," he said. "But we have to move fast. We have to get away from here as soon as we can."

His friends looked at him without at first speaking. Their awareness of the scene that was unfolding around them (they were to tell him later) seemed disarranged. Their faculties for quick-witted perceiving were as battered as their bodies. Yet they kept resisting the pain roused by their struggling gait and by Benoît's broken arm. That he had rescued them so unexpectedly and only an hour before their torturers were going to kill them was both astonishing and mind-boggling.

"Don't worry about us," Raoul said, tough-willed and self-pitiless. "We'll keep up with you."

In silence thereafter, while Marc assisted his wounded friends, the three of them stumbled away from the crypt vaults and away from the dead bodies of Fabien and Gaston. Raoul and Benoît were prepared to fight their way into an escape. They had armed themselves with Fabien's Bren gun and with Gaston's Colt revolver. Only when they were making their slow and painful way to the long, narrow passage that would bring them to the secluded alley from which Marc had entered the basilica did Benoît permit himself to speak.

"If any Nazis stop us," he said in a jagged, whispering voice furling into itself, "I'm ready to shoot them."

"So am I," said Raoul, in a voice no less halting and pain-racked. "It will be a pleasure."

Marc had a different plan.

"We won't shoot unless we have to," he said. "We're better off if we don't leave any traces of where we are headed."

His two friends nodded in agreement. Clearly, in this matter of their escape from the crypt vaults and their securing safe passage out of Montmartre, they regarded Marc as their leader. Their journey to a farmhouse in Sancerre, a hilltop town in central France, would be fraught with new dangers.

They knew the plan that Marc wanted them to follow. Each of them was carrying false identity papers and ration cards. Beneath his raincoat, Marc was still wearing the uniform of a German major. That he spoke fluent German, had traveled widely in Germany before the war, and was carrying a German handgun validated the persona that on this journey he would inhabit. Benoît and Raoul wore the clothes of Belgian laborers. Born and raised in the French section of Belgium, they spoke with conviction the specific inflections of that region.

Under cover of a rain-swept August night, they made their way in the Mercedes-Benz. Dark scattering streets, looking haunted because they were empty, rose up to meet the flare of their headlights. In the proximate distance, the booms and volleys and roused flashes of night bombing were overtaking Paris. But never did the allies' bomber aircraft fly above the streets of Montmartre or above the long, rural roads on which they were traveling.

Their luck also stayed with them through every checkpoint where German officers or patrolmen stopped them. That Marc was disguised as a major exempted him from the curfew imposed upon civilians. Each time the three of them were stopped, he explained that, on a week's leave from the war, he was driving his two friends to their homes in Belgium. They were recovering from injuries they had received when British aircraft strafed a Paris hospital in which they were repairing the master furnace.

The three of them were not going to Belgium, though. They were headed for a farmhouse in Sancerre. That town had become a regional command center for the French Resistance. Within the expansive vineyards of the area, a woman who was Raoul's and Benoît's friend was hiding from the men who wanted to kill her. Among those men were more of the double agent's henchmen, who went in search of her right after he had devised the arrest of Raoul and Benoît.

Marc was eager to arrive at the farmhouse in Sancerre. There, Raoul, Benoît, and he would be out of harm's way temporarily. Within that tenuous safety, they would conceal themselves until the night that their squadron sent a Lockheed Hudson or a British Beaufighter to bring them back to London. In Sancerre, he might dispel his lingering uncertainty about Raoul and Benoît. He might also discover from them or from a woman who was their trusted friend the clues that could lead him to the double agent.

Chapter Two

Uncertainties

The first weeks in Sancerre rose upon Marc's awareness without incident. But his ingrained realism compelled him to receive this nearly calm period as temporary—a will-o'-the wisp the Fates had designed to throw him off his guard. The expansive mosaic of fields and orchards, of trees and vineyards and flowers wakened his ease. While he scanned the territory on a dun-colored Criollo, they taught his eyes to experience once more as a fleet, tenuous joy the quickened rush of being at home in the world.

In this landscape, colors flourished and roused his comprehension of bronzed sienna meadows, golden yellow haystacks, and a teal-blue lake. From the dark, hidden waters of that lake, rainbow trout—with purple and pink stripes rippling across their sides and with black-spotted backs and tail fins—jumped and somersaulted with aerialist symmetries. In the distance, also along the southern margins of this farmland, tidy lavender fields billowed and swayed as if they were floating in the late summer breeze. Nearer than that, a strawberry tree-lined road was hurrying toward the nearest village. Within the sun-mist of afternoon light, a tractor path meandered westward near vermilion-red and yellow-gold wild flowers and then disappeared at the crest of a chrome green hill. Beyond that hill, inside the heave and surge of wind-tossed woods, white-tailed hawks with long pointed wings and pale gray plumage were hovering and kiting above the scarlet of pomegranates, the blue-grayness of Leyland cypresses, and the burgundy redness of the common beech.

The tangy scent of clean barns and stables, of ample paddock and granary, and of smooth leather saddlery also gave him back the imagery of long-ago happy days. Then, while a youth vacationing with his great-grandparents on their retirement farm about ten miles from this property, he rode his favorite Tobiano over turf-laden forest paths and across undulating roads at the foot of the jagged protrusion of mountains. Sometimes, as an expression of his rugged physicality and while working alongside the field hands he had befriended, he helped to harvest the burgeoning vineyards.

Now, as a man of twenty-four, bonded though he was with war-time combat, he was too practical to resist the benefits of these different days that kept offering him their apparent solace. The benefits included a return to the vineyards and farmlands he had loved since his boyhood and a renewal of the many friendships he had cultivated whenever he found himself visiting the area. At the same time, he refused to accept these days as anything more than a tentative stay against the danger that was waiting to trap him and trap the two men whom he had just rescued. He could not help thinking that these nearly peaceful days were a trick—a ruse meant to put him off his proper course. Even within the more enjoyable hours of his stay in Sancerre, his matter-of-fact appraisal of things kept telling him the hard truth of his situation. This period of near-calm was merely an artifice unleashed by the workings of Blind Chance. It was a stratagem composed by whatever Fates deceived beleaguered men and women.

Always, he remained aware of the danger that was coming toward him and toward the comrades he had rescued. That danger was coming as well toward the family that was providing them this tentative refuge. Whether he was fine-tuning the motor of his Mercedes in the roomy garage not far from the stables or when, with a curry comb and perfect circular motions, he was removing dried mud and loose hairs from the gray coat of a Sorraia that stood, docile and attentive, in a well-kept stall or, while with long sturdy clippers, he worked within the teeming foliage of an orchard, pruning the leaves of olive and walnut trees—always, his anticipation of danger as a steadfast and imminent reality governed his senses. His negotiations with the apparent calm of things were taut and understated harmonies.

There was the danger, first of all, that French military police who represented the Vichy regime and who were collaborating with the Nazis would appear without warning. They would arrive suddenly to inspect the main residence and the six cottages that housed the families of the men and women who worked the vineyards and orchards and farm. The police (who were usually sadistic and murderous) would search for Jews who might have found a tenuous harbor here. With Lugers and Derringers, they would quickly shoot them and shoot the family that had been concealing them. These French police, with their borrowed Nazism and their betrayal of their own people, would search as thoroughly for wounded Allied soldiers and pilots or for Allied secret agents who had narrowly escaped their would-be assassins.

There was also the danger of German soldiers overtaking the property and using it for a few days or for more than a week as their barracks.

He was not certain that the unknown double agent had linked him to the killing of Fabien and Gaston. His rescue of Raoul and Benoît might very well call him to the mind of the traitor. But he was certain that this double agent had already sent out a squad of his henchmen to find and kill Benoît and Raoul, whom he would blame for killing Gaston and Fabien. Those henchmen might eventually find their way to this farm. There was that danger, too.

The farm belonged to Pascal and Marcelle Grenier, whom he had known for two years now. Even so, he always learned something new about them every time that he paid them a visit. Their main residence was a renovated nineteenth-century two-storied manor with a handsomely carved sandstone façade. The house faced south and found sweeping views of vineyards and vegetable gardens and orchards that kept fanning outward to a neighboring lake of the Loire River as well as to the hills beyond. The Greniers' estate, which encompassed one hundred-twenty acres, was called Domaine de la Croix de Saint Jeanne. The title signified that their vineyards produced a more-than-ordinary wine.

Though to some the title might sound exclusive and predominant, there was nothing pretentious about Pascal and Marcelle Grenier. Earthbound and matter-of-fact, they brought to their love of the land a robust proficiency and a life-loving enthusiasm. Pascal stood nearly six foot. During the First World War, he had fought bravely as a captain assigned to the French Second Army at Verdun. It was there, alongside the artillery troops he led, that he fell wounded after long and unforgiving days of battle. The skill of meticulous surgeons restored his shattered left leg, fractured pelvis, and broken back. The long, painful road to recovery did not diminish his steadfast self-belief or his confidence in the future. Even now, at the age of forty-eight, he was a rugged and indomitable man who wore with blunt authority his silver hair, cragged features, and sun-bronzed skin.

The freedom fighters who from time to time came down from the mountains to pick up a new supply of weapons, food, and other provisions sometimes sought his advice or his encouragement. Even before they spoke, his quick, studious glance would inform him whether any one of them had grown weary of killing Nazi soldiers and Vichy collaborators. He would regard their downcast expressions and taciturn manner as reliable signs that they had become uncertain of their powers as guerrilla fighters. Perhaps it was his tough-skinned, resilient appearance or his own war-ravaging experiences that persuaded these men to confess their self-doubts and their anxiety.

"I know what you are feeling," he would tell them. "I have made the same journey. But you must never give in to your fear. The important thing is to allow your courage to lead you."

That he was one like them confirmed their trust in him and reignited their willingness to go forward to do the things that needed to be done.

Marcelle Grenier, who was forty-four, stood five feet-eight inches tall. Strong-bodied and tough-minded, she knew how to fire a Bren gun with a swift accuracy that equaled that of her husband. He had taught her how to dismantle and clean the rifle and how to load and fire it. She could fire as skillfully a Beretta pistol and a Colt snub-nosed revolver. She had also learned how, with one lightning stroke, she might kill an adversary with a V8 Stiletto. She could not with certainty tell herself that, in the heat and flare of danger, she would be able to kill her adversaries. For years now, she had melded her inherent assertiveness with the motherly instincts that had brought her the love of her four sons and that had strengthened her bond with her husband. This balance of assertive and maternal had also won her the loyalty and trust of her neighbors.

Her full-bodied appearance suggested this balance. Her gray-flecked brown hair, which she combed back so that it could form a coil at the nape of her neck, suggested an honest simplicity. Her oval face, with its light brown eyes, turned-up nose, and full lips, wore expressions of kindness and courtesy. A direct and attentive gaze and a quiet, temperate voice inspired respect and friendship. All these natural affinities, which anchored themselves to peaceful associations, left her with misgivings about her ability to kill her enemies, if it became necessary for her to do so. As much as she probed her conscience to find her proper bearings concerning this matter, she was—even after long and rigorous hours of self-searching—left with her misgivings and left with insufficient knowledge of the dangerous part of herself. Each time that she emerged from the privacies of her search, she had to admit that she did not know whether she could kill.

But she did know that she would do all that she must to save the pilots and other freedom fighters and the Jews that, while being pursued by the Nazis, had found refuge in her home. Thus far, during these years of war, she and her husband had effectively assisted more than forty Jews and twenty wounded pilots and freedom fighters. These men, women and children, eluding their German enemies, would hide inside the ample granary or, disguising themselves as farmhands, would work in the vineyards and orchards and in the stables. They would be carrying false identity cards and would be thoroughly rehearsed in the smallest details of their fictional biographies. Eventually, the Resistance fighters would return to their posts in the hills and mountains. With the help of British and French pilots flying Lockheed Hudsons and Bristol Beaufighters at night, the Jews would find asylum in the villages of Switzerland or in the countryside outside London.

The Greniers had assisted the French freedom fighters and the British and American allies in other ways. They had offered their property as a key site for parachute drops of weapons and other supplies that would enable the fight against the Nazis to proceed successfully. At night, pilots flying Avro Ansons and Bristol Blenheims and guided by Pascal and Marcelle shining three red lights upward from a pre-arranged location, would parachute heavy cylinders into the north hayfield of the Greniers' property. These cylinders or canisters contained hand grenades, plastic explosives, detonators, wrenches used for loosening rails, and British Sten sub-machine guns that were easy to use and could be quickly broken down and hidden. With their farm staff and two large trucks assisting them, Pascal and Marcelle would conceal these canisters within the haylofts, granary, and wine cellars of their property. Soon thereafter, the rural bands of Resistance fighters who called themselves maquisards would arrive from their posts in the nearby hills and mountains to collect the supplies and to carry forward their war against the Nazis.

In all these useful and brave things, the Greniers freely participated. But, despite the raw courage and unhesitant impetus of her risk-taking, Marcelle continued to worry about her capacity to kill her Nazi enemies, should they suddenly overtake the comfortable home and the fertile land that she and her husband had so carefully cultivated. Of her misgivings, which goaded her peace and left her believing that she was, after all, a stranger to herself, she never spoke to her husband. She did not care to burden him with her worries or to revise his image of her as a strong and self-reliant woman. Nor did she tell the good women who assisted her in the maintenance of her large house and in the care of the home fields.

It was to Marc that she revealed the worry that had made a fault line inside her confidence. He was in the stables, saddling up the same dun-colored Criollo that he rode whenever he was reconnoitering the area. Once he was firmly astride its cantering energies, the sturdy, compact horse would bring him to further scouting for enemies and then back to his work in the vineyards, now that the lunch hour was over. Dressed in a faded blue denim shirt and trousers, he had the look of a strong-bodied field hand. Already, in the weeks since he had been here on the Greniers' farmland and vineyards, his summer tan had deepened and in these early September days had given to his dark-haired handsomeness an even more burnished intensity.

Because he stood alone beside the horse, Mrs. Grenier approached him without hesitation. Her husband and the men and women who assisted them had already returned to their work of harvesting the vineyards and the orchards. None of them would hear the words that would tell him how it was with her. She was pleased that, while she spoke the words that were so difficult for her to say, he did not pause in the task of adjusting correctly the horse's stirrup irons. While pulling them downward, he kept them away from the horse's sides so that they would not bump him. His carrying forward the action that he had already initiated seemed natural and understated. The gesture made her words seem just as natural and deflected whatever emphases her dismay might have otherwise aroused.

When he had heard all that she needed to tell him and because he had finished adjusting the stirrup irons, he turned to observe her directly. There was in his expression a respect and an empathy that quietly eluded the sentimental.

"When the time comes," he said, "you will do whatever needs to be done. You will do it because you won't be thinking about yourself. You will be thinking about saving the lives of others."

With matter-of-fact friendliness, he patted her shoulder. He was reminding her that they were comrades in war. The rules had changed. Although she belonged to no army, she might have to kill her enemies.

Only after he brought his Criollo out of the stable and found his place in the saddle did he speak the other words that he believed would keep her on her proper path. By this time, a tight grimace had leeched away the softer aspects of his demeanor.

"Keep remembering what the Nazis did to Nicolas," he told

her. "Keep remembering what they might do to your other sons."

Mrs. Grenier stood silent before the blunt rhythms of his counsel. The grimace that had taken hold of his features took hold of hers, as well. She needed no reminder that the Nazis had shot down the plane that Nicolas, her youngest son, had been piloting while he and his crew bombed the cities of Hamburg, Berlin, and Munich. Nor had she forgotten that her three older sons were fighting the Nazis as maquisards in the mountain of France. If the Nazis ever captured her sons, they would interrogate and torture them, and then they would kill them. This thought roused her fear and her fury. It brought her face to face once more with the obligations that the war had imposed upon her. She would have to accept those obligations without hesitation and without counting the cost to her safety.

In days to come, she was to tell him so. The effect of his words upon her, incremental and forceful, would fire anew her willingness to do whatever the war asked of her. Today, though, she stood immersed in the silence that overtook her upon hearing his counsel. Enclosed within the mandates of her stillness, she watched him as he brought his stallion to trot. Reliable and confident in the saddle, he squeezed both of his legs actively against the horse's sides and softened his hands forward so that the horse felt free to increase the pace and to go forward into the trot.

As he was riding away to his afternoon assignments, he saluted her with ingrained militant poise. She, in turn, saluted him. This gesture had become a bond between them. They had shared it occasionally during his recent visits. It was his way of reinforcing her awareness that they were fighting the same ongoing battle.

He did not think that his blunt manner had displeased her. If anything, it put to rout the ambivalence that had chipped away her confidence. It dispelled the ambiguities that had been assailing her perception of things.

That he could not dispel the ambiguities yoking themselves to his own understanding of things dismayed and angered him. These first weeks of being here on the Greniers' farmland with Raoul and Benoît had revealed new ambiguities that shrouded the truth of an unfolding mystery. He had to admit that there were gaps in his knowledge of Raoul and Benoît, even though they had fought alongside each other as pilots and as intelligence agents for the Resistance. He had not yet met their trusted friend, Valérie Moreau, because she had arrived here ten days earlier, when he was away from the farm with Pascal, helping him to transport ammunition and food to the maquisards in the distant hills. For more than a week, he had joined these hardened fighters in night raids against the Nazis in their barracks and beer halls within the neighboring villages they had overtaken. He wondered whether, like Raoul and Benoît, Valérie would appear to his eyes as wily and enigmatic. While he was with these three here in Sancerre, he would need to decode the gestures and the language that concealed more than revealed who they really were.

First, he would do the things that needed to be done right now. He would ride forward to the strategic hills that offered him a panoramic view of the villages and the towns below and of the rugged roads along which the Nazis might hurry toward the Grenier property. Then, after he had determined that no Nazi parties were in sight, he would return to the vineyards and orchards. Once there, he would activate his role as a farm laborer in the employ of the Greniers. Later, when he completed his work for that day, he would visit the wounded Raoul and Benoît, who were convalescing within a secret room inside the granary.

He would also pay a visit to Valérie Moreau, who—he had been told upon his return from the commando raids against the Nazis—had already made herself a valuable addition to this farm that had become their hideaway. Part of the time, she was an efficient nurse to Raoul and to Benoît. At other times, she worked in the vineyards and in the orchards. She also assisted Mrs. Grenier with cooking and housecleaning. She painted and decorated the cottage where she planned to stay for a few weeks before she returned to London. From time to time she also used her wireless radio (a 3 Mark II Suitcase Transceiver) to intercept Nazi military correspondence and to transmit these messages to RAF and Free French Air Force agents and to Allied army commanders.

Hearing all these favorable reports about her, he would never deny that Valérie was useful. But he did not know whether she was trustworthy. Before she left Sancerre, he had to find out. He had to find out, too, whatever truths that Raoul and Benoît were concealing.

The Greniers had hidden Raoul and Benoît on the upper floor of their granary, within the living quarters under the eaves of the double-sloped roof. They believed that there, inside the granary, the two wounded men would have a better chance of remaining undetected. This nineteenth-century brick structure, capacious and teeming, overlooked the southerly orchards and also observed the far-distant home fields. If the Germans sent their soldiers to reconnoiter the area for deserters or for wounded enemies, as they occasionally did, even such malevolent enemies might accept a granary for the thing it was made to be: a storehouse brimming with September's early harvest.

During the first week of their concealment there, Raoul and Benoît benefited from a well-monitored care. Noah Hoffmann, a Jewish doctor whom the Greniers were hiding from the Nazis, had set in their initial stages the repairs of Raoul's dislocated shoulder and lacerated kneecaps and ankles. After realigning the broken pieces of bone, he had also placed a plaster cast around Benoît's fractured right ankle and around his fractured left arm. (Noah, Marc observed, looked exactly like his twin brother Franz. His own parents, Henri and Marianne Roussillon, had rescued Franz from the Nazis a few years earlier and then brought him, with his wife and daughter, to England.)

The motherly, gray-haired women who for years had shared with the Greniers the duties of the farmland and vineyards now shared nursing duties with Marcelle Grenier and with Valérie Moreau. There were big-boned Celeste, petite Honorée, and rail-thin Delphine. These women—always in pairs and never more than two at the same time—provided for the wounded men days and days of spotless refuge and reviving baths, nutritious meals and restful beds. They would enter the granary in a horse-dawn cart that was overflowing with baskets of apples, oranges, and pears that had been picked from the nearby orchards earlier that day and were ready to be stored in the granary. During each of these visits, the apples and oranges and pears in two of these baskets occupied only the circumference of an upper lid placed near the top. Hidden carefully below the lid, within a wide and deep interior, were fresh linen and blankets and steaming food.

Occasionally, the husbands and sons of these women paid brief visits to the two pilots. Alphonse, Xavier and Pierre, defined by their grizzled features and manes of white hair now, had (twenty-five years earlier) fought at the Marne. Their sons were brawny, olive-skinned Quentin; hulking, ruddy Yannick; and wiry, sun-bronzed Régis. They were farmers by day and sabotage agents by night. These young men and their fathers would share with Raoul and Benoît anecdotes about horseback riding, fishing, soccer, hunting, and skiing. Sometimes, they would ask the two pilots about the aeronautical precision of an Avro Lancaster or a Vickers Wellington. But never did they ask them to recall their experiences of bombing German cities, airfields, and harbors. Tough-spirited and unsentimental, they understood nonetheless that no man or woman enjoys re-living a scene of conflagration and massacre.

This afternoon, after assuring himself that the Nazis had not infiltrated the area, Marc rode with cantering agility across dark-green, undulant hills and over wide riders' paths that led him to the granary. He was careful to dismount at the entrance to the apple orchard that stood, sequestered and productive, next to the granary. From the orchard, he took a large basketful of apples that Alphonse had left there for him to carry as he entered the granary. This carrying of apples gave to his being there a convincing authenticity. He was a workman with a valid reason for entering the building.

Stepping inside, he saw huge bins of golden grain and tightly-bound bales of wheat and rye waiting their turn to be threshed. He also saw equally deep bins overflowing with oranges, pears, and apples that were to be packed into crates and brought to the markets of neighboring villages. All these things he had seen during his visit to this cool, well-insulated place on the preceding day. The orderly arrangement of the space and the fruit-scented cleanliness never failed to impress him. But only for a moment would he permit this thought to linger upon his apprehension. Quickly, he poured into an empty bin the apples that he was carrying. Then, keen-eyed and efficient, he turned to find the secret door that smoothly blended with the opposite wall. When he pushed forward the correct cedar panel, this door opened to an ascending stairway and to a sequestered loft beneath the eaves of the roof.

With swift, athletic poise, he climbed the stairs and made his way into the loft. What he saw first of all were Raoul and Benoît aiming a Bren gun and a Colt revolver at him. Rays of light streaming in from a trio of miniature windows in the cedar wall or welling up from a gasoline lantern cast an eerie haze around them. Dressed in the clean shirts and trousers of farm laborers, they were sitting in two pallet beds while leaning against an ample support of pillows. The light showed his eyes that their long, muscular bodies—enclosed in part by plaster casts or harnessed to shoulder slings—dominated each of the pallets, which were placed side by side.

But the same light, with its vaporous and murky swirls, concealed their faces. Only after they recognized who he was and put aside their weapons did he step forward to observe them more closely. Only then did he see their tense and furtive expressions. He might have given no notice to their tension, because his sudden appearance in their hiding place would naturally have aroused their uncertainty and their wariness. Combat-trained, they would have reached for their weapons the moment they heard him ascending the stairs. But, even after he whispered a greeting to them and gave them the cigarettes and brandy he had stored in his travel bag two weeks earlier when he had been in London, they remained uneasy. Whether by chance or by intention, they leaned back further into their pillows and moved out of the light.

Their concealing themselves from his view did not so much surprise as disappoint him. Had he made a mistake about them? Were they, in spite of their heroic efforts on behalf of the Allies, in league with the Vichy government and with the Nazis? Or were Raoul and Benoît compromising their roles as Free French Air Force pilots and as Resistance fighters by protecting a friend who they refused to believe was a traitor?

Neither Raoul nor Benoît wanted him to see their faces or to observe their expressions as they answered the questions that he had come to ask them. He imagined that they were anticipating variants of the questions he had been asking them for three weeks now. On each occasion, because his questions had intimidated them, they had offered him answers that were both elliptical and evasive. They were not yet ready to tell him the important things that they had failed to do and the impulsive things that they had done which had endangered themselves as well as others.

Here in Sancerre his questions were more complicated than the ones he had asked them four weeks earlier, when they were being tortured within the crypt vaults of the Basilica of Sacré-Coeur. The newer, probing intricacies of his questions sought to discover not only the identity of the double agent, but also the roles that Raoul and Benoît may have played—by willful choice or because of an inadvertent blunder—in divulging crucial military information to this secret agent who might be their friend.

Before he began questioning them today, Marc tried to put them at ease. He poured brandy into the cups that they used to drink coffee. He was glad to join in this bit of camaraderie and, with no reluctance whatever, gave himself over to the warm kick of the liquor upon his senses. After the second round, Raoul and Benoît appeared to relax. They leaned into the light and allowed him to observe the openness of their faces.

"Drinking with friends like this brings back my best days," Raoul said. "If Piaf were singing to us in this room, or Chevalier or Josephine Baker, I might imagine that I was having a good time in a Paris nightclub or inside one in Montmartre."

For a moment, Benoît mused upon his words. Then, he decided to resist their nostalgia.

"Those days are gone forever," he said. "They will never come back."

Marc smiled pensively. He appreciated Benoît's realism. But he did not care to revive the tension that had made his two friends secretive. So he hurried to put a happier spin on the thoughts that they were exchanging.

"You are right," he agreed. "Those days are past us now and will never return. But, if we are lucky, we may live through a few days that are even better."

He had chosen the right words. No sooner had he spoken them, than his two friends permitted themselves to laugh.

Now Raoul raised his cup while inviting them to join him in a toast.

"Let each of us promise to persuade those days to invite us to the party."

"Done," Marc said, almost believing in his lightheartedness. "Those days will belong to us first of all."

The three of them laughed again. Then, while his two friends drank more brandy and consented to their casual engagement with the hour, Marc began questioning them.

First of all, he asked them to identify—as they had on the two preceding days—the man that they believed was the double agent. For weeks, not only Raoul and Benoît, but also Valérie Moreau had worked to ferret out of his secrecy the traitor who was placing their entire Resistance group in jeopardy.

"We think that he is Hans Mueller," Raoul said matter-of-factly. "We are not yet certain that he is the traitor. We haven't enough proof. We don't often see him unless we are flying out of London on the same bombing mission. When he is in France, on assignment as an agent for the Resistance, he usually operates out of the Vichy sector. He has also made London, Lausanne, and Bergen his contact stations. Everything we've found points in his direction. He is the one man on our team who could very well be collaborating with the Nazis."

Marc pushed him forward with a pertinent question.

"Exactly what have you found?" he asked.

Raoul hesitated, though not because he needed time to

calculate an appropriate answer. He had already answered this question on those other days when Marc had come to the granary.

Now Marc urged Raoul to go forward nonetheless to the words that would clarify the information that he and Benoît, as well as Valérie, had gathered about the suspected traitor.

"I know that we've gone over all of this before," he said. "But I want you to tell me again. Yesterday or a week before that, you may have left out something important. Maybe today you will say everything that you need to say."

With a nod of his head, Raoul agreed quickly to summarize once more the information that he, Valérie, and Benoît had thus far discovered about Hans Mueller.

"His name came up every time we checked the roster of agents who were assigned to our sabotage teams. Hans Mueller was aware of the important maneuvers that our teams were planning against the Nazis. Every one of the maneuvers that involved his approval or his participation ended in failure. They cost the Resistance and our Allies hundreds and sometimes thousands of lives."

Now Benoît spoke up. There was a bitter edge to his husky voice.

"If Mueller is the double agent, we know this much about him. He enjoys killing," he said. "He also enjoys telling the

Nazis when and whom they should kill. He'd have his own mother killed, if he thought that Hitler would pin a medal on him afterward."

Raoul hurried to denounce the traitor who was working in their midst.

"We believe that, just three months ago, he led the Nazis to our Resistance people who were sabotaging telephone lines and intercepting military messages which they passed on to British spies operating here in France. He was the catalyst in the deaths of all six hundred of those workers."

Grim-faced and accusatory, Benoît spoke up again.

"Two months ago, a man who may very well be Hans Mueller gave the Nazis the names of the four hundred French railroad workers who belonged to an underground organization called The Iron Network. At no little cost to their safety, these men and women had been diverting Nazi freight shipments to the wrong locations. They caused derailments by not operating the switches properly. They destroyed stretches of railroad tracks and blew up railroad bridges. Each one of them was helping us to win the war."

"The Nazis killed all of them," Raoul said. "But, before they could round them up in Paris and machine gun them in the courtyard outside La Santé Prison, they needed someone like Hans Mueller to give them the names and addresses of these people."

"Last month Mueller probably gave the Nazis top-secret information about Allied troop movements," Benoît said. "He is one of the few men in the Resistance who have access to the schedule of troop trains. A day later, the German Air Force bombed the trains that were carrying thousands of our troops to the front. We lost eight hundred men."

Marc pondered what they were telling him, even as he studied their morose faces. They looked displeased with themselves and even guilt-ridden. This unexpected response aroused his interest. So he pushed forward.

"The two of you know more than a little about Hans Mueller," he said. "Yet you say that you don't socialize with him very often."

"We are never on leave at the same time. Apart from our occasionally sharing bombing missions with him, we met him most recently in Lucerne last November," Raoul said. "When we were skiing there with our girlfriends, Mueller joined us for a week-end. Lucien Chardonne and his girlfriend had invited him."

"He was a friend of Lucien Chardonne?"

"We were all friends," Raoul said. "We went to law school together in Heidelberg."

Marc probed further, still directing his inquiry to both men.

"You still called Hans your friend, even though he was a German."

Though the brandy had subdued their tension, their furtiveness had not left them. He felt that they were toughing out this hour with him. They were calculating how much they should tell him and whether their telling him all the essential things would alter his regard of them.

Raoul poured himself another brandy and swallowed it roughly. Then he hurried to the words that might clarify things for himself and for the two men watching him.

"We always thought of him as the Hans Mueller that we knew before the war," he said. "To us, he was always a good German. Even during the few times that we met him after the war began, we told ourselves that he was the same Hans we knew when we first met him at the University of Heidelberg.

"Both mentally and physically, he was imaginative and adventurous. He was an original. He was the friend who would steer you in the right direction if you'd taken a wrong turn. He was the one who'd always put in a favorable report on you, even if it meant that he'd have to stand out of the limelight for a while. That was the Hans we remembered. That was the image we imposed upon him in those later meetings. We told ourselves that, in spite of the war, he had not changed in any of the important ways. He was still the Hans Mueller who had been our loyal friend long ago.

"We were lying to ourselves, of course. The war had changed everything for him.

"When the war began, he understood all too clearly the rotten political landscape that the Nazis were building. His days were numbered if he remained a Jew. At first, through Benoît's and my recommendation, he tried to become an RAF pilot. But the British distrusted his background. Both his father and his grandfather had fought against the Allies during the First World War. At Cambrai and at Neuilly, they died bravely for the Germany that eventually produced Hitler. The RAF dismissed the favorable words that we had written on behalf of Hans. There are, the team of officers reviewing Hans' application told us, many Muellers who are fighting today for a world dominated by the Nazis. They couldn't afford to take a chance on this Hans Mueller. The chances were strong that he might turn out to be a Nazi.

"Those RAF officers meant well. But their experience of war had turned their hearts to stone. They told themselves that they were being stern realists. War had taught them to trust no one. In their eyes, Hans was a Jew who belonged to a foreign country. But, before that, he was a German who might betray whatever trust they placed in him. As far as they were concerned, he was none of their business. So they left him to his grim fate."

Raoul paused, musing bitterly upon some remembered incident he was not yet ready to share.

Sensing his reluctance to go on with his story, Marc offered him a cigarette as well as another brandy. He offered the same to Benoît and to himself. Then, as though his main purpose for being there was to put them at their ease, he found the casual words that might persuade Raoul to resume his narrative about Hans Mueller.

"Joining the RAF was the right thing for Hans," he said. "But having that path closed off didn't leave him defeated. For a time at least, he made other things work for him."

Still reluctant to take up once again the story he had been telling, Raoul—with gravelly timbres and blunt terseness—accepted his level-headed point of view.

"Yes," he agreed. "Hans made things work for a little while."

Having said so, he withdrew inside a pensive stillness. He did not care to say anything more about a subject that he found so forbidding and so grievous.

Aware of his friend's somber mood, Benoît continued the narrative that meant to tell Marc who Hans Mueller was and why he had fallen under suspicion.

"Hans's fate had made him a German Jew," he explained,

"but he was determined to make the best of things. After the RAF turned him down, he entered Germany's *Junkerschule*—a rigorous and even brutal Officer Candidate School. Within eighteen months, he was a second lieutenant in the *Waffen-SS*. He had concealed his Jewish background and, on those terms, would play out the hand that had been dealt him. He was hoping the gamble would pay off. He wanted to use the war to win a better life for himself. Unlike most men, he went into the war not because his country told him that was his obligation. He joined up because the British had turned him away and he had nowhere else to go. Since he had to return to Germany, he planned to convince others, and maybe himself most of all, that he was not a Jew.

"For a long time he stayed lucky. When he was training to be an officer, the physician who periodically examined him never revealed that he was an uncircumcised man—a telling sign that he was probably a Jew. This physician had known and respected his father.

"This luck stayed with him when he was on the battlefield. Even during the fiercest combat, he suffered no life-threatening wounds. But after three years of hard fighting and after all the killing, he no longer wanted to be a Nazi. Maybe he'd found out what the Nazis were doing to his Gentile friends. Maybe he learned for certain what they were doing to the Jews. Maybe what they were doing to the Jews influenced him to turn away from the Germans. What influenced him most of all, we'll never know for certain. But we do know that one day he declared to himself and to a British intelligence unit that he was no longer a Nazi. That is the day he became a Jew once again. On that day, he decided to become a German who was not a Nazi.

"He began working in secret for the Resistance and for British intelligence. Three years earlier, British officers had turned him away when he asked to be one of their pilots. Now, at a secret meeting with him in Belgium, they regarded him differently. They decided to use him as one of their agents. They persuaded him to become a member of *Abwehr*, the German intelligence network. No longer did he fight on a battlefield. After his training, the German High Command sent him forth to kill Jews and French Resistance fighters, as well as British and American soldiers and pilots.

"We do not know whether he ever killed any of them, so that he could maintain his cover as a secret agent for the British. We do know that he intercepted important information about German troop movements, combat locations, military train schedules, aerial combat schedules, and the names of Nazis who had infiltrated the French Resistance. Everything that he was doing helped the Allies to win a battle in the air or to take an important hill on some remote and unforgiving field or to ford a strategic river."

Understated and specific, Marc interrupted the narrative. He thought that Benoît should revise his interpretation of Hans. He was leaving out something important.

"All that you have said may be true," he began. "But facts are facts. Hans was involved in the killing of those eighty-one freedom fighters in Brittany."

Quickly, Benoît countered his remark.

"Hans didn't kill any of them," he said. "He wasn't even at the scene. But Gaston and Fabien were there. They were probably the Nazis' henchmen. They led fifty storm troopers to our guerrilla forces who were maintaining their posts in the mountains. They bombarded them with grenades and heavy machine gun fire. The Germans lost twelve men, but they killed every one of those freedom fighters."

Now Raoul came back into it.

"After they captured Lucien Chardonne and the two captains who had always been loyal to our side, Gaston and Fabien blamed them for the massacre in Brittany."

Marc frowned. A question and an assertion both incisive and tough-minded rode upon the influence of that frown. He anticipated Raoul's response. But he wanted to hear nonetheless all the words that composed it.

"Why would they kill Chardonne and the captains?" he

asked. "Those three men had fought the Nazis bravely. They always helped the Allies."

"Gaston and Fabien had a very good reason," Raoul said. "Lucien Chardonne and the two captains discovered that Gaston and Fabien were Nazi spies. They may even have discovered who their leader was. The French traitors couldn't afford to have Lucien and the other two men stay alive."

Hearing the words that did not surprise him, Marc studied Raoul with an even more penetrating gaze.

"You speak with uncertainty about this leader."

Defensive, Raoul hurried forward with words that were as anguished as they were impassioned.

"I am uncertain. I don't have any real proof yet. I only have a few words that were spoken to me many months ago. At Lucerne, Lucien tried to warn me against Hans. 'Be careful of him,' he told me. 'He's not really one of us. He's not on our team.' But I wouldn't believe Lucien. I thought that he was mistaken. I had seen Hans killing Nazis. I was there the many times that he saved men and women who were part of the Resistance.

"Even after Lucien warned me against him and after I saw Hans kill two of our best fighting men when he convinced our group that they were Nazi spies, I still believed in Hans. During those years in Heidelberg, Hans, Lucien, Benoît and I were brothers-in-spirit. We would have died for one another. As far as I was concerned, the war hadn't changed any of that for us."

"But something did change your mind. Something or someone."

Raoul paused. He was not enjoying any of this. Re-tracing his uncertainty made him edgy and grim-faced.

"Valérie has worked with me to put Hans to the test. She has entered the secret path that, as a Resistance fighter, he has made for himself."

Though this news surprised him, Marc held himself—reliable and steady—within the privacies of understatement.

"How did she manage to do that?"

Once more, Raul paused. He took a drag on his cigarette and swallowed more of the brandy. With a sullen acceptance of the moment, he glanced first at Marc and, after that, at Benoît, who all this while had listened uneasily to a story he probably knew well. Then he spoke the words that, Marc thought, must have been very hard for him to speak.

"A year ago, a few months after they met, Valérie made a special bond with Hans. She made the same bond with Lucien, too, and with Benoît and me. He, too, finds her an extraordinary woman. He respects her for the years that she spent as a nun and for the courage she has demonstrated in this war. Like Lucien, Benoît, and me, Hans has always stood a bit in awe of Valérie.

He regards the agreement that we made with her as a pact that must never be broken—not even after the war, when Valérie chooses the one man among us that she wants as her husband.

"The pact that Valérie made with us became a law that we promised to follow as if it were part of our religion. While the war lasted, Valérie would be a sister to all four of us, with no strings to bind her to any of us afterward, except to the one that she chose when the war was over to be her lover and husband. To make this beautiful woman a close friend without sleeping with her was an altogether new experience for all of us. At first, it intrigued and even puzzled us. After a while, we felt liberated. In her company, we had no need of romantic games. We could be ourselves—straightforward, matter-of-fact, and authentic. That we consented to such a friendship with her does not seem so surprising to me now. Valérie, after all, had been a nun before the war. She left the convent to fight the Nazis. For that and for her courage, we respected her. We still do. Her seductive disguise as a nightclub singer didn't change our opinion of her. We thought of her as a good girl. Like most of us during this war, she was carrying the burden of all her losses. But she refused to be destroyed by whatever the war had done to her. We all fell deeply in love with her. Maybe Hans fell in love with her most of all. At least, that is the way we saw him. But, in the past few months, he changed. Valérie noticed the change at the same time that Benoît and I did. But she understood it first of all."

Raoul hesitated again, before all the words he would need to say if they were to make sense of his uncertainty.

Marc waited. He imagined that Raoul sought in these words that were so difficult for him to say not an echo of his condemnation of himself for having failed to resolve the identity of the double agent. He wanted his new words to grant him a clarified awareness.

When he resumed his narrative, Raoul spoke briskly, as if he were hurrying toward whatever clue his words might reveal to him.

"Four months ago, Valérie saw everything that I had seen," he said, "and that I had refused to connect to Hans. She saw that the Nazis were winning too many battles in the sky, bombing too many of our troop trains, and killing too many of our men fighting them in the mountains. But she saw even more than that, because she was in frequent contact with Hans. She knew him well and knew what she would have to do first of all, if she wanted to find out whether he was a double agent."

"What was that?"

A taut stillness hovered about Raoul, even as he found the essential words that might push him toward some hard-earned resolution of his uncertainty.

"Four months ago, without sharing his bed, Valérie intensified her friendship with Hans. She convinced him that it was he whom she loved more than she loved any of us. She used that lie to disarm him. When he was with her, he became even more alive. Away from his combat flying and his secret missions for the Resistance, he was once more the man he used to be before the war. Valérie began to know him well."

From these words, Marc perceived new complications and different layers of uncertainty. Yet his blunt inflections gave no evidence of his uneasiness.

"Four months, you say. It has taken her a long time to find out whether Hans is a secret Nazi."

Raoul pondered this response for merely an instant. Then, with the emphases of renewed conviction, he continued his troubled narrative.

"Valérie has worked very carefully," he said. "She does not want to send Hans to his death, unless she has to. Thus far, he appears to be in the clear. She has checked all his correspondence, listened in on his telephone calls, and intercepted his wireless radio communications. He has even brought her into the group of persons he calls his special friends. Always, he has done the things that a good freedom fighter should do."

Arbitrary and abrupt, Raoul stopped himself in the midst of

his defense of Hans. A vague bitterness took hold of his rugged and handsome features. The next words that he chose, he anchored to ambivalence.

"Until lately, Valérie had grown certain that Hans was not the double agent that we need to kill."

Marc noticed the ambivalence and probed matter-of-factly.

"And now something has made her less certain."

This time Raoul answered without hesitation.

"Lucien Chardonne made her less certain about Hans. In these last weeks before his death, Lucien was tracking every move that Hans made. Every time there was an aerial bombing of an aircraft plant or the sabotage of a bridge or a railway track, Hans may very well have been involved. He had access to all the information that the Nazis and their henchmen needed for the aerial bombings and the sabotage.

"Over and over, Lucien kept explaining to Valérie all the facts that worked against anyone's believing that Hans was innocent. But Valérie brushed his facts aside as coincidences that she refused to take seriously. After a while, Lucien stopped mentioning Hans when he was in her presence. She began to feel that Lucien must have found out that she had been right to believe in Hans's innocence. She grew uneasy, though, when a week later Lucien told her that he had discovered the identity of the double agent and was going to London to make his case to the MI5 office there. Unfortunately, he did not tell her more than that. Whatever secrets he discovered died with him when Nazi agents killed him. After that, Valérie began to look at Hans in a different way. Even then, in spite of her doubts, she insisted that Hans was innocent.

"The double agent—whoever he is—sent Gaston and Fabien to kill Lucien Chardonne when Lucien discovered who he was. At the same time, because he was convinced that Valérie knew who he was, he sent other assassins to kill her on stage at the nightclub where she had been singing. Dressed in a form-fitting beaded gown, she was standing by the piano while she sang 'Frankie and Johnny.' She looked like the beautiful American film star Lana Turner.

"Suddenly, from the shadowy, candle-lit tables where they had been sitting, the two assassins sprang into the spotlight. They were wearing swastika armbands and carrying Mauser semi-automatic vest pocket handguns.

"'Here is a present from Hans Mueller,' they shouted.

"No sooner had they called out these words, as though they represented an official edict of execution, than Valérie shot the two of them with the snub-nosed revolver she had quickly taken from the beaded purse she had placed on the piano. Her training as one of our agents paid off. She hadn't really expected anything to happen that night, at least not at the club. But she was ready."

Benoît came into it again.

"I know a young married couple who had been there, watching Valérie's show. When the shooting occurred, a hush fell over the audience—there were more than a hundred people who had come to see Val that night. At first, everyone thought that the shooting had been faked, that it was part of the show. The pianist—a cool-headed black man in his thirties who had once seen his best friends lynched by a mob in Mississippi— kept playing as if nothing unusual had happened. But, when the two men who'd been shot didn't get up and when the spotlight caught the blood spilling from their bullet-torn skulls, the crowd went wild.

"A group of Nazi army officers who had come to hear Val sing were rushing to the stage when the club manager turned off the lights. Whether the Nazis meant to protect her or to arrest her, nobody at the club knew for certain afterward. What they remembered were the tables and chairs being overturned, a dozen or so fistfights breaking out, and somebody firing pistols into the air. By the time the lights came on again, Valérie and the pianist had cleared out."

Raoul offered a coda to this narrative.

"Valérie has been on the run ever since—first in Annecy, then in Grenoble, and now here in Sancerre. She won't stay here long, because she doesn't want to endanger the Greniers or their staff. She understands that her safety in this place is only temporary. She'll keep moving on, until the day she comes face to face with her assassins."

Marc hurried to find out more.

"Is Hans one of them?"

A taut ambivalence coiled itself about Raul's answer.

"She keeps telling me that she is not certain. She says that she has no way of knowing whether Hans sent those men to kill her while she was singing in the night club."

Now Marc saw how it was with Raoul.

"You don't believe her."

To his blunt assertion, Raoul responded with careful understatement.

"She may know more about Hans than she is willing to admit—to herself and to every one else."

A hint of anger quickened Marc's next words.

"Why would she not tell you?" he asked. "Her silence allows the Nazis to kill thousands of men and women who are fighting on our side."

For an instant, Raoul held back his answer. He swallowed more of the brandy and then, with a surly intensity, withdrew momentarily to the privacies of his bitter thoughts.

Marc saw that Raoul was weary of the uncertainties that had

raveled themselves around his perception of things. He sensed, too, the subdued wiliness that kept him on his guard. The wiliness and the guardedness influenced Benoît as well. It made a bond between them. He was not surprised that Benoît, upon observing his friend's momentary furtiveness, also withdrew to the mysteries of his own stillness.

Nor was he surprised when Raoul challenged him to take the next step needed, if they were to discover the identity of the double agent.

"You will have to ask Valérie to explain herself," he said. "She may be able to do that far better than I can. Maybe you will even persuade her to tell you all that she knows about Hans and all that she feels."

Chapter Three

Turmoil

It was not until a week later that Marc, upon returning from another round of missions into the mountains, discovered that Valérie Moreau was none other than Simone, the beautiful wife whom he still loved and from whom he was estranged.

During those brief times when he was at home with the Greniers, he had wondered why this woman that he had been told was Valérie Moreau never appeared at the lunches and suppers where the Greniers and their staff of devoted workers gathered, all of them as affable and life-loving as hard-working people can be during a time of war. She was, he had sometimes been told, resting in one of the Greniers' cottages, where she was staying in the secluded southwest corner of their property. At other times, he had been told a different story. She had spent her day working in the apple orchard and had sprained her ankle when she had fallen against a boulder that jutted from a shadowy alcove inside the large grove of trees. Or she was bringing her nursing skills to a sick child in a nearby village.

Or, as a nurse and a friend, she was conferring with Raoul and Benoît inside the secret apartment within the granary and preferred that their meeting remain private. That mere chance or a wily plan of her making prevented him from seeing her roused Marc's curiosity and his suspicion. He wondered why she was avoiding him. Her continued withdrawal from his presence now compelled him to watch her from a distance.

During these first weeks in Sancerre, he had sometimes observed her working in the orchards and in the vineyards while, on his favorite Criollo, he was reconnoitering the area in search of Nazis. But he did not recognize that she was his wife because of the wide-brimmed straw hat that concealed her face or, at least, partially hid it in shadows. She wore the hat and the dark green corduroy jacket and overalls as though she were a young woman who belonged to the farm. Her assured movements as she worked in the vineyards gave evidence of agrarian skills that she had honed to a sharp precision. Twice he had seen her at mid-day when, with Quentin, Yannick and Régis, he was returning in the Greniers' largest farm truck from a night's journey into the mountains. To the guerrillas waiting there for them, he and the three others had carried Bren sub-machine guns and US M3s, Lee-Enfield rifles and Winchester semi-automatic carbines, Webley Mk IV revolvers, American Colt automatics, British Mills grenades, the Gammon grenade (which was a lump of plastic explosive covered in a cloth skirt with a detonator on top), and Fairbairn-Sykes knives. Two weeks earlier, the British had parachuted the weapons, which were stored inside heavy cylinders, into the north hayfield of the Greniers' property. But the Nazis' night bombings of the area had kept the Greniers from sending their couriers into the mountains with the weapons.

On those two afternoons, when he was behind the wheel of the big truck that brought him and the three others back from the mountains into the Greniers' home fields, he saw in the sun-fused distance the woman that he believed was Valérie at work in the vineyards. But, even though he carefully watched her, he did not yet recognize her as Simone. She was picking large bunches of grapes from the vines, and her broad-rimmed hat concealed her features. Because he stopped the truck momentarily at the top of the distant hill that sloped into a homebound road, he and the three farm hands could observe her privately. He saw at once how agreeably she worked with two or three teenage girls from the village. On the second occasion when he chanced to see her, she and these girls were softly singing romantic ballads in French, English, and Italian. The singing provided a sensitive and melodic counterpoint to the good-natured camaraderie that he and his three friends had been sharing on their ride back to the main house. Even then he did not recognize her. Her singing voice, which to his ears had always before been distinctive and lilting, was lost to him because it was so smoothly blended with the voices of the village girls.

In this second sighting of her, there in the vineyards, he noticed that, in the midst of her singing, she suddenly broke away from the song. She left the two younger girls to carry forward the plaintive or heartening or ironic message of the lyrics. At this time, she halted momentarily her task of plucking the grapes with cautious ease from the vines. He imagined that a weary sadness was slowly overtaking her face, which still concealed itself in the shadows cast by the September light because of the large, broad-rimmed hat that she was wearing. She would search the wide expanse of the vineyards as far as her troubled eyes could perceive them. Then, not finding what she sought, she would scan the distant hills and mountains. She was (Marc imagined) waiting for someone to arrive. Whether he was her enemy or her friend, only time and the episodes unfolding their ambivalent surprises and their apparently inevitable surfaces would tell him.

On one Sunday, just a few minutes after his visit to Raoul and Benoît, Marc saw her without seeing even a fleet impression of her face, there in the distant haze of the sun. She was standing with her back to him, self-possessed and helpful at the entrance to the practice track. There, in the sun-misted glow of early afternoon, she was teaching nine-year-old Guillaume and eight-year-old Ariane how to ride their bay-colored Welsh Mountain Ponies more smoothly. The boy and the girl, dark-haired, long-bodied and slender, were the children of Nicolas Grenier, the Free French Air Force pilot who had been killed three months earlier while flying in a combat mission over Berlin. That this woman who, he had been told, was Valérie would take the time to help these children to become more proficient riders impressed him. Her being here on the turf-covered practice track not far from the Greniers' stables revealed to his watchful eyes a new layer of her existence. He saw how patient and teacherly she was as she guided the children. The glamorous and sensual imagery that (he had been told) usually adorned her personhood belonged to a different version of herself. He imagined that her adventurous life did not often allow her to activate this more wholesome presentation of who she was. Or, possibly, she chose to activate only on rare occasions what she perceived to be a safer and more conventional imagery.

As Valérie was dressed, so Guillaume and Ariane were dressed protectively in hard hat and chin harness, in long-sleeved sweatshirt and comfortable breeches, and in boots and gloves. He liked the confidence of the children as they sat on their ponies, which were a blend of palomino spirit and docility. They had learned well that one sits with the weight of one's body in the center of the saddle, thereby allowing one's hip joint to be open and one's legs correctly positioned as close as possible around the pony's sides. On this sun-bright autumn afternoon, while all the time they were attuned to Valérie's effective supervision, they held their hands correctly, with palms facing each other and their thumbs uppermost. Without using their arms, they clasped the reins by wrapping their fingers around them and almost closing their hands to make a fist. It was as though arms and reins belonged to the pony, the better to follow its motion.

He watched teacher and students with unobtrusive attention. He had just emerged from the stables with his reliable Criollo. While he was there, within the well-kept and comfortable surround of the building, he had applied exercise bandages to the horse's legs to protect them during the fast-paced ride that would bring him to the edge of the far-away hills and mountains. First, he had placed padding around the Criollo's legs, making certain that the edge of the pad lay between the tendons on the outside of the leg. He had started below the knee and finished below the fetlock joint. With equal skill, he had applied the bandages over the padding so that they would be neither too tight, nor too loose. If they were too tight, the bandage wraps (a melding of white and red fabric) could damage the horse's tendons. If they were too loose, they could cause the horse to fall.

Now, seated on his Criollo outside the stables, he continued with casual-seeming ease to observe Valérie as she taught the Grenier children how to improve their riding techniques. He was not the only one observing her. Pascal and Marcelle stood in the distance by the paddock fence. With beaming eyes, they were watching her with their grandchildren. Not far from where they stood, Quentin and three or four other field hands were comfortably perched upon the cedar smoothness of the fence. All the spectators there were enjoying this leisure hour that their Sunday schedule had granted them. Occasionally, any one of them might call out a word of encouragement or signal with a clap of hands an unconditional approval. For all of them, this scene of the children testing their mettle as riders was very special.

Deliberately, he held himself apart from the scene. With a tug of the reins, he kept his Criollo from moving forward while, keen-eyed and unobtrusive, he studied the scene unfolding before him.

He was favorably impressed when he saw Ariane poised erect and responsive upon her pony. Bright girl that she was, she walked the agreeable horse by using her leg nearest Valérie (around whom in a circle she was riding) to create a superior forward gait. She used her other leg to hold the hindquarters in place. The pony nodded its head to balance itself, and the girl sat alert and companionable in the saddle, so that her body in synchronous rhythm absorbed the horse's impulsion.

He found as much pleasure in watching Guillaume asking his pony to go forward into a canter on the left rein. Newly effective while he sat on his pony, he kept circling Valérie, who from time to time guided him with her instructions. He sat deep and pressed his inside leg (the leg nearest her) on an Atherstone girth, the fine leather band contoured about the belly of the pony to keep the saddle in place. In the next instant, the boy asked more actively with a squeeze or a nudge of his outside leg back behind the girth.

A few minutes later, Valérie gave Guillaume and Ariane further instructions. This time her voice was low and confidential, so that her words were lost to his hearing. Her students listened to her, keen-minded and determined. Gamely, then, brother and sister raced each other around the practice track. Marc enjoyed watching them collaborating with their ponies' kinetic energies. Each of their ponies lengthened out its body and its neck and fully extended its legs as they powered forward over the ground. Riding with commendable ease and with the seat taken out of the saddle, Guillaume and Ariane tucked their upper body in behind their horse's neck and extended their arms forward as with each stride the horse stretched his neck forward. That afternoon, they were riding with shorter stirrups, the better for their weight to be lifted out of the saddle. Through the reins they were always keeping contact with the horse's mouth in order to help balance him.

Although Ariane was becoming a very fine rider, Guillaume had attained a more consistent mastery. Yet, as he was finishing the race, he held back. He lightly squeezed his legs inward against the pony's sides, spoke to him in a soft but insistent voice, and pulled firmly on the neck strap until the pony slowed down. These were gestures both subtle and deliberate. Guillaume was giving the race to his sister, whom he had been easily outdistancing. He wanted her to win.

"Well done," Valérie called out, after Ariane and (a minute later) Guillaume reached the finishing line. At least, those were the words that he thought she had spoken. The medley of other voices had overtaken her voice, so that its distinctive sound eluded him. But, with a more defining clarity, the lilt of the voice told him that Valérie was elated.

Marc heard elation in Ariane's lighter voice, too, and he watched it brighten her face. But still Valérie's face eluded him. He noticed, though, what Ariane had not. Her teacher had directed her words of praise to Guillaume, too. She was, Marc imagined, saluting his courtly gesture. Winning the race was less important than influencing his sister's happiness. He was not surprised by Valérie's empathy for the gesture that defines itself by *noblesse oblige*. Nor was he disappointed that her appreciation of a boy's courtly deference to his sister grew out of her matter-of-fact awareness that even well-meaning gestures anchor their intricacies to subtle calculation.

Once again, before leaving the scene, he tried to discern Valérie's elated face. The elation, he imagined, must have given to her blonde sensuality a tincture of the ethereal. At that moment, while Marcelle and Pascal and several field hands were gathering around the two children to confer their words of praise in a mixture of laughter and high spirits, Valérie met his gaze. It took her a moment to remember who he was and to understand that, with wary and sharp-eyed inquiry, he was watching her.

It was now that he recognized who she really was. The beautiful woman standing with the two children there in the distance, surrounded as they were by the Greniers and their field hands, was Simone, the wife who had left him a year ago. In this moment of mutual recognition, he did not move, mounted as he was on his docile Criollo. Not for the first time, he willed himself to maintain a stoic demeanor that concealed his surprise. His stillness, hard-won and steadying, gave him time to guess that MI5 had assigned Simone to a mission that had put her on the paths of Raoul, Benoît, and Hans Mueller.

He waited for her to make the next move.

For an instant, Simone held him inside her gaze, as though she regarded their mutual sighting of each other as a tenuous bond between them. But no longer did elation touch her face. Instead, a troubled expression overtook the happiness she had borrowed from an extemporaneous occasion. Her blue, uneasy eyes recognized him as an obstacle that she would need to get past or, at the least, as the known identity that she would have to reinterpret.

So he imagined.

What he saw as a palpable influence upon her senses was the frown that creased the pristine beauty of her forehead. It was this frown which most clearly revealed the struggle that, with stoic propensities, she was waging between tough-minded resilience and quiet despair. But he had underestimated her capacity to surprise him. No sooner had he expected her to hurry toward him in angry inquiry about his too-studious attention, than she chose an altogether different strategy. After a taut stillness held her to itself and as though she were summoning familiar powers that dispelled all brooding and hesitation, she brought a laughing smile to her lips. Now she turned quickly away from the sight of him and gave herself to the merriment around her.

Though he was eager to speak with her, drawing from her if he could the answers to all the complicated questions that her presence here on the Greniers' farm roused in him, he kept himself from riding forward to her. He did not want to unsettle Simone or to call attention to his special relationship with her. As far as the Greniers and their field hands knew, Simone was Valérie Moreau, and Simone, his absent wife, was in England, fighting alongside the British.

Instead of riding to her, he signaled his Criollo to go forward to the walk and into the trot and on into the canter. Though he did not turn his head to see her, he felt that Simone had looked up once again to find him galloping toward the hills and the mountains and the more sequestered places where he searched for the Nazis who might be coming to arrest or to kill all of them, because they were an active part of the Resistance. In these moments, no words had passed between him and Simone, who smoothly wore her latest disguise as Valérie. Yet he believed that their sighting of each other was an essential preface to their meeting later that afternoon.

In this conjecture, he was not mistaken. Around three o'clock, shortly after he returned from his surveillance of the town roads and forest trails through which their Nazi enemies might hurry toward them, she came to him in the paddock nearest the stables. He had led his Criollo there, after unsaddling him and after removing the bandage wraps from his sturdy legs. Freed of the wraps and of the adept rider who asked so much of him, the horse cantered with lighthearted vigor toward his stable mates. They were grazing in the distance or, with playful agility and as a group of six, racing each other around the panoramic expanse of the paddock.

It was against this backdrop that Simone, temporarily discarding her role as Valérie, approached him with an easy affability. Her loveliness glowed in the September light that, a half-hour ago, had turned cloud-darkened and storm-fused. He saw at close range now and with new admiration the riding clothes that she wore so well: a mint-green shirt and a tan quilted jacket, brown jodhpurs and summer-cool boots, and cobalt-green protective hat and gloves. Even against his will, he was roused by the traceries of her glamour and by the modulated rebelliousness of her ironic manner.

"So it is starting all over again," she said, "our being here together and not really wanting to be."

He met her words with low-keyed inflections that made what he said sound intimate and even anguished.

"Speak for yourself," he said.

As if she meant to eclipse both his intimacy and the suggestion of anguish, she drove her light-heartedness forward.

"Those Criollos have the right idea," she said. "You get to know a lot about your new friends and even about long-ago friends when you find yourself racing next to them."

She was inviting him to ride with her. Because the storm would not arrive for a few hours, he accepted her invitation with brisk and natural-seeming courtesy. They would, he imagined, ride vigorously until they found some private place where they would dismount and where she would answer directly or parry skillfully the questions that he was waiting to ask her.

They chose to ride dun-colored Sorraias, with black eel stripes making handsome imprints down the center of their backs and zebra markings enhancing the long lines of their legs. The horses were waiting within their stalls inside the stable. That she had, with the assistance of a field hand, already applied exercise bandages to their legs and saddled them up properly intrigued him. She had anticipated this meeting with him and, in fact, was hurrying them into it.

Their ride increased rather than relaxed the tension that had stayed with him through all of the ambivalent days he was compelled to spend on the Greniers' vineyards and their adjoining farmlands. He saw in Simone's ingratiating manner a wily effort to undermine or subvert his distrust of her. That, because of her emotional attachment to Hans Mueller, she might be drawing Mueller and his fellow assassins to the

Greniers' home left him doubtful and vigilant.

For the next half-hour, with her beside him, he rode tensely over the arcs and curves and canted configuration of the land. Allied nonetheless with his spirited Sorraia, he hurried through the fleet apparition of a montage that to his eyes seemed as excited as it was menacing. All around him there were intensity and momentum and progression. There were ambiguity and shadowy surfaces and concealment. There was the stippled imprint upon his senses of the paddock and stables and barn wheeling past him then, vertiginous and soaring. Past him too was the gleaming main house, its sandstone façade a spun velocity inside their seeing. In cantering motion, he glimpsed vineyards and orchards and, in the faraway distance, the intricate, coiling forest. Farther than that, beyond the amorphous line of the horizon, he sighted a confluence of soot-darkened storm clouds overtaking blue-grey cirrus clarities. He saw as well a fellowship of glaucous-winged gulls, skyborne and azure-white and hastening.

On his reliable stallion, while holding his body well forward and over his knees so that his horse's back was not carrying his weight and could move freely, he (with her keeping pace with his skill on her own Sorraia) ascended green northerly hills and skimmed by lavender fields. Once more he rose to the trot. Lightly, he balanced his feet in the stirrups, and, with his lower legs, urged the horse forward. Relaxed in the ease of his proficiency, he rode past winterberry holly, sedum, and sweetspire and past oak leaf and hydrangea and permisetum grasses.

At this time, he squeezed his legs inward against the horse's sides and decreased the forward movements of his hands to negotiate a smooth and proper halt. He arrived at the edge of the untamed woodland and paused before the cultivated gentility of a flourishing grove of trees that the subtleties of a new-borne wind were gradually stirring into restlessness. Once he and Simone dismounted, they permitted their horses to graze in a meadow of ornamental grasses that was enclosed by a split-cedar fence. Appearing sober and reflective, he accompanied her into a portion of the property that only an hour earlier must have displayed an early autumn sumptuousness. Now burgeoning dark clouds were draining the grove of its colors. All about them, tall and breeze-tossed laburnums showed pendulous and cloud-dimmed sprays of cascading yellow. In uncertain union with the sudden chill of the darkening afternoon, equally tall and decorative hawthorns suggested roiling propensities as stronger breezes disarranged flowers pink and white and red. Tamarisks billowed as well with the tangle and heave of rose-tinted plumes and vulnerable, feathery leaves.

At the entrance to the grove, they paused while watching in

silence the swaying ascensions of the trees. Then, as if in unison, they turned to read the language of each other's expression. Marc's gaze was matter-of-fact and direct. Simone's glance was self-possessed and ambivalent.

She was the first to speak. Her smoky voice made her words sound both intimate and guarded. She knew why he was there.

"What is it that you need to know?"

He was standing very close to her now, as if with clarified eyes he would apprehend the truth that she was concealing. When—after a moment—he spoke, his words wore an undisguised bluntness.

"I want you to help me find the double agent who has infiltrated our group."

For an instant, she continued to meet his gaze. Then, as though it was a natural and unremarkable gesture, she turned away from him to observe the two Criollos in the meadow nearby. When she turned back to face him once more, she answered him with precise and quiet inflections.

"I can't help you," she said. "I haven't met him yet."

A rough energy drove Marc's new words.

"I think that you have," he said. "He sent his henchmen to kill you while you were performing in a nightclub."

In spite of the push of his words, her blue eyes gave no evidence of her uncertainty.

"I don't know who he is," she quietly insisted. "I told you that I have never met him."

"You've met Hans Mueller," Marc said. "You know him well."

At the mention of Hans, she became very still. She used the stillness to retain the self-control with which she answered him.

"Yes, I know him well. I know him too well to call him a traitor. Only a fool would believe that he is a secret Nazi."

Marc challenged her further.

"I don't call you a fool because you believe that he *might* be a Nazi. Isn't that the reason you resumed your relationship with him? You wanted to find the evidence that will prove he is a Nazi."

There was anger in her eyes now. She liked neither his questions, nor the path onto which he was drawing her.

"You're wrong," she said. "I wanted to prove him innocent. I wanted to show Raoul and all the rest of you that Hans is the real thing. Every day, he puts his life on the line. He is loyal and selfless and patriotic."

"He may be all of those things," Marc said, "but not for France or for any of our allies—and not for you. He sent his henchmen to kill you, because he has the heart and mind of a Nazi."

Still she maintained her self-control. But her straight-back posture stiffened, and her eyes revealed a spark of defiance.

"I don't believe that. In these months when we have come to know one another, Hans and I have created a very strong bond. It is, in important ways, even stronger than the bond that I made with Raoul, Benoît, and Lucien Chardonne."

Was her bond with Hans more than the romance she said she had fabricated so that she could discover whether he was a spy? Marc wondered. He intended to find out. But first he would point out the darker probabilities of their situation.

"If Hans is the double agent," he reminded her, "he has already shown us that bonds of friendship mean nothing to him. He had his assassins finish off Lucien Chardonne. They would have killed Raoul and Benoît, too, if I hadn't stopped them."

This time she held her voice taut and clipped inside the anger of her protest.

"Hans would not have sent assassins after Lucien or Raoul or Benoît," she said. "I tell you that he never would."

Abrasive and unyielding, Marc pressed forward.

"What if he did?"

At first, his question drove her back to the ambiguous emphasis of silence. Then, seeking perhaps to dispel his doubt of her or to invoke his empathy, she placed the graceful smoothness of her right hand over the rugged strength of his own.

"You don't know how it was with the five of us in London during this past year."

He did not resist her touch. Nor, after she withdrew her hand, did he refrain from meeting her blue-eyed, troubled glance with his own gaze. In this instant, his neutral regard of her gave no evidence of his skepticism or of the tough-minded appraisal he would make of all the words that she would say to him.

"Tell me about it," he said.

She did not tell him her story right away. Whatever words she would choose to tell him, she kept inside a silence that observed its own idiosyncrasy, contrasted as it was by the occasional rush of the wind and by the whinnying of the Criollos. Instead, she walked with him back to the meadow of swaying grasses where their horses were grazing. When they reached the cedar fence that enclosed the meadow, she turned to face him directly. Her blue eyes still held their mysteries, but her smoky voice now shaped words both intimate and confiding. She wanted him to be on her side, and she wanted him to believe that she was telling him her secrets.

She told her story swiftly, as though the subtexts of its meaning might be discovered within its momentum.

"In London, even while the war was raging, Raoul, Benoît, Lucien, Hans, and I were free spirits. We were discarding the worn-out rules and imprisoning conventions that the Old World had devised. The rules and the conventions we had once lived by, as we were growing into the persons we thought we could be, now seemed like tricks to dissuade us from our natural impulses. They suppressed our creativity. They denied us our freedom. Living outside the rules made the war-torn world a tremendous possibility and made our being in it an ongoing adventure.

"I met Hans Mueller first of all. I was singing at a night club called The Lorelei, where RAF pilots and agents for the Resistance used to come on the weekends, when they were in search of a good time and of young, available women. I'd gone out with a few of them, but I never shared my bed with them. We made the night exciting without that. I gave those fellows pleasure just by being with them. We danced together. We sang together. We drank together. We told each other the stories of our lives. I, of course, told them the story that belonged to Valérie Moreau. We shared confidences. We comforted each other. All of that gave them and me the excitement we needed to keep on going. Ours was an amicable arrangement. There were never any arguments spawned by jealousy or by the need to dominate the partner who feeds one's desires. There were never any pledges of sensual fidelity or long-lasting love. There wasn't any romantic love at all. 'A platonic enterprise,' I used to call it. They gave me brotherly kisses, and I shared the pleasure that came with that. It was a very natural transaction that carried no liabilities and no recriminations.

"Then something happened that changed everything."

Simone paused, her voice tremulous with the implications of what she had decided to tell him.

He, in turn, regarded her silently, always trying to decipher the subtleties of her motives, hidden as they were inside this confession that she was willing herself to make to him.

"You will not like what I am going to tell you," she said. "But we have always tried to be honest with each other. I'm not willing to change the rules to soothe your ego or to avoid another angry scene. Besides, you are bound to find out soon enough."

Summoning whatever energies she needed to explain this new self that she had acquired, she hurried forward to speak the words that, in spite of his anticipation, surprised him.

"I broke the pact that I made with the four men. Unknown to the other three, I fell in love with Hans. I fell in love with him because of the extraordinary man that he is and because he looks so much like Gerhard. I knew for certain that I loved him when we hurried away from the war for a week of skiing in Switzerland. There were times in Lausanne when I even called him Gerhard, so much did he appear to be Gerhard. When we spent two days in Graubünden, as Gerhard and I had once done,

I was certain that he was Gerhard. Whenever I saw him coming toward me from a distant snow-capped hill or in the glow of a moonlit hotel terrace, I saw him not as himself, but as Gerhard. He was a ghost made visible. He was Gerhard come back to life."

Still Marc held himself to tight-lipped stillness. There was a part of him that did not want to hear the words that she was telling him. But the anger that his silence carefully harnessed compelled him to listen. It was a familiar anger that devised stratagems, tactics, and maneuvers to overcome his adversaries and, in this complicated episode now unfolding, to win back Simone's love that once belonged to him alone.

Simone hurried now to tell him more, as if the telling were giving her the sort of pleasure that conspires with bitterness. The telling, he felt, was meant to punish him. She had not forgiven him for what he had done to Gerhard and for what he had made her do to him.

"Being with Hans was different," she said. "I think that I began to fall in love with him from the moment I met him, and I think that he started to fall in love with me at the same time. He is one of the handsomest men I have ever met, and he is very good in bed. But, even though looks and sex mean a lot to me, I fell in love most of all with his gentleness, with the courage and poetry that define his character, and with his razor-sharp mind.

He has a wonderful mind. He knows how everything works. He can explain so clearly the engine of an automobile or of an airplane. Once, he described to me the best way to build a house if it was located near the sea. In his spare time, before the war, he helped one of his friends to build such a house. He also assisted friends in building the engine of a car that was to be used in the Le Mans auto races.

"The amazing thing is that all these interests were ancillary to his study of corporate law. He believes that the world of bankers and other power brokers is a mess. It is a scenario of greed and corruption. He wants to do his part to clean up the mess. He wants to make a difference for the better.

"But he did not want to fall in love with me. He did not want his love to appropriate the freedom of my life. Nor did he want my love to subvert his own freedom. He told me so outright. By falling in love with each other, we were breaking the promise we had made at the beginning of our relationship. We would not permit ourselves to fall in love. There were too many things each of us wanted to do in the world without the other. There were so many roads we planned to travel as individuals. There were so many mountains we needed to climb alone.

"So we decided that we would see one another less often.

"Our separation was a hard thing to live through. As though I wanted to prove that I could go on without him, I immersed myself in my work. But I also made time for my friendship with Raoul, Benoît, and Lucien. They were Hans's friends. Their bond with him kept his presence alive, even though it could not compensate for Hans's not being there with me, in our day-to-day exploits and in the exciting nights when he shared my bed. For a whole month, Hans stayed away from me. Eventually, though, because of his need for me or because of the ingrained realism that told him that we were meant to be together, he did come back to me. We have had a wonderful time together. He grew to trust me and to tell me all the important things that I needed to know about his background. When I came to know all about him, I did not love Hans any less, but I learned to understand him so much more. I know now how much he has suffered and what a brave man he is.

"When the war came, Hans hurried into it, though not in the way that he had planned. At least in the first years, Hans chose to fight for Germany, because no other country would have him. Raoul, Lucien, and Benoît joined the Free French Air Force and at the same time became agents for the Resistance. I joined them in their Resistance work a year ago, when MI5 persuaded me to become Valérie Moreau. That was right after a squad of Vichy assassins killed my aunt and my uncle.

"I imagine that you already know what happened to my aunt and my uncle. For many years, you may remember, they managed a theater in Montparnasse. After the Germans entered Paris, my aunt and my uncle used their theater to awaken the patriotism of their French audience. They hated their government leaders for allowing the Nazis to overtake France without any resistance. Night after night, my aunt and my uncle presented plays that exposed the Nazi regime as a tyranny and France as an all-too-willing victim—a country that had lost touch with its courageous past. My uncle directed the plays, and my aunt designed the sets. Sophocles' *Antigone*, Shakespeare's *Julius Caesar*, and a stage version of Kafka's novel *The Trial* became lacerating critiques of the Nazis, of Hitler, and of the French president's collaborative government.

"My aunt and my uncle knew that the war they were waging with the Nazis would cost them their lives. But they went on fighting it, anyway. That final night, they were aware of what was about to happen, and they accepted it as their fate. But they played out the last scene of their lives on their own terms.

"The Nazis had already wrecked the theater, and now they were hurrying to my aunt and uncle's brownstone to beat them savagely and to arrest them. After that, they would haul them away to hours and even days of brutal interrogations and to a death camp. Those were the orders that the six storm troopers were carrying forward with their usual sadistic fury. They must have been very surprised when, after breaking down the front door and rushing up the main staircase, they saw my uncle and my aunt at the top of the stairs, aiming Sten Mk II sub-automatic machine guns at them. My grim-faced uncle and aunt and the machine guns must have been the last images they understood before the bullets tore into their foreheads and faces and chests.

"As soon as they killed the soldiers who had come for them, my aunt and my uncle ran to the second-story windows and threw grenades upon the two military cars that were waiting to carry them away. The cars exploded, and the Vichy spy and his two bodyguards who were standing by the car were killed instantly. My uncle and aunt threw more grenades and watched two other military patrol cars blow up. They must have seen the bodies of the occupants torn apart, their dismembered corpses scattered along the street that was heaving up its debris.

"In what was probably the next instant, a German armored truck lumbered through the broken road, aimed its 47mm gun at my parents' house, and fired repeatedly. The smooth stone of the house crumbled and fell in a heap straight downward. Flames shot up from the ruined interior and ignited smaller explosions, like ricocheting bombs. At the same time, other flames spewed and spurted out of the bodies of my aunt and my uncle as their flesh and bones burned away.

"An old woman, a retired journalist who had been a friend of my uncle and aunt for many years, saw all of it from a window in her home across the street. Even four months later, when by chance I met her in Lausanne, she did not want to tell me what she had seen. Only at the end of our meeting, after I prodded her with a show of emotion and after I made the promise that I would avenge my aunt and my uncle, did she tell me what had happened. 'Take special care,' she warned me. 'Remember that you are fighting monsters.'

"After they killed my uncle and my aunt, the Nazis came searching for me. I've been on the run ever since—but not as some weakling who is willing to sell her principles for a bit of safety and not as some fantasist who thinks the war will go away if she waits long enough. Right after the Nazis killed my aunt and my uncle, I asked for the most dangerous assignments that the Resistance could give me. As an agent who knows how to use a wireless radio, I've been the catalyst more than a few times in the defeat of the Nazis in aerial combat and on the battlefield.

"Through all these wretched months of war in the year since you and I separated, I've worked with many brave men and women. Among the men, Raoul, Benoît, and Hans take the greatest risks and never count the cost to themselves. They know how to make even the most intricate plan workable. They know how to win every battle. Lucien Chardonne was just like them. In different ways, the war has taught me so much about them. Benoît and I have worked together on many dangerous assignments. So have Raoul and I. We have seen a great deal of each other, even now when a new assignment has brought me back to Hans.

"At first, I wanted no part of the assignment. Our Resistance team asked me to put Hans to the test. Basically, they are on his side. They are well aware of all the important things that he has done for the Allies. But they want me to find out whether Hans is on the level. They want to make certain that he has not become a Nazi again. 'Find out how he lives and who his friends are,' they told me. I would have regarded the assignment as less difficult if I had not loved Hans so much. Imagining that he was a mysterious stranger helped me maintain a rigorous detachment. I judged him not by what I already knew about him. I discovered his past as if it were new to me, and I experienced first-hand the current incidents of his life that he shaped or that shaped him.

"I have been telling you all of these things, I suppose, to convince you that I am a reliable witness. I've been with Hans long enough to know that he is not a traitor."

With these words, Simone, still coiling her identity within the mystery that was Valérie Moreau, retreated to the cool stillness that gave to her presence an indeterminate quality, as if there were hidden behind her lovely exterior an alternate self that could not be easily defined. The wind, restless and furtive, went on stirring; the trees in the grove—with threatening inclinations—billowed; and, inside graceful aptitudes, the ornamental grasses wavered. The hardy Criollos still grazed, and the lowering sky appeared to watch everything.

With his keen-sighted scanning glance, Marc saw all of these images as if they were caught in a kaleidoscope or in a kinetic montage. Simone influenced their meaning for him and dominated the scene with the subtle emphases of her poise and the hint of an unease that held her to its arbitrary mandates. He continued to study her carefully. Her enigmatic face, with its blonde sensuality that today traded the intricacy of its powers for a carefully contrived wholesomeness, met his gaze directly. Maybe she really believed everything that she had just told him. Maybe she had allowed her nostalgia to dispel too quickly whatever doubts about Hans might have flared their warnings to her. Maybe her love for Hans compelled her to revise or even cancel all other allegiances.

If she were concealing a darker truth about Hans, he needed to uncover it. He began questioning her again. At the start, his husky voice was brisk with inquiry both firm and probing.

"You say that you've continued to love Hans. Does he still love you as much? Or are his feelings a wily sort of pretense?"

She answered him obliquely.

"What do we ever really know about another person's feelings? Hans tells me very often that he loves me. The words he says to me make his love seem very real."

Marc pressed forward.

"Do you believe him?"

Her reply was cautious, yet not without confidence.

"Yes."

There was a harder edge to his next question.

"Is he still good in bed?"

She tried to turn from him before she gave him her answer. But his rugged hands were grasping her arms now and keeping her from turning away. At his rough handling of her, she searched his face with a mixture of resentment and apprehension. She did not like his question, but she chose to answer him with decorous understatement.

"He's very good, I suppose."

Furious and caustic, Marc snarled out another accusation. At the same time, he shook her until, for a few moments, her body no longer resisted his pinioning hold of her.

"You enjoy being in bed with him."

He paused, only to see that her eyes were showing a new contempt for him. She was going to tough out the jagged uncertainty of this scene.

"Of course, I do. But I'm still doing the job I was sent to do."

More furious now because she was once more resisting him, he slapped her face so hard that the impact sent her reeling. Her body fell back into the fence, against which she leaned momentarily until—with his rough handling—he pulled her forward. Now he slapped her again and again. His angry voice rasped out his own contempt of her.

"In spite of everything that points to his being a spy for the Nazis, you let yourself fall in love with him."

Still she resisted him, throwing away his accusation with the tattered edges of her voice, which was momentarily lost to her because of his hard slapping of her face.

"No."

She tried lifting her right arm and hand so that she could punch or slap him. But, with his strong left hand, he held down her arm, and with his right hand he began slapping her again. His face a mask of brooding rage, he snarled once more his bitter accusation of her.

"You love him, even though he's a Nazi."

Pinioned and mauled, yet always struggling to free herself from his hold upon her, she began screaming her protest.

"He is not a Nazi."

He slapped her again.

"You love having a Nazi's cock inside you."

Once more she screamed her protest.

"He is not a Nazi."

His beating of her had tossed away her rider's hat and had loosened her blonde hair from its neatly arranged coil. Her hair, caressed by the wind, was flowing about her head and face. Red bruises were bringing an unnatural blush to her otherwise flawless skin. Even with her show of toughness, she looked vulnerable and lost.

"You love when he fucks you."

Her face was bitter now with her hatred of him.

"Yes."

He slapped her again.

"You're working with him in secret. You've given him information about military train schedules and aerial combat missions."

This time the slap left her breathless for more than an instant. She began coughing and gagging. Her mouth opened wide and tried to draw air inside her. When she recovered, vaguely tremulous and badly shaken, she defended herself with a quiet, level voice.

"I would never do that. Everything about my life should tell you that I would never betray our people."

He felt no pity for her. He slapped her again.

"You've led him to the towns where the Resistance is working effectively. You've given him the names of the leaders there and have virtually signed their death warrants."

Again she reeled from his slap, which this time was more like a punch.

"No. No. No. I never have and never would help the Nazis. They killed my aunt and my uncle. They killed Lucien and so many other friends."

"You would betray any of us, if Hans asked you to do it."

She began to cry softly. Her beautiful face was disarranged now, twisted into a painful grimace.

"He never would ask. He's honest and brave and good."

This time Marc did not slap her. With his rough hands, he drew her to himself so that he could stare into her eyes and so that she would see very clearly his antipathy and his distrust.

"Look! Look at him without lying to yourself, you lovesick bitch. He sent his squad of killers to shoot you down in the night club where you were singing."

He threw her against the fence now and stood with rancorous watchfulness apart from her.

She used the moment to summon a new energy and a stitched-together calm. She invoked the calm (he imagined) to make her words sound reasonable and even persuasive.

"Hans had no part in that. You are the one who needs to

look at him honestly. You've got the whole thing wrong. You are looking at a patriot and a hero and seeing a traitor. You *want* him to be a traitor, so that you can prove how right you are."

Her calm words did not persuade Marc. He thought that they were spawned from her clouded judgment of Hans. In his own way, with blunt and callous words, he told her so.

"Hans's assassins aren't finished with you yet—not until they do the job right. They've placed you high on their list of people to kill."

She answered him quickly. Her voice was still calm, yet it could not hide completely its strong emotional textures or the turmoil within herself that she was working hard to suppress.

"I know Hans far better than you do. I believe in him."

"That may be your undoing," he said.

He looked hard upon her now. He was not sorry that he had roughed her up. He only regretted that he had not brought her back to a realistic sense of things. She was too eager to believe in Hans. He had to admit, though reluctantly, that she could be right about him. But she needed more proof. Maybe the only plausible evidence in Hans's favor would be their finding that the double agent was somebody else. Maybe the easiest solution to this dilemma would be to kill Hans quickly. But that would not be the best solution. Hans had won many battles for the Resistance. He appeared to be an intrepid leader in the fight against the Nazis. To kill him without absolute proof that he was a traitor would compromise the solidarity of their membership. All the other agents would believe that they were no longer safe from unverified accusations or from wrong-headed suspicion.

These were his thoughts as he turned away from Simone. He hurried into the meadow now and, with athletic ease, mounted the Sorraia that had earned his respect and his admiration. As he rode out of the meadow, intent upon cantering onward to the workman's cottage he had made his temporary home, he saw Simone as a fleet image falling away from his cursory glance. She was standing by the fence, wary and forlorn. Yet her lithe figure had regained its straight-back posture, and her blonde hair—though wind-blown and disarranged—still conferred upon her presence an enigmatic radiance. The brightness gave her the appearance of a wraith or an apparition. His eyes saw her brightness as false—a will-o'-the-wisp meant to conceal the confusion within herself. The brightness would not alter the course of the storm hurrying toward them. Nor would it keep their enemies from overtaking these vineyards in some unexpected and furious hour.

Chapter Four

Combat

His thought was a prophecy of the turmoil that unleashed itself upon all of them two days later. In the dawn of that Tuesday morning, when he returned from a night's journey into the mountains, he expected to find the familiar calm that had always received him as he made his way into the Grenier farmlands. Hours earlier, under the cover of night, he had delivered a truck-load of weapons to the maquisards that British airmen had dropped from a Lockheed Hudson into the Greniers' southwest meadow on the previous evening. Returning, he saw from his perch at the top of a hill overlooking the north field that French Nazi henchmen had overtaken the place.

His keen eyes told him that fifteen officers of the Milice française—a paramilitary force collaborating with the Nazis— were at that moment rushing upon the main house and the various cottages. Four of them were storming the vineyards, orchards and lavender fields. Two were entering the red brick building that housed the cool, vaulted cellars where the Greniers made their wine. Another three were hurrying toward the granary that concealed Raoul and Benoît. They had come in four Citroën U23s. These two-ton trucks were sturdy enough to travel across the most rugged terrain and large enough to carry Milice troops as well as captive men, women, and children suspected of working for the Resistance.

His first thoughts were of Simone and of the danger that was surrounding her. He was going to do everything that he could to rescue her, if she needed his help. But, in this instant when danger was hastening toward the good farm people who were unarmed and had no way of withstanding the militant invasion that was rising against them, he was counting on Simone's wiliness to save herself. Simone was a proven soldier. She was a formidable agent. Disguised as Valérie Moreau, she was smart enough to expect that the Nazis would be sending their Vichy henchmen to kill her and to kill the farm people who had provided her refuge. Unlike most of these good farm people, she knew how to fight the Nazis and their henchmen. She knew how to fire a Sten Mark II submachine gun. She was more than proficient at throwing a grenade so that it would hit the necessary target. Silently approaching her enemy from behind, she could—without hesitation or the compunction that stymies a less confident agent or soldier—plunge a Fairbairn-Sykes knife into her enemy's back. While pinning back his arms with a viselike grip, she could use the same knife to gouge his throat or to slice across it with an even stroke, so that, in the seconds before he gagged and the raw sound of gurgling fell suddenly away from him while blood spurted out of his mouth and gushed from his wound, the neatest cut across his throat gave no other evidence that he had been instantly killed.

Yes, he knew Simone well. He trusted her ability to disappear from her enemies until she chose the right moment to attack them. Though the danger that had come upon her left him with a tightened unease, he willed himself to do the things that needed to be done right here and now. The farm people needed his help. In this very moment, his eyes showed him their peril. Moments after he sighted the three soldiers riding toward the granary, he saw two other persons riding in the same direction. They were not the troops of the Milice. Nor were they riding in a two-ton truck. One of them was Xavier, the grizzled veteran of the First World War and, for years now, a loyal farmhand and carpenter in the service of the Greniers. He was mounted on a sturdy, chestnut-brown Lusitano. Only minutes before, he must have left his work in the vineyards to ride alongside his wife—good-hearted and petite Honorée, who was one of the housekeepers overseeing the maintenance of the main house and of the cottages. In a wagon drawn by a bay-colored Dartmoor pony, she was bringing Raoul and Benoît their breakfast, which was concealed beneath the upper lid of a basket of apples that appeared to have been gathered in that early hour from the branches of an autumn tree. This delivery of breakfast was one of their first assignments of the day—one that they especially enjoyed, because it gave them an opportunity to share conversations with the two brave men who were fighting their Nazi enemies in the sky and on land.

He saw at once that neither Xavier nor Honorée was aware that the Milice were overtaking the Greniers' farmlands. Their bringing food into the granary would alert the Nazi collaborators that fugitives they were pursuing were being hidden somewhere inside the building.

His instincts drew him to the granary, which stood a quarter of a mile from the hill upon which, at the wheel of his farm truck, he had quickly scanned the scene below him. He would not arrive there before the Milice did. But he was going to try, nonetheless, to save Benoît and Raoul, as well as Xavier and Honorée. Shifting into low gear, he raced down the green-gold hill and over the gravel road that brought him to the apple orchard that was flourishing a hundred feet away from the granary. Swift yet cautious, he concealed his truck near the scarlet foliage that had grown lush and protuberant outside the orchard. Then, armed with a Sten Mk II sub-automatic machine gun, a Beretta pistol, and a V8 stiletto, he ran toward the granary.

En route, he heard the report of a revolver. Almost simultaneously, he heard the report once again.

He did not enter the granary right away. Instead, crouched at the edge of the grove of apple trees, all the while concealed by the thick foliage and by the dark shadows of the interior, he studied the imagery before him. A Milice lieutenant, as callow as he was brawny and grim-faced, was standing as a sentry by the closed door of the building. He was holding a MAS-38 submachine gun in his right hand and staring in his direction, though apparently not seeing him. The Citroën U23 was parked a few feet from the entrance to the granary. A hundred feet to the left of it, tied to a hitching rail at the edge of the orchard, stood Xavier's Lusitano. Tied to the same rail was the Dartmoor that was still harnessed to the wagon which had brought Honorée to this visit with Raoul and Benoît.

He might have used the wagon for cover, until with his Sten gun he could get a proper bead on the lieutenant. That was his first thought as he began moving out of the orchard while using a militant, crouching position.

But chance worked in his favor, so that he could take action against his enemy more swiftly than he had anticipated. A barrage of gunfire exploding from the granary caught the sentry's attention. Made uneasy by the repeated shots, he opened the door to the building while raising his revolver. He was about to step inside and assist his cohorts, if they needed him. At that precise moment, however, Marc called out to him while aiming his Sten gun at his head. He did not want to shoot him in the back, nor did he care to take him prisoner.

"Drop your gun," he commanded.

The lieutenant spun around and was already firing his MAS-38 when a bullet from Marc's Sten gun tore into his forehead. The bullet blew out the back of his head, as blood and flesh and tissue sprayed across the whiteness of the open door of the granary. For an instant, the body of the lieutenant buckled and wavered, and then it dropped straight down upon the turf-laden ground.

In the instant afterward, Marc took cover at the side of the open door. He held his body taut against the red brick wall of the granary. With a stealthy proficiency that made his every move both cautious and defensive, he kept his Sten gun cocked and his trigger finger ready to shoot. But no French Nazi rushed out of the building firing a MAB Model D pistol or a MAS-38 submachine gun. Nor did Xavier and Honorée appear, their hands raised in defeat and a Milice lieutenant pushing them forward with the threat of the gun or pistol he was aiming at their backs. Instead, an eerie stillness overtook the place, as though it had taken captive whoever still lived within its vast agrarian spaces.

Not only silence had entered the granary. Death had come there, too. Of that, he was certain.

As swift as he was accurate, he rushed into the granary. The secret door in the wall stood ajar. There, at the foot of the stairs that led to the loft where Raoul and Benoît had been recovering from their wounds, he saw the bodies of Honorée and Xavier. He imagined that the Milice had noticed the two of them carrying baskets of supplies into the granary. When they did not return to their horse-drawn wagon in a timely manner, the Milice must have entered the building in search of them. For a moment or two, the lieutenants or sergeants or whoever was there would have been caught surprised to discover that the middle-aged couple had disappeared. Yet surprise would have only briefly touched them. The French Nazis would have quickly understood that the two persons who had entered the building were still there, though not anywhere within the flowing surround of the main floor. They might have even heard the whispering voices that from some secret room or alcove carried traces of momentary contentment here.

In the midst of the bins of golden grain, the equally deep bins filled with oranges, pears, and apples, and the bales of wheat and rye, the Milice must have waited. They would have waited, militant and cautious, until Honorée and Xavier opened the door in the wall after they had completed their visit with Raoul and Benoît. Perhaps, upon seeing the Milice standing there with raised pistols or machine guns, Honorée first cried out in astonishment. Possibly, Xavier cried out, too. But neither of them would have cried out in fear. They would have summoned their cries of anger and dismay to warn the wounded men hiding in the loft that their enemies were here in the building.

It was this cry of warning, Marc imagined, that ignited the fury of the Milice. They opened fire upon Honorée and Xavier, whose bodies lay riddled with bullets. Blood spilled out of their foreheads, their eyes and mouths, and their chests. It stained their skin, which was still bronze from their work beneath the summer sun. It bleached their salt-and-pepper hair. It ran in rivulets out of their prostrate bodies along the otherwise spotless path of the concrete floor. But only for a moment did he allow his furious eyes to scan their crumpled bodies. Instead, while aiming his Sten gun at the space ahead of him, he ran up the stairway that would bring him to the loft.

Halfway to the top, he paused. There, just beyond the entrance to the hidden room, he saw the bodies of two young Milice lieutenants sprawled across the enshadowed floor. As he hurried forward, he saw close up their long ruined bodies. Machine-gun fire, targeting his forehead, had blown out the back of the head of the lieutenant who had fallen a few feet inside the room. His hand still grasped his MAS-38. Bullets from a revolver, fired rapidly, had torn into the heart of the other lieutenant, who lay—used up and discarded—deeper inside the room. His MAB Model D pistol had fallen a few inches away from his sun-bronzed, rugged hand.

Right away, Marc understood that Raoul's Bren gun had killed the first lieutenant and that Benoît's Colt revolver had killed the other one.

In the next instant, he wondered whether Raoul and Benoît had also been killed. He wondered, as well, whether a Milice officer, hidden inside the loft, was waiting to shoot him down as he entered the room. Accepting the risk that an enemy might answer him with gunfire, he called out to his two friends.

"Benoît! Raoul! It's Marc. Answer me!"

At first, no one answered him. He was aware only of the silence that enclosed him inside its own mysteries. So he called to his friends once again.

"Raoul! Benoît! I'm here to help you."

Now Raoul answered him. His voice was weak and pain-racked.

"It's all right. Come inside."

He did not enter the room immediately. Instead, he called out other words to Raoul.

"I'll be there in a minute," he said.

He ran down the stairs and closed the door in the wall. If any other Milice officer entered the granary, they would see the bodies of Xavier, Honorée, and the lieutenant. But it was unlikely that they would discover the door in the wall. By closing this door, he was concealing his friends and himself from the enemy. Only after taking this precaution did he hurry up the stairs and enter the hidden room.

Raoul and Benoît were lying on their pallet beds. Propped against their pillows, they were aiming their guns at the entrance to the room. Even now, after they had heard his voice calling out to them, they were uncertain whether he or one of their enemies would appear. In their shoot-out with the Milice, each of them had received new, life-threatening wounds. Bullets fired from the MAB Model D pistol had grazed Raoul's right temple and his spleen. Benoît had sustained equally painful wounds, when bullets from the MAS-38 ripped through his right lung and his left leg.

Grim-faced and stoic, both of them were resisting the pain that was overtaking their rugged bodies. They had toughed their way through the aftermath of other wounds. They were prepared to do so now. The pallor that had insinuated itself upon their ruddy complexions suggested the rigorous battle they were fighting. Yet, as they studied him carefully while he waited for them to tell him how it was with them, there was in their expressions neither complaint nor remorse. Their hardened view of things resisted self-pity and regret. Nor did they hold in high regard the praise that might come to them because a few minutes ago they had killed two of the Milice. They had done the thing that needed to be done. Once again, they had killed their enemies. They had met them as savages. In days to come, if they survived the war, there would be those men and women who would call them heroes. But "hero" was a word they resisted as much as they disdained self-pity and self-lying. War had made them savages. They had become beasts prowling their battlefields with sub-machine guns and revolvers, grenades and daggers, and bomber aircraft.

Marc knew Raoul and Benoît as well as any man can know another. He knew how they thought. About their raw courage and their trenchant perception of the world, at least, he knew more than a little.

He was not surprised that they did not ask about Xavier and Honorée. They would have heard the shouts of the humble farm couple that saved them. They would have heard the blasts from the French Nazis' sub-machine gun and from the revolver that killed them. There would be no words at this time that they cared to say. Xavier and Honorée had met the fate that was meant for them. Their cries of warning had increased the possibility that Benoît and Raoul could overcome the enemies rushing up the stairs to kill them. Maybe the word "hero" could legitimately apply to each of them. They had carried no weapons, yet they had fought an unflinching battle. They had died without becoming beasts.

The words Raoul and Benoît summoned referred to those valued persons who might still be alive and were in danger.

"Help Valérie and the Greniers, if you can," Raoul said.

His words were a tightened whisper. Marc imagined that the bullet that had grazed his temple left him initially stunned and afterward depleted of his energy. For the first minutes after he had been shot, he must have wavered in and out of consciousness.

Now alert and vigilant once more, Raoul urged him to hurry forward to the persons who would need him. This time he willed himself to speak above a whisper. But his stoic determination could not keep back the frown of pain that crossed his brow.

"They will need your help," he said. "You must go to them quickly."

Marc sought to ease his friend's realistic apprehension. He knew the odds were against all of them. Chance might arrange her random powers so that the Milice would capture them. They would interrogate and torture and then kill them. But, despite the odds, Chance might favor him and his cohorts. He preferred to believe that Chance would favor him and his friends. Yet neither he nor they would rely upon her perverse workings. They would rely upon themselves and upon their well-trained aptitudes for combat.

"Don't worry about Valérie and the Greniers," he said. "They know how to take care of themselves."

His words did not alter the frown that revealed Raoul's pain. Nor did they ease his apprehension. Benoît also noticed his friend's dismay. So he brought forward his own words of petition, which hovered about a brusque and militant suggestion.

"Go to them," Benoît told him, as if with his raspy inflections he were deliberately echoing Raoul's remark. "Go to the others and help them."

Marc respected the militant brusqueness. Had he been the one wounded, he would have spoken in the same manner.

"I'll do my best," he promised.

Then, because here and now he wanted to be of some use to them, he pushed himself into a series of tasks. Taking blankets from a chest of drawers that stood opposite the pallet beds, he covered both men. It was important that they stay warm until a physician could attend them. He also applied to Raoul's wounded head a cool compress, which he had made out of a large face-cloth that he soaked in spring water from one of the many bottles that the Greniers and their staff had left with the two men. With medical gauze that he had found in the bathroom, he made a tourniquet to stem the bleeding of Benoît's leg. Aware of the pain that was afflicting his friends and wanting to allay it, if he could, he considered injecting each of them with a dose of morphine. Both a hypodermic syringe and the morphine were stored in a medical kit inside the bathroom. But the morphine would make them drowsy and place them at greater risk. They would not be able to fire their guns accurately, should other Milice officers discover their hiding place. Instead, he brought out one of the flasks of brandy that he had left with them most recently. With careful skill, he held the heads of both men while they sipped the liquor that would work to revive them.

All of these things he did while he assured them that he would kill as many French Nazis as he could. Never in these seven minutes did he reveal the tension that was churning inside him or the doubts that were assailing him. That the Milice might kill him as he attempted to rescue the Greniers and Simone did not worry him. That he might fail to achieve his mission did rouse his concern. The thought also stirred his hatred of his enemies and his determination to kill them before they had a chance to kill him.

Stepping around the bodies of the French Nazis, he hurried down the stairs and closed the door in the wall behind him. With soldierly precision and with an energy renewed by the thought of what he had to do, he moved across the main floor, scanning once more in the distance the deep bins of apples, pears and oranges; the huge bins of golden grain; and the tightly-bound bales of wheat and rye. Much nearer than those, he passed by the bodies of Xavier and Honorée and, outside the door, the body of the fallen Milice lieutenant. Always, he held his Sten gun before him. Always, he summoned the reconnoitering perceptions that would enable him to sight and quickly shoot a concealed enemy. If his combat skills served him well, no other enemies would enter the granary—at least, not while Raoul and Benoît were hiding there.

Outside the granary, he decided to ride to the main house on the Lusitano, rather than in the farm truck. The motor of the truck would alert the Milice to his presence far more quickly than would the hooves of a fast-moving horse. He unhitched the Lusitano from the rail and smoothly mounted it. With tough-minded resolve, he cantered across a wide and sequestered trail that no stranger to these farmlands could easily discover. This southerly trail allowed him to make his way quickly toward the main house, where the Greniers and their house staff would ordinarily be preparing breakfast. Simone, in her role as

Valérie, might be there, too, because she wanted in various ways to be of use to her hosts. Just as likely, she might be enclosed within the cottage that had become her temporary home. There, while working at her transceiver wireless radio, she would be sending a message to London or intercepting the Nazis' military communication.

On more favorable days, he would have enjoyed riding the Lusitano. He always liked bringing his horse into the gallop. He would have found an immense pleasure in the leap and rush of their collaboration. Even on this precarious morning, he admired the agility of the Lusitano, now at full stretch with body and neck lengthening and each leg fully extended as he powered across the winding trail. Behind this superb horse's neck, he tucked his upper torso precisely and fused the outline of their forms. He lifted himself out of his saddle, so that he could drop his weight down into his heel and push it further back, allowing his upper body to tuck in behind the neck of the horse. As he went galloping through the trail, he rode with shorter stirrups to make it easier to lift his weight out of the saddle. He kept his lower legs on the girth and kept his arms extended, as his horse stretched his neck with each stride.

Rows of strawberry trees flanking the path rushed past him now. Flashing past him, too, in the faraway distance on each side of the path, was a familiar montage of agrarian imagery:

bronzed sienna meadows, golden yellow haystacks, and a teal-blue lake; tidy lavender fields billowing and swaying as if floating; chrome-green hills and wind-tossed woods; and a tractor meandering westward near vermilion-red and yellow-gold wild flowers. The brawny youth driving it was unaware of the danger that was rising all around him.

As he galloped out of the rider's trail, Marc saw the danger in a new way. There, within the flourishing vineyards two hundred yards from him, two Milice lieutenants (tall and big-boned and sadistic) were pointing MAS-38 sub-machine guns at Alphonse and Pierre, as well as at their teenage daughters. With methodical timing, they pushed the long barrels of their guns into the foreheads of the men and the girls as they interrogated each of them. Even from that distance, he could hear their guttural threats and their rapid-fire questions. Neither the men nor the girls were providing the lieutenants with the incriminating answers they wanted to hear. Their furious grimaces suggested that at any moment they might take a few steps back and, in scanning movements, shoot all of them.

Only at the last moment, when it was too late, did the lieutenants hear him galloping onto the path of the vineyard, where they were standing with their prisoners. Only then did they see him, a poised and aggressive muscularity riding a Lusitano and raising his Sten Mk II submachine gun to fire at them. He kept riding as he fired at them. The bullets shattered their heads and their faces and tore into their chests. The thud of the 9mm bullets lifted their bodies and held them, caught and suspended by the impact, until he stopped firing his gun. Then their bodies folded into themselves and fell straight down. Blood spewed out of their heads and faces and chests and quickened into red pools.

He kept riding onward, leaving behind him the dead lieutenants and the startled farm workers whom he had saved.

Because, with firm control and a nudge of his right leg, he was always urging him to go forward, his horse had no inclination to stand up on its hind legs out of fear or to bolt because of the threatening imagery that he was already racing past. Compatible and effective with his Lusitano, he galloped faster and faster toward the main house. The sky was still on fire with early morning's ascension—a melding of blue and gold and crimson emphases. A rougher wind was scattering layers of cumulus and cirrus into sun-blanched hills and waves. Navigating in and out of these clouds was a squadron of flamingos. The pink flame of their wings was a flush or flare upon the floating sky.

He sped past barns and paddocks and stables, past a sea of ornamental grasses and a forest of oak and elm trees. He sped past fields of wheat, rye, and lavender and past the southwest vineyards. He sped away from an imagery of three youths and a fatherly man harvesting corn in one of the smaller southerly fields. He was hastening into the home field when in the distance, a hundred-fifty yards to his left, he saw Régis and Yannick shooting and being shot by two of the French Nazis. His newly acquired farm friends were wielding a MAS-36 rifle and a Sten gun. The Nazis were firing MAS-38s.

The four men were waging their battle outside the red brick building which housed the cool, vaulted cellars that were so important for making an excellent wine. For several days now, Yannick and Régis had spent long hours cleaning the intricate machinery which pressed the grapes into a promising liquid that would be allowed to ferment within giant casks and, later within vats, before being bottled. He imagined that, as the Milice officers drove up to the building in their Citroën U23, Yannick and Régis must have rushed out upon them, firing their weapons. The French Nazis, who had come there to interrogate and then kill these two farm laborers that they thought were unarmed, had just emerged from their truck, which they had parked by the side of the building. As overconfident as they were brutal, they had already cocked their MAS 38s and were hurrying into the building. Yannick and Régis met them with a fusillade of bullets.

Speeding by on his Lusitano, he saw—from that distance of a

hundred-fifty yards ahead and to the left side of him—the blood exploding from the chests and faces of the Nazis as they were thrown back and then fell heavily down upon the turf-laden ground. He also saw Régis and Yannick thrown against the stainless steel door to the brick building. Still holding their weapons before them, they remained standing there for an instant before they stumbled back into the place where they had been working. Although they were wounded, they were prepared to defend themselves against any other enemy who might storm the building.

All these images he saw as swift flares upon his perceptions. But he did not stop for any of them. Instead, he continued to gallop toward the main house.

Now he approached the paddock that stood three hundred yards behind the house. He pushed his lower leg forward while squeezing both legs against his horse's sides. He braced himself against the stirrup and shortened up his reins all the while putting into the neck of his horse the hand that held one of the reins tight. He used his other hand to keep a strong hold on the second rein, as the horse started to listen and to slow down. Only after he entered the paddock and brought his horse to a complete stop did he dismount. Then, leaving the Lusitano behind him to join the company of six other stallions, he hurried out of the paddock and stepped onto the undulating path that would bring him into the rear entrance of the Greniers' house.

The path first brought him through a meadow of silver-feathery miscanthus grass, its flourishing height and wind-blown density camouflaging his presence. He had assumed a crouching posture and, with a firm grip on his Sten gun, was running with militant agility through the seven-foot grass. When he reached the edge of the meadow, he peered through the long wavering leaves of the grass and observed the tile-roofed farmhouse and the two expansive courtyards surrounding it. An eerie stillness hovered over the place. No one was in sight.

Now, seeing his chance, he leaped out of the grass that had concealed his passage and ran toward the house. No sooner had he stepped onto the wrap-around patio, than he spotted his next adversary. He was a brawny Milice captain who was about five foot ten inches and may have been in his early forties. Methodical and sinister as he carried a MAS-38 on his right shoulder, he was patrolling every inch of the patio. Every so often, he would look away from his post and out toward the panoramic imagery of meadows and fields, vineyards and orchards, and the workmen's cottages. He was searching for any farm hand that might have eluded the brutal intrusion of his fellow French Nazis.

When he came around the southwest corner of the patio, the

Milice captain saw him holding himself taut against the sandstone wall by an open window. But he saw him too late. He had no time even to swing his machine gun off his shoulder and, with sprung-coil accuracy, aim and fire at him. Marc shot him quickly and paused only long enough to notice that the bullets had torn off the top of his head and blasted through his startled mouth. Then he climbed through the open window and made his way into the house.

Swift yet furtive, he hurried through a gallery of well-appointed rooms that included the Greniers' bedroom, the dining room and the kitchen, and the living room.

No French Nazi confronted him in any of these rooms. Nor did he see the Greniers or Simone in her disguise as Valérie.

But when he ran, fleet-footed and stealthy, into the parlor, he heard an angry voice spewing its threats from a place outdoors. Right after that, he heard a cry of protest rising from another voice and the flattened thud of a rifle against a body that was being beaten.

He approached the window of the parlor and quickly assumed a crouching, militant posture. The wide window was slightly ajar, and the pleated drapes were pushed to the sides so that the bracing autumn air could enter the spacious room. He placed the barrel of his Sten gun at the rim of the open window and carefully surveyed the scene. Two hundred feet ahead of him, a Milice captain was interrogating Xavier and Honorée's son, Quentin. He was also questioning Quentin's girlfriend, Denise Perrault. Standing ten feet behind them, with two Milice lieutenants hovering at their sides, were four equally young farm laborers whom the Greniers had recently hired to help with the autumn harvesting. Like Quentin and his girlfriend, the four of them were members of the Resistance who used their farm work as a camouflage for their activities of laying mine fields on railroad tracks that were transporting Nazi enemies to their next battle stations and on bridges over which the Nazis and their heavy artillery tanks would be traversing.

Next to them, dressed as field workers and standing arm-in-arm, were Noah Hoffmann, the neuro-surgeon who was in hiding because he was a Jew; his fragile, raven-haired wife, Esther; and their three children—two steel-hearted, good-looking sons who were ten and eleven and tall for their age and a quick-witted daughter who was twelve and already a lovely girl with dark curly hair and an alabaster complexion.

The Greniers had been hiding this family in one of the two secret apartments within the first and second floors of their large home. During those days when the Greniers' surveillance of their land discovered no oncoming platoon of Milice, Dr. Hoffmann and his family often worked in the orchards and in the vineyards. They understood the risks they were taking. But, rather than confine themselves to their apartment, as comfortable as it was, they chose to be outdoors, in the warmth of the sun. They wanted to lend a reality to their impersonating farm people, and they wanted to help the Greniers, who had taken them in as though they were valued relations.

The captain had not yet interrogated the farm laborers or Noah and his family. The danger for them, in spite of their callused hands and the deep tan of their skin, was that the captain or the two lieutenants might perceive that their identity cards were not genuine.

It was in this instant, right after he had taken note of the men, women, and children who were being treated as the prisoners of the French Nazi officers, that Marc recognized the captain as Léon Varot. He had crossed his path once before, during a February night seven months earlier when he, Raoul, and Benoît had lobbed grenades at 44 rue Peletier, the Paris headquarters of the Milice. There, he and his friends had then machine-gunned the nine men who were running out of the first floor of the exploding house. The leader of these men was Varot, whom he remembered from a photo in the files that the Resistance had been building against him—one of the most notorious of the French Nazis. Varot had fallen as if he were dead. Blood spilled out of the left side of his head and out of his shoulders and his chest. That night, Raoul and Benoît and he had hastened away from the scene in a hearse that belonged to the owner of a funeral parlor. They were wearing the somber clothes of morticians and, thanks to the owner who was on their side, carrying identity cards that made them plausible.

Driving the hearse swiftly past the exploding house and the suddenly deserted street, he thought that he and his friends had killed all nine men. But, he learned much later, the captain had not died.

A tall, gaunt man in his mid-thirties, Varot was using these war years to hone his sadist's appetite for apprehending and then torturing, maiming and murdering Jews who had been in hiding; Allied pilots whom the Nazis had shot down; and agents of the Resistance who for many months had been eluding him and his brutal henchmen. A wide beret concealed most of his jet-black hair. A blue uniform coat and matching trousers, a brown shirt, and brown leather boots gave to his rangy physicality a militant bearing. His brown, glacial eyes noticed even the smallest detail in a crowded street or inside a bombed-out building or in the face of an apprehensive prisoner. His aquiline nose and the hint of a sneer reinforced his proprietary manner.

At this moment, Captain Varot was firing out a command at Quentin. As he spoke, he was lashing Quentin's face and his hands with a rider's whip.

"Tell me that Valérie Moreau is here," he shouted. "Tell me that first of all."

Quentin's face and hands were streaked with blood. Already, the Captain had inflicted several lashes upon them.

As the whip cut through his skin once again, Quentin winced and, nearly losing his balance, stepped backward. He looked directly into the cold, brown eyes of the Captain and carefully modulated the contempt that he felt for this enemy. Then, with brusque and matter-of-fact energy, he threw out the same words that he had spoken three times before, whenever the Captain had paused in the lashing of his face and hands.

"I do not know any Valérie Moreau," he insisted. "Wherever she may be, she is not here."

Captain Varot observed him with impatient hatred. Now, with an even harsher lash of his whip, he struck Quentin across his mouth. Blood spilled out of his lips and welled up over his teeth.

"She *is* here," he said. "Yesterday at dawn someone from the village saw her riding a Tobiano along the northern road of your property."

This time, the lash of his whip caught Quentin's forehead and once more pushed him, staggering, backward. Racked with pain, Quentin took a full minute before he found new words to answer Varot.

"You are wasting your time," he said, his brooding voice hovering at the edge of insolence. "She has never been here. Your village spy is mistaken."

To these words, Captain Varot said nothing. Instead, with an even fiercer hatred, he lashed Quentin across the mouth and watched more blood spewing from his lips and through his teeth. After that, he clipped his riding whip to his belt and allowed his right hand to pause momentarily upon his MAB Model D pistol before drawing it out of its holster.

A dangerous stillness overtook the scene once more. Everyone there thought that the Captain was going to shoot Quentin. But he turned to Quentin's girlfriend, Denise, instead.

Her red hair, blue eyes, and sun-tanned complexion made her look exotic and glamorous, even though she was wearing her working clothes. She was dressed in a light blue flannel blouse and a navy blue cotton jacket. Her beige slacks, a blend of cotton and light wool, were tucked inside her brown-leather work boots. She wore, as well, a feminine delicacy that she had learned to use as a disguise for her tough-minded efficiency as a freedom fighter.

The toughness—with its realistic underpinnings about the way things are in a war-torn world—served her now, as Captain Varot approached her. He was pointing his revolver at her right temple. In a harsh voice that rose from a barely-controlled anger, he was delivering his judgment upon her.

"Tell me that Valérie Moreau is here," he said.

He kept his gaze fixed upon Denise while he directed his words at Quentin.

"Tell me now, or I'll kill *her*."

Quentin stood silent. His fleet glance first took in the imagery that was Denise holding herself taut and stoical before the barrel of the MAB Model D pistol pointed at her head. Then, in the moment just before he began to speak, he stared at Captain Varot.

Whether his words could save Denise or himself or any of the others, Marc did not wait to discover. From the window of the parlor, he fired his Sten gun at Captain Varot. Seconds before he pulled the trigger, the Captain suddenly moved out of the line of fire, toward Quentin. The round of bullets did not kill him. But they did tear into his left shoulder, into the right side of his face, and into his chest. Varot fell down, gravely wounded. Yet, in spite of his pain and with a fierce grimace, he maintained a solid grip upon his revolver. This time he pointed it at Quentin.

He never fired it.

Another bullet from Marc's Sten gun ripped Varot's forehead open. The impact pushed his eyeballs out of his head, their viscous remains scattering across his cheeks. As if in slow motion, his body—already fallen upon the ground—keeled over.

The swift trajectory of the next minutes altered the meaning of the scene.

No sooner had Marc fired the shot that killed Varot, than he saw Pascal and Marcelle Grenier and Simone leaping from the southwest wing of the house. He guessed that they must have been hiding in the secret apartment within the second floor of the house. The French Nazis, in their search of the house, had not discovered them. Rushing across the courtyard, a flash and flare of aggressive motion, the Greniers and Simone were firing MAS-38 submachine guns at four of the lieutenants who were guarding the Jewish surgeon and his family and guarding as well the four Resistance agents who were disguised as farm laborers.

At the same time that Marc's bullet killed Varot, the French Nazi lieutenants saw the Greniers and Simone hastening toward them. It was too late to take cover inside the tall silver grass that stood, wind-roused and billowing, at the rim of the courtyard. The four lieutenants fired their MAS-38s as they ran to meet their adversaries.

Pascal, all primitive fury and speed, shot two of the lieutenants quickly. His bullets ripped through their lungs, their mouths, and their heads.

Marcelle shot the third lieutenant through the heart. In her, there was none of the hesitation that she had feared would thwart her capacities on the battlefield. Her need to avenge the Nazis' killing of her first-born son in an air battle over London had sharpened her combat skills. As formidable as she was unflinching, she made her kill and then hurried onward to seek out another adversary.

She saw the fourth and brawniest of the lieutenants firing his MAS-38 at Simone.

"Bitch!" he snarled. "Here's a present from your boyfriend."

Fired wildly in the mêlée rising around him, only one of his bullets hit her. It grazed her left shoulder.

The impact pushed her back, but not before she fired her Sten gun. She fired accurately, and the bullets caught this lieutenant in his forehead, his right eye, and his heart. She killed him instantly.

Marcelle hurried to her, all the while wielding her rifle defensively before her.

Simone remained standing, in spite of her wound. Alert and tough-spirited, she held her gun steady and scanned the courtyard for other enemies.

Marcelle hovered nearby to protect her.

"Don't worry about me," Simone said. "Take cover. I'll be all right."

Her blonde hair flowed in the wind and her blue eyes were intense with a bitter hatred. Her alabaster complexion made her look ethereal and even ghostly. She looked like a woman who kept company with lightning. Perhaps, she was thinking of the adversary who had tried to kill her. Or, more probably, she was reflecting upon the blunt meaning of his words, which told her that her boyfriend had sent him to kill her.

(Mrs. Grenier was to tell all of them so in the rough days that were to follow.)

Only two French Nazis remained.

The first of these had taken Denise Perrault as his hostage right after Marc's bullet had killed Captain Varot and after the Greniers and Simone had rushed onto the courtyard. His strong left arm holding her against his body, he kept backing into the path that would lead him inside the tall grass. At the same time, he began firing his MAS-38 to keep back his adversaries.

From his post at the parlor window, Marc aimed his Sten gun and waited for the lieutenant to turn his head slightly to the right. When this French Nazi did so, he could fire a round of bullets into him.

But something happened that he had not anticipated.

Denise began struggling against the hold that the lieutenant had upon her. She elbowed and kicked him and kept twisting her body to get free of his hold on her. So powerful was his grip, she could not break free of him. But her struggling put him off his balance and interfered with the accurate firing of his gun.

For these reasons, he pushed her away from him. Tough-hearted and fatalistic, he accepted the risk of not having her as a cover. He did not shoot her. Nor did he look at her. Instead, with a grim acceptance of the moment, he backed into the tall grass quickly. As he scanned the territory before him, he held his finger on the trigger of his weapon. His rugged physique pushed the tall grass away to each side of him while, backward moving, he stepped into its path. The grass accepted him and, each time he stepped backward, would have sprung forward to conceal him.

But he had time to take only a few steps into the grass. There, before him, stood Quentin, who was already firing the revolver that he had grabbed from Captain Varot's clenched hand.

"Come and get it, you bastard," Quentin said as he shot a bullet into the lieutenant's chest.

The lieutenant fell dead.

In the same instant, the last of the lieutenants sprang out of the tall grass firing his MAS-38. One of the bullets pierced Quentin's right hand. His gun flew away from him and left him enraged and vulnerable.

The lieutenant, expecting to die, moved toward Quentin and

Denise. He wanted to kill them before he died. He wanted to kill them face-to-face.

But Noah Hoffmann, the Jewish surgeon, surprised him.

At the start of this battle, Noah had hurried his wife and their three children into the tall grass. Because of the rapid fire of enemy bullets targeting him, he was prevented from following his family into the concealment of the grass. Instead, he fell to the ground and, maintaining that prone position, hugged the cobblestones while the fighting continued. Minutes later, a Milice lieutenant fell dead beside him. Without hesitation or fear, Noah grabbed his enemy's gun. Rising from the ground, he hurried to help his friends.

He saw the lieutenant shooting Quentin's gun out of his hands. He saw Denise moving to scoop up Quentin's gun. He saw the French Nazi lieutenant as he was about to press the trigger of his gun.

That was the moment in which he shot him.

Then, looking about him cautiously, he saw what everyone else there was noticing. There were no other French Nazis to kill in this hour.

Quentin, determined to resist surprise or sentimentality because Noah had rescued him, anchored the moment to matter-of-fact words.

"You shot well," he said. "You saved our lives."

Noah offered him a brotherly smile.

"We all saved each other," he said.

Carefully, he was examining his friend's wounded hand. He was a doctor once more, come there to heal his patient.

All of these things Marc saw from his post at the window. The scene that had unfolded within the ten minutes since he had arrived on the Greniers' farm left a trail of disarranged fields and disfigured corpses.

Now he hurried to do the things that needed to be done quickly, if he and the others were to avoid the retaliation of the French Nazis. With the Greniers and their loyal staff, he lifted the bodies of the captain and his lieutenants into their two Citroëns. Then, he helped to collect the bodies of the other fallen Nazi officers, scattered as they were across different parts of the Greniers' property. Only after that, with two of the farm hands armed as sentries in the cargo section, did he and Pascal drive the trucks onto the forest paths that would bring them to an old and little-used cemetery at the northern edge of town. Another farm hand drove the truck that would return them to the Greniers' land.

Strong winds were hurling themselves against the tall trees of the forest. In the proximate distance, a deer leaped across the shadowy path into the privacy of wild-flowering greenery. Two squirrels scampered up a pine tree, and a fox—with its flare of red and brown colors—peered out of a tangle of bushes. In his speeding truck, he saw all of these images as if they belonged to a kaleidoscope. Even the light of the sun seemed a scattering motion. The wind howled, and the formidable powers of the trees rose skyward, billowing. It was as if the wind were turning the forest into a sea that was rising around and over them.

So, he imagined, understanding that the memory of his early morning battle—with its brutal finalities and its promise of still other battles—was influencing his perceptions.

They reached their destination within forty-five minutes. But, aware that daylight would expose them to their enemies, they waited. For several hours, they stayed inside the seclusion of the forest. Only when darkness fell around them did they drive to the deserted cemetery. As silent as they were furtive, they dug a mass grave and buried the bodies of the fifteen Miliciens whom they had killed.

Afterward, he and Pascal drove the Miliciens' Citroëns and their guns and ammunition into the mountains. Once again, one of the farm hands drove the truck that would bring them back home. Hearing their story of what had happened, the maquisards cheered them for their courage and their luck. But neither he nor Pascal nor the farm hand felt any joy in their praise. As for himself, he believed that the massacre which had spattered the Greniers and him with its blood had stolen a little more of their humanity. He felt no pride in having killed his enemies.

When they returned to the farm on the following morning, he saw that Mrs. Grenier and her loyal team of workers had imposed upon the place its well-kept order. No field gave evidence that men had fallen dead within its autumn-flourishing space only a day earlier. The granary also stood without the dark stains of blood, and the cobblestones of the courtyard outside the main house gleamed as brightly as they always did on a sun-lit and wind-tossed morning. Horses grazed or cantered in the ample paddock. Men, women, and children worked to harvest the fields of wheat and rye and the vineyards. Tall boys on ladders were picking apples from the orchard. Women in the kitchens of the workers' cottages were busy bottling preserves of orange marmalade and strawberry jelly. In the kitchen of the main house, Marcelle Grenier and two assistants were cooking the sea bass, quiche, and lemon meringue pies that they would serve at the noon meal.

Nothing appeared disarranged. Nobody wept or grimaced with anguish. They exchanged ordinary platitudes and even managed to laugh once in a while. Most important of all, they kept working at their tasks. Work tested and sharpened their aptitudes. It roused their hope in a future and validated their belief that, in spite of the war raging around them, they might yet experience some remembered joy or discover the surprise of a new one.

Their days did pass with a few differences. All that week, Marc and the other men stood armed and ready to face a new group of adversaries. They wondered whether the French Nazis would trace the passage of Captain Varot and his team of men to the Greniers' farm. That Varot and the lieutenants had vanished did incite the Milice to scour the countryside for any signs that the people of Sancerre had killed them. But, when a group of Milice officers, led by Captain Georges Lugand, came to the farm, they found the Greniers and their staff busily harvesting the land. Politic and respectful, the Greniers invited the men to share the noon meal and to visit the barns, stables, paddocks, and vineyards. They urged them to ride their best horses as they surveyed the property. They accompanied them into the brick building to study the process that would eventually turn the grapes from their vineyard into an excellent wine.

The French Nazis accepted their cordiality. Whatever suspicions they harbored before they arrived at the farm were, for this day at least, dispelled.

Pascal and Marcelle, as well as the men and women who assisted them in the running of their large farm, loathed these French men who had betrayed their country by joining the

Nazis. But, subdued and cooperative, they played with conviction the scenario they had devised so that the French Nazis would not discover the persons they were hiding.

All went well. By the end of their visit, Captain Lugand and his men believed that the Greniers were apolitical. They, too, would join the team that won the war.

After Lugand and his men left, the Greniers conferred with one another privately.

"Maybe one day I'll have the good fortune to kill some of those men," Pascal said.

Marcelle was just as bitter as her husband. Their perilous situation had compelled them to serve their food to the French Nazis, to share their horses with them, and to allow them to observe all the significant buildings and landmarks of their property.

"I hope that I'll be there when you kill them," she said. "I hope that I have the chance to help you."

They told Marc how they felt a few hours later. They were not sorry that they had treated the French traitors so well. By so doing, they had dissuaded these enemies from searching too carefully every building on their land. Raoul, Benoît, and he had remained safely concealed in the secret apartment within the granary. Simone, Quentin, and Denise stayed undetected inside the secret apartment on the first floor of the main house. There in the main house, though on the second floor, Noah Hoffmann and his family also hid themselves quietly.

Noah had tended the wounds of Simone, Raoul, Benoît, Yannick, Régis, and Quentin. Simone, whom the doctor—like everyone else on the Grenier farm—knew only as Valérie Moreau, would recover quickly. But the others would need several weeks to convalesce. Their expected recovery was, nevertheless, another reason to cheer. So Noah reminded the Greniers and Marc when they first paid a visit to them.

Days earlier, when Quentin had rallied from his wound and was able to be there, the Greniers held a private funeral for his parents, Xavier and Honorée. A priest from the village, who worked in secret for the Resistance, officiated at the Mass that was held in a small chapel within the Greniers' home. The men and women who helped the Greniers maintain their farm, as well as some of the friends to whom the Greniers were offering refuge, attended the brief ceremony. On that morning, in spite of their painful convalescence, Benoît and Raoul willed themselves to join the group. They felt it was important that they pay tribute to the humble couple. By crying out to them that the French Nazis had discovered their hiding place in the granary, Xavier and Honorée had saved their lives.

But Simone could not attend the funeral because of the chance that other Nazi officers, sent there by the surviving men in Varot's squad, might barge into the ceremony and kill her. For a few days after she had been shot, she remained secluded. During this period, only Marcelle and one of her housekeepers entered the secret apartment on the first floor of the main house where, still disguised as Valérie Moreau, Simone was staying. There, after the minor surgery which the doctor had ably performed upon her shoulder, she stayed alone, devising—Marc imagined—new plots to overcome her enemies and to keep him at bay.

It was four days before Marc was allowed to visit her. On that afternoon, her blue eyes glowed with cautious inquiry and tough-minded perceiving. Propped against her pillows, she was studying him with a shrewd awareness of why he had come to see her. She knew him well enough to anticipate the questions he was going to ask her.

At first, she deflected his questions.

"Give me a cigarette," she said.

He hesitated.

"The doctor said 'no.'"

With a well-practiced feminine grace, she held out her hand to him. She contrived a smile that was very appealing. Even with the discomfort of her wounded shoulder, a special radiance touched her. Not only the blueness of her eyes, but also the fair skin of her face glowed. Her wound had not kept beauty from remaining her friend. Aware of her powers, she invited him again to give her the cigarette. Her voice, melding the playful and the intimate, was coaxing him.

"Give me one. One isn't enough to kill me."

He resisted the intimacy and the playfulness. He had come there with a serious purpose, and he would not let go of it. With a smooth gesture, nonetheless, he gave her a Patagonian cigarette and lighted it.

"I hope that you know what you are doing," he said. "You need to stay well. We have many more battles to fight."

He had made his remark matter-of-fact and practical, rather than playful. He could see that she did not care for his words. She did not want to be reminded of oncoming battles. Nor did she want to answer his questions about Hans. There was, suddenly, nothing intimate or playful in her reply to him. Instead, there was a blunt cynicism, and there was a vague distrust of his reasons for being there. She did not yet permit anger to fuse her next reply. But he sensed that anger was waiting, poised at the taut sounds of her new words.

"We've survived this latest battle," she said, as she exhaled the tangy fragrance of her cigarette. "If we want to keep living on this stinking planet, all we have to do is to train for the next battle."

He observed her with brooding interest before he allowed his hard, brown eyes to meet the blue elusiveness of her own. Only then did he push his first question toward her. He was daring her to answer him honestly.

"Do you think that you'll make it?"

She met his words with her own question—one that was rhetorical and brusque.

"Why wouldn't I?"

It was now that he reminded her of the words which one of her Nazi assailants had thrown out at her just before he shot her.

"'Here's a present from your boyfriend.' Those are the words the Milice lieutenant shouted to you when he tried to kill you."

It was her turn to pause now before she answered him. She was weighing the words that might persuade him to believe as she did.

"The lieutenant was a fool," she said. "He didn't know what he was talking about."

He persisted.

"Hans sent him."

Again, she protested.

"No."

He stood by her bed, formidable and determined as he peered down at her.

"He sent Captain Varot, too. It was Varot who kept asking

everyone whether you were here."

"Hans didn't send him."

"He sent all of them to kill you."

"He didn't. He never would."

She had risen from her pillows as she spoke, crying out her anger and her conviction. The intensity of her belief in Hans did not altogether conceal the apprehension that had begun its bond with her and that had come there to observe her almost imperceptibly.

"Varot did not need Hans to send him here," she said, even more determined to persuade him that Hans was in the clear. "Varot had his own reasons for coming here. He came because he was jealous and because he wanted to kill me."

Marc became very still. The word *jealous* was a clue leading him to a path that he did not want to enter.

"You and Varot were lovers."

"We were. That was the only way I could draw out of him the information that has saved many of our allies. It was through Varot that I learned about the schedules of the Nazi troop trains carrying infantrymen to distant battlefields. It was Varot who, after we shared a few rounds of scotch, would tell me the specific days and locations of Luftwaffe bombing missions over London, Manchester, and Hertfordshire and over any other British city or town where there were aircraft factories. It was this same Léon Varot who, whenever I slept with him, gave me the names of secret Nazis and Vichy Frenchmen who had infiltrated the Resistance as double agents."

Simone paused. Her memory of Varot left her sullen and bitter.

"Varot found out about you and Hans Mueller."

"Yes, but not right away. At first, he thought that Lucien Chardonne was my lover. So he had his henchmen kill him. Afterwards, he convinced himself that Raoul and Benoît were my lovers. I told him that it wasn't true. He was my only lover. But he would not believe me. His jealousy knew no bounds. He ordered Gaston and Fabien to kill Raoul and Benoît. Fortunately, you saved them. Varot would have gone on to kill any other man to whom I gave even the slightest attention."

"He did not try to kill Hans."

"Hans is very smart. He does not make himself easily accessible to his enemies."

"Maybe Hans is Varot's friend. After all, Varot came here yesterday to kill you. He was not looking for Hans."

"Varot was Hans's enemy just as much as he was mine. He was an outspoken enemy of the Resistance. He is the man that you should have been hunting down. But now he is dead. He is no longer a danger to us. We can move on to do battle with other dangerous men."

"Hans is still alive. He is a danger that we cannot ignore."

"Don't do this, Marc. Don't lie to yourself. Don't contrive reasons for killing Hans."

"I have never met Hans. But everything that I know about him warns me that he is a traitor."

"You are a master of lying. Lying gives a cutting edge to your malevolence. But this time MI5 will not listen to you. They have been finding out everything that they need to know about Hans."

"I'll find out what they need to know about Hans Mueller. That's a promise."

"Hans is innocent, I tell you."

He decided not to push her any further. His abrasive words would not alter the bond that she had made with Hans. Nor would they draw from her the confession that revealed Hans's duplicity. A part of him loathed her for lying about Hans and for convincing herself that her lie was the truth. Yet he also empathized with her. He knew the perverse influence of obsession. His obsession for her had destroyed their marriage. It had compelled him to destroy the man who had cast his spell upon her. In that year, obsession had also ensnared Simone and her lover. It had made a prisoner of all three of them.

There was a remote chance that Simone really did not know

whether Hans had leagued himself with Varot and was serving the Nazis as a double agent. Whatever the case, he determined in this moment that, if he were to discover who Hans Mueller really was, he would need to devise other ways to draw Simone into his plan.

Now he chose temperate words that would preface his quickly taking leave of her.

"You may be right," he told her. "Hans may be in the clear."

Then, because he preferred to tether his softer remark to a realistic scenario, he added other words that echoed his determination to prove that Hans was a spy.

"I'll find out soon enough."

His words helped her to retrieve her calmer self. With traces of sadness and apprehension, linked as they were to her resilience, she managed a smile. Since there was nothing else that they wanted to say to one another, he hurried away.

The imagery of her apprehension might have stayed with him for many hours. But bad news compelled him to other thoughts. In the courtyard of their military barracks, which were located in the center of the town of Sancerre, the French Nazis had killed twenty teenage youths whom they suspected of being sympathetic toward or giving assistance to the guerrilla forces who made the neighboring mountains their fortresses as well as their headquarters. They killed them in reprisal for the fifteen

Milice officers who were still missing and whom the Nazis believed had been killed by cadres of the underground Resistance that were attached to the town, hills, and mountains of Sancerre.

"There is nothing we can do for the boys they killed," he told the Greniers. "They were caught because they were careless and over-confident."

He had known all those youths. He had admired and respected them. They were fine athletes and brave patriots. They were pleased to think of themselves as young men who could save the world. Once, not so long ago, he had been like them.

He refused to mourn them. Only by staying tough-minded and unsentimental, would he be able to go on to the things that he needed to do.

"We'll just have to fight harder," he said. "Otherwise, their deaths won't mean anything."

Under the dark cover of a night at the end of that week, two Lockheed Hudsons came for him, for Raoul, Benoît, and Simone, and for Dr. Hoffmann and his family. They were going to England. Raoul and Benoît would be spending a few weeks in the 28th Station Hospital in Sudbury, a village in the county of Derbyshire. Noah had been invited to join his twin brother, Franz, as a surgeon in the same hospital. He and his family would be living in their new home in Sudbury. Simone was going to report to an air base to which she had been recently reassigned, after she convinced the MI5 team that an agent who was not romantically involved with Hans Mueller should find out whether he was a Nazi spy.

For a few days, before he returned to aerial combat, he would stay with his parents in their home in Derbyshire, which was located about a hundred fifty miles outside London. While he was on leave, he would visit his estranged wife at her air base. There, with the consent of the MI5 team, he would try to persuade her that she was the best agent to help the team find out the truth about Hans Mueller.

Chapter Five

Summoning Ghosts

Marc's plot to discover whether Hans Mueller was a Nazi spy might turn intricate and dangerous. In spite of the evidence that, thus far, pointed to Hans's innocence, he kept telling himself that Mueller was guilty. He wanted him to be guilty. He wanted to have a valid reason for killing him. That he was drawing Simone further into his murderous plan seemed inevitable. If he could make her believe that Mueller was a Nazi spy, her being involved with his plan would make her an accomplice to the killing of Hans Mueller. There had been other times when he had persuaded her to risk everything so that they might save the life of a heroic friend or rescue a team of their beleaguered comrades or trap men who appeared to be their enemies. Always, he had shared the risk with her. He had been there, ever vigilant and often invisible, to track her moves and the moves of their enemies. At times, he might alert her of an oncoming peril by sending her a wireless message through his Mark II Suitcase Transceiver. Or, at an elegant party to which in disguise she was being escorted by one of the German enemies, he might appear in an equally adept disguise to convey with the white carnation placed in the lapel of his tuxedo the important news that could save her. Once in a while, in a crowded Paris train station or at a fashionable Swiss spa or on a Belgian farm, he might confront her as though they were meeting for the first time. Then, while inhabiting an identity as fictive as the one she had recently made her own, he would casually speak the guarded words she needed to hear if she were to stay alive so that she could kill her enemies.

Whenever with coiled and activated energies he had partnered with her openly in these uneasy missions, he had been there beside her to hurl grenades into official Vichy windows and to detonate car bombs that instantly killed whole teams of German officers. Together, he and Simone had blown up essential bridges across which truckloads of Nazi infantrymen were hastening. Sometimes Simone and he had found themselves face to face with their enemies. On those occasions, hurling themselves inside swift and furious motion, each of them had plunged a Fairbairn-Sykes knife or a V-42 stiletto into the hearts of the men who had been sent to kill them. More than a few times, when they were besieged and outnumbered, they had fired their Sten 9mm submachine guns, their Colt Vest Pocket semi-automatic pistols, and their Enfield revolvers into the chests and faces and foreheads of as many as ten Nazis who were rushing toward them while wielding StG 44 assault rifles, Luger PO8 pistols, and Walther P38 semi-automatic revolvers.

Through all these brutal years of war, Simone had been not

only brave and resilient, but also clever and resourceful. In Sweden, she had worked with her father to decode (by means of a Siemens and Halske T52 teleprinter cipher machine) the messages that the Germans had been sending to one another about their plans to bomb Allied cities, ships, and air bases. Made aware of their enemy's intentions and the locations of their aircraft, ships and railways, the British, French and American Air Forces moved swiftly to bomb German air bases, munitions factories, shipyards, rail lines, and harbors.

Shortly after that, while on a night-time mission to Denmark and while guiding imperiled men, women, and children to concealed ships and boats that would carry them across the Danish island of Zealand to the Swedish province of Scania, Simone and her father helped to save thousands of Danish Jews from the Nazi storm troopers who were pursuing them.

In France as an agent for the Resistance and within the secrecy of subtle disguises, she had intensified her murderous aptitudes. Sometimes, she poisoned or stabbed or shot the well-educated and cosmopolitan Nazi officers who had imagined that they would enjoy her company in bed as much as they had in the night clubs, the opera houses, and the theaters to which they often escorted the disguised imagery that had become so completely herself. That imagery, usually blonde and glamorous and alluring, made plausible and exciting the scenarios that she and her fellow agents had devised for her playing. Occasionally, she killed these courtly Germans, who in her eyes appeared both sinister and proprietary, with a French Resistance thumb dagger or a hat pin dagger or with a 6mm pipe gun or a plate knife that she had concealed in the heel of one of her fashionable boots.

In England, while working with the Air Transport Auxiliary in a non-combat role that sent her nonetheless into the danger of air battle conditions, she ferried new or repaired aircraft from factories and assembly plants to trans-Atlantic delivery points, to active service squadrons, and to airfields. By doing so, she made these fighter planes available to combat pilots. Early in her assignments as an aviator, she often supported secret sabotage work in Scandinavia by flying to the north of the Shetland Isles plane loads of detonators, explosives, and electric wiring, as well as the commandos who would carry forward widespread and crippling attacks against the Nazi that had invaded their countries. More than a few times, because of the need for additional combat flyers, her base commander sent her unofficially into bombing missions. On those occasions, she would pilot Avro Lancasters, Handley Page Halifaxes, and Bristol Beaufighters. With a steely precision that matched her determination and her courage, she hurried into the conflagration. Those hours were ignited by the bullets that she fired into the wings and the engines of enemy planes and by the bombs that she dropped upon Berlin, Dresden, and Hamburg.

Never did she flinch from the things that needed to be done. Never did she allow herself to fear dying or to feel remorse that the bombs that she fired from her plane were blowing up whole towns and cities and killing or maiming thousands of human beings. The war had taught her well that life is a tenuous experiment and that morality—one's own as well as that of one's government—involves pragmatic actions and hard-hearted casuistries.

That she was fighting for the freedom of her country and of the countries of her European allies made the bombings and the killings acceptable to the power brokers who manipulated or revised the rules. But, unlike those leaders who eased their consciences with words such as *hero, patriot, and freedom fighter*, she refused to lie to herself. The war had made her a killer. Even now, the war was displacing the worthwhile aspirations that had for all the earlier years of her life intensified her belief in herself. This belief in her singular aptitudes and in her realistic possibilities had convinced her that, through her skill as an interior designer and as a landscape architect, she would one day make the world a more beautiful experience. But the war had altered her perspective. No longer could she persuade herself that, if she survived its atrocities, she would reclaim the uncompromised and optimistic identity that had been Simone Bergman Roussillon.

From this time forward, she would forever be a stranger to herself. She would struggle in vain to find her way back to the person that she had been creating. After the war and after the bombings and massacres were behind her, the woman that she would see in her mind's eye and perhaps in her mirror would no longer have the familiar face that had reflected her girlhood hopes, her quiet inspiration, and her occasional exhilaration. That earlier face would now exist as a momentary flash of memory, a will-o'-the wisp in her private seeing, or a face hidden behind her present face, as though—like an image painted beneath the revised face on an artist's canvas—it was an original and displaced conception.

So, in these years when she felt betrayed by him and when they were struggling to save their marriage, Simone had told Marc.

That their marriage was in trouble had as much to do with his obsessive need of her as it did with the war. He could not say with any certainty that they would regain what they had lost. But his frequent recollection of their happiest years together, which burned through his soul like a loss that was both irrevocable and anguished, taught him in new ways what he had done wrong and why—even though their fates had brought them once more onto the same path—she had turned away from him.

Together, they had enjoyed six years of happiness. They were happy while he was a student at Le Rosey, a private school in Switzerland, and while she was enrolled nearby, at La Combe. They were happy later, while he studied architecture at the École des Beaux-Arts and while she studied languages and literature at the Sorbonne and also joined him in studies at the École des Beaux-Arts. In every one of those years, she had been his most exciting pleasure and one of his most loyal advocates. Intimate and authentic, she had been his stay against the confusion that sometimes overtook him in the year when his father had become distant and withholding.

Everything changed for them when the war arrived. But it was not the war alone that changed things for them.

In September of 1941, the Germans captured his best friend and fellow aviator, Jean-Claude Jourdan. After a Messerschmitt Bf 109 shot down his Spitfire and after German farmers pulled his severely wounded body from the burning wreckage, well-trained physicians saved his life so that Nazi agents could eventually torture and interrogate him. Brutally treated once he had been restored to good health, Jean-Claude never divulged any information about his French Resistance cohorts or about the RAF war plans that he had helped to carry forward. Because he was a symbol of the Allied fighters who were working to overthrow Hitler, the Nazis alternated their weeks of interrogating and torturing him with days of hospital care that kept him alive. They wanted to break his spirit. They wanted him to divulge essential information about the Allies' war plans. Then they planned to kill him.

As soon as he heard that Jean-Claude was alive, Marc persuaded his squadron commander to send him and other combat pilots on a mission that might rescue his friend. But, before he and his squadron could activate the rescue, the Nazis moved his friend to an unknown prison. Determined nonetheless to save Jean-Claude, who had been like a brother to him all through their adolescence and their young manhood, he now drew Simone into a plot that was both daring and unforgiving. At the start, though, Simone hesitated before the plan. She believed that the odds were against their making this mission a success. But when he explained that Jean-Claude Jourdan was the pilot whom they would try to rescue, she agreed unconditionally to collaborate with him.

While they were at their schools in Switzerland and later when the three of them were studying in Paris, Jean-Claude had also been her friend. In spite of his handsome individuality, though, she had never regarded him as a romantic partner. The Fates, she told herself, had sent him into her life as a man she must regard as a brother and as her lover's best friend. Nor had

Jean-Claude ever permitted himself to regard her in a romantic way. She was, he said, the sister he had never had. She was the one girl he would never try to seduce, because his best friend was her lover.

"Each of you completes the other," Jean-Claude told him as well as Simone during an especially happy summer when, with his latest girlfriend, he had joined them on a vacation in Tahiti. "You will never be happy with anyone except each other."

Marc remembered how, with openhearted affection and keen-eyed respect, Simone had smiled at Jean-Claude, who was studying the two of them while, hand-in-hand, they were walking on the tawny sands of the beach. Jean-Claude had glanced at them only fleetingly, right after the hurl and heave of the waves had playfully hurried him and his equally playful girlfriend onto the shore. His best friend understood the intensity of their love for one another. That sensitive awareness had pleased Simone very much. She was pleased, too, that Jean-Claude accepted the platonic nature of his friendship with her.

Later, within the privacies of their rooms at the hotel that stood on a hill overlooking the moonlit serenities of the sea, she and Marc spoke of Jean-Claude's loyalty and the life-affirming spirit of his friendship.

"He's always been on my side," Marc told her. "He's always been an essential part of my team."

Simone praised Jean-Claude, too. He was, she said with an affection that anchored itself to nostalgia and to the specific history of their friendship with him, an extraordinary human being whom she admired because of his intellect, his originality, his courage, and his empathy.

Two years after that vacation in Tahiti and while death was hovering about him, she worked efficiently to do all the things that needed to be done if Jean-Claude were to be rescued from his Nazi captors. Without hesitation, she pledged herself to a secrecy that kept knowledge of the plan even from her father, Knut Bergman. Had her father been told of the danger into which she was being drawn, he would have found some way to hold her back from it and to place himself in the danger, instead.

Marc remembered that time as a series of clever ruses and understated cunning. Many days and many nights drove their subterfuge through furtive glances, sinister ploys, and wary intrigue. It was a year of calculated measures, of pretext, and of trickery. It was a year when, to save Jean-Claude, he pushed Simone onto the path of Gerhard Hauptmann, the Nazi officer with whom she fell in love. It was the year when he set a trap for this man who was stealing away the love that Simone had given to him alone, without qualification and without deviousness. It was a year of bleak endings and equally dark beginnings. It was the year when he lost the Marc Roussillon that he thought he had known well.

Now, two years later, Simone's grieving for Gerhard had become as silent as it was insistent. Sorrow enclosed itself within the ambiguous privacy that was her troubled self. That she still loved Gerhard, there was in his mind no doubt. That she loved and desired and hated him, Marc Roussillon, the first man she had taken as her lover and as the only man who was meant to be her husband, he was also certain. Their decision to remain together for so many months after Gerhard's death surprised neither of them. They had always been each other's lifeline. They had, together, been a fierce and enigmatic alliance. They had been a tremendous and unyielding obsession. Or so they kept telling themselves, reluctant to yield to the bitter truth that hovered, brooding and accusatory, about them. That truth turned their memories of the persons they had been for each other into an imagery that was as ghostly as it was melancholic.

So they drifted apart, weary of all the uncertain days and the anguished nights that had made their love a bleak ambivalence. Always, though, even when he had reluctantly agreed to their parting, he believed that their separation would be merely temporary. He could not envision a life without Simone. In this first year without her, he kept telling himself that she felt the same way. She would come back to him.

Even now, two years after the Gerhard episode was over and nearly a year after their separation, Simone had not come back to him. In that first year after Gerhard, he felt that he still knew her well. Now he knew, as if it were a certainty that he was condemned to witness whenever he was in her presence, that something important had died in the love she still felt for him. No longer was there joy in her eyes when she looked upon him. No longer did a romantic lilt touch her smoky voice as she spoke to him. Her words sounded matter-of-fact and semi-detached, as though, while she spoke to him, she was a woman other than herself listening to a conversation that belonged to some woman who was merely a vague acquaintance.

Nor did she accept his intimate glances whenever his discerning eyes were probing her muted discomfort or studying her with his familiar, sensual need. He noticed, too, how—whenever he caressed her shoulders or touched the delicate skin of her arms or held her close to his body so that he could breathe the fragrance of her hair or fondle her ample breasts or lightly kiss her lips—she would stiffen, held taut by what she now received as the surprise of his intimacy, as if he too were a stranger.

Even when, in those last months together, he made love to her she was different. No longer between them were the smooth and natural rhythms of their bodies together, their teasing and constant momentum, and the protracted joy of their climaxes. Their intercourse had become a shared and perverse tension. Whatever pleasures remained were part of an unsentimental biological act. Gone was her roused elation when, naked and erect, he would enter her—vigorous and adept. Gone, too, was his belief that she belonged to him alone. Yet they desired each other no less. That desire, a wayward fuse to their self-loathing, fed the furious and masochistic rawness of their lovemaking.

Then, a year ago, she left him, promising that in her own way she would be loyal to him and would always be his friend. She was, he felt, trying to find her way back to him. He wondered whether Hans Mueller was merely an experience that she would have to live through, if she were ever going to find her way back to the happy life they had shared before Gerhard. In his heart, he wanted to believe that Simone could never really love any man except him. But his realistic perception of things, melded as it was with his cynical understanding of the world, compelled him to face the truth. Simone *had* loved another man. She had loved Gerhard. In this year when she was rebounding from the death of Gerhard and from her separation from him— Marc Roussillon, the lover and husband to whom she had once pledged herself, body and soul—she had fallen in love with Hans Mueller.

Now he wanted to draw her further into a new plan that involved his killing another rival.

He wondered whether his ambivalent feelings for her were driving his efforts to secure her consent to the plan. She might be killed if, with hair-trigger capacities, the scenario he was devising to trap a spy recoiled upon her. Possibly, he was testing his own influence over her and the proficiency with which he drew her to his will. Or, perhaps, he wanted to find out whether her romantic nature would compel her once again to go on loving a man such as Hans Mueller, even if she discovered that he was a dangerous enemy. Whether one of these motives was influencing him to draw her into his plan, or all of them, he could not say with any measure of certainty. His experience had taught him that the mind sometimes withholds its truth and that the private language with which we interpret its messages deceives ourselves even as it attempts to mislead others.

For most of the time, when with an accurate and impassive assessment he reviewed her qualifications to play an essential part in this dangerous assignment, he told himself that she was the best woman for making plausible the intricate episodes she would be navigating. By the well-proven evidence of her training, she increased and accelerated the likelihood that she would succeed in her mission. She was, after all, an expert wireless operator and a first-rate marksman. She was a daring pilot, a skillful code-breaker, and an effective saboteur. Just as important, she was a beautiful young woman who might—if any woman could—insinuate herself into Hans Mueller's confidence.

To do so, she would have to continue to be Valérie Moreau, the daughter of Pierre Moreau, who until his death a few months earlier as the Vichy Regime's Minister of Information and Propaganda, had been one of the most notorious leaders of the Milice française, the French militia who were fighting the French Resistance. Moreau and his paramilitary forces took no prisoners. They often killed their captives quickly, after they rushed upon them in their homes within the suburbs of Paris or dragged them away from their classes at the Sorbonne or breached their secret rooms within the churches, theaters and museums of the Marais, the Champs-Elysées, and Montmartre. They would kill them just as quickly after they surprised them in the cafés and restaurants of the Luxembourg Quarter and of St-Germain-des-Prés or when they broke through their makeshift hideouts within Provençal farmlands. Rarely did they take the time to interrogate and torture these suspects. For Moreau and his fellow assassins, the war was a dark and unforgiving labyrinth that required swift and lethal actions and a constant hurrying forward to the killing of all the other enemies (most of them unarmed) who were trying to elude capture.

A traitor to the egalitarian ideals of his country and to the inherent patriotism of most Frenchmen, Pierre Moreau had been shot down with his latest mistress in the bedroom of his palatial hotel apartment on the rue Solferino. The two men who shot them were agents of the Resistance. More specifically, they were members of the Maquis, a paramilitary group. Usually, they were stationed in La Tresorerie within Boulogne. But, among the best fighters of the Resistance, they had been carefully selected to make their furtive way to Paris to assassinate the Vichy minister who was responsible for the deaths of so many innocent men, women, and children.

As crafty as they were proficient, these two maquisards had quietly entered the hotel dressed in the blue uniform coat and trousers, brown shirt, and wide blue beret of Milice officers in the pre-dawn hours of a November morning. The Vichy security guards who greeted them in the foyer of the luxurious hotel thoroughly checked the authentic-looking military orders that the two men were carrying with them. According to the official-looking orders, they were assigned as escorts of the minister, who would be traveling in a Daimler-Benz limousine to an important meeting of Vichy and Nazi leaders that was to take place in Brussels. With an equal thoroughness, the security guards observed the two members of the Maquis army who were as young as they were and who, according to their affable and casual remarks, shared their passion for soccer, boxing, and mountain-climbing, as well as for sailing, hunting, and fishing. Only then, after their blunt inquiry had yoked its purpose to discovering the enemies of the Reich, did the guards allow them to enter the elevator to report to Monsieur Moreau. It helped the maquisards that the minister was expecting the arrival of the Milice officers whom an hour earlier they had intercepted and killed en route to the hotel.

With no betrayal of reticence or fear, the two men went up to the minister's room and, firing their MAB Model D pistols, quickly killed him and his nightclub paramour. The bullet that killed Moreau shot away the top of his head, which was silver-haired and had a large brow. The nightclub girl, who was only twenty and whose surface prettiness masked a weary disillusionment, died when a bullet pierced her heart. The maquisards left the room quietly and would have hurried away from the hotel without any further incident. But, having heard the loud reports of the shooting, the two security guards were already racing up the stairs to confront them. These guards had cocked their Luger PO8 pistols and were about to fire upon them. But the maquisards, who minutes before, had shared a lively conversation with them about their mutual athletic pastimes, fired their weapons first and killed them instantly.

It was the minister's daughter whom Simone was impersonating because she had agreed to become part of the plan that aimed to catch a spy.

Pierre Moreau's wife had died of a brain tumor sixteen years earlier. Their only child was this daughter who, when she was six years old and shortly after her mother died, was sent away to a convent school in Belgium. Her name was Valérie. That she was not a son who would carry forward the name of Moreau worked against her. Not caring to be her father, Pierre Moreau for the most part shut her out of his life and by means of a willed and adamant forgetfulness out of his memory. Only when it served his career-minded purpose did he mention her to his associates. Year after year, he mentioned her when it was important that European power brokers and their wives regard him as a dutiful father who had placed his only child in the meticulous care of nuns. He also mentioned her if a newspaper reporter or a cardinal visiting from the Vatican or a rich widow whom he was with subtle charm courting asked about her.

To their compassionate inquiries (they had known and respected her elegant and well-born mother), Moreau would invariably allow a melancholic frown to touch his brow before he explained how his daughter was receiving a first-rate education from the commendable nuns. Thus far, Valérie had expressed a heartfelt interest in the religious life as a potential vocation. She had also demonstrated scientific aptitudes that might draw her into a career in medicine. As he told his inquiring friends and acquaintances all these things, he was careful to mention how lovely she was. She had curly blonde hair, soft blue eyes, a turned-up nose, and a radiant yet demure smile. She was tall for her age, and she was as quick-witted as she was articulate. During these rare times when—prodded by his closest friends and by other more impersonal associates—he mentioned her, he would also describe his most recent visits to the convent in Belgium and the enjoyable excursions that he and his daughter (now a self-possessed young woman) had shared while visiting the parks, museums, and opera houses that gave to Belgium a well-earned cosmopolitan and aesthetic identity.

But he never mentioned the tension with which the exemplary nuns permitted him to take the girl away from their guardian care. Nor did he mention their studious and ambivalent regard of him, because—he guessed—they had discovered that he was in league with the Nazis. He did not know that the tension of the nuns derived as much from their concern that he might become aware of the many ways in which they and his daughter were working for the Resistance.

Nor did he notice the tension in the latest version of his daughter that, after the most recent absence of three years, he had come to witness so that he would present a more humanized imagery to the wealthy Europeans (many of them in self-imposed exile in South America and in Switzerland) who were wavering in their support of the Vichy government. The thought never entered his mind that Valérie might be repulsed by the murderous reputation he had made for himself and by his proprietary and arrogant manner. That she was repulsed by all that he represented, an aged nun who had for a few days survived the later bombing of the convent verified when maquisards and a nurse linked with the Resistance questioned her. With a palsied and frail body that appeared to be overwhelmed by the large, makeshift hospital bed in which she lay and with rheumy brown eyes and raspy voice, this nun (whose name was Sister Antoinette) told them more.

"Valérie had come to us vulnerable and alone," the dying nun said. "She had no sisters or brothers, and both sets of her grandparents had died from pneumonia or cancer or heart disease, shortly after she was born. But even on that first day she did not cry. She had already learned the uselessness of weeping over the past and regretting things that she could not change. She had a tough spirit even then, when she was only ten years old. We Sisters became her family, and she accepted us gratefully. But I believe that, despite our guardian love of her, she never quite escaped from her belief that she had to face the world alone. We told her that God was standing beside her and that he would always help her. But she resisted that thought. It made things too easy. It was passing most, if not all, of the burden to God. It was giving her an excuse to wait for somebody else to rescue her. It was making respectable the whole idea of standing still and doing nothing. She knew better than that. Though God was watching her, He refused to play the magician who soothed His audience with pleasing hat tricks or miraculous levitation. As demanding as He was unsentimental, God expected her to meet the fallible and shifting world with honest yet artful devices.

"'He will not help me unless I try to help myself,' she told us. 'God does not favor cowards or leaners.'

"We were glad to hear her speak those words. They were tough-spirited and realistic words. They were not unlike the words we too would have spoken, if we had been in her situation. But she was so much younger than we were, and her courage even at that age was even fiercer than ours.

"Our Valérie was prodigious. She was strong-minded and patriotic, too. She had only contempt for Pierre Moreau—this crafty stranger who called himself her father, this distorted facsimile of a human being, this failed parent, this *pére manqué*. But, whenever she was in his presence, she played a gentle and deferential role which enhanced the daughterly impression that, with the skill of a trained actress, she made upon him. It gave her pleasure to know that she was outwitting the man who had condemned her to a nearly anonymous existence which was almost completely disconnected from his own.

"It pleased her even more to guard as a life-saving power the truth that she and the nuns whom she had grown to love as though they were her blood relations were doing their part to save innocent lives and to advance the work of French patriots and their allies. Had she lived, she was going to take a leave of absence from our convent. She believed that for as long as the war lasted she needed to be in the world. She intended to join the Resistance as a wireless operator, as a ferry pilot, and as an intrepid agent who could plausibly disguise herself so that she could enter the territory of enemies and discover their military secrets.

"She would have done wonderful things, had she lived," Sister Antoinette said. Her voice was weaker now and barely audible. But with the same tenacity that had through the many years of her life defined all her efforts, she compelled herself to rise from her pillow and to speak still other words about Valérie.

"She was extraordinary, I tell you," the good nun said. "She had a mind that was more scientific than conventionally religious. But she was a searcher of the Spirit nonetheless. She would have been a fine physician and a helpful teacher. She would have become a nun who was capable of leading our order into the modern world."

All these things, the dying Sister Antoinette told the maquisards and the other Resistance fighters who visited her in the Nissen hut that served as a hospital during the last hours of her life. From these specific words and from all the other words that summarized Valérie's biography, Marc perceived even more clearly the character of the brave woman whom he hoped that Simone would continue to impersonate.

Under the tutelage of the Sisters of Saint Joseph, Valérie Moreau had become a well-trained nurse at the hospital which they served effectively and which carried the name of their order. She had rarely left the convent, because she was being carefully trained to be not only a nurse, but also a nun. Eventually, after the Sister Superior of her order received the consent of the local bishop, she was going to enroll in a Swiss medical school to become a physician.

During the sixteen years she had spent at the convent, she had also become a brave young woman. Ever since the war began, she and the equally brave nuns had been hiding Jewish families within the sequestered rooms of the convent and in the rooms of the adjacent buildings, which included their hospital and their parish church. She and the good nuns who had influenced her to be as compassionate as she was courageous had also tended the wounds of Resistance agents and of Jews who had narrowly escaped being captured or killed by Nazi storm troopers and by Vichy spies. When these men and women had recovered from their wounds, Valérie and the nuns arranged for their safe passage into Switzerland, into Spain, and into England.

Perhaps the Nazis had discovered that the Convent of the Sisters of Joseph had become not only a safe harbor, but also an embarkation point for the rugged escapes that were bringing the enemies of the Reich to other countries. Or possibly the Luftwaffe had sent in reprisal one of its bomber squadron to strafe random areas in Belgium, as a warning that many more squadrons would be sent to bomb even larger areas of the country, if its citizens continued to assist the men, women and children who were enemies of Germany. Whatever the case, the Junkers JU87 Stukas, the Messerschmitt Bf 109s, the Heinkel He 62s, and the Arado Ar 234s laid waste to both industrial and suburban sections of Belgium. Their bombs completely destroyed the Convent of the Sisters of Saint Joseph, as well as the school and the hospital that the nuns had so efficiently administered.

Among the two hundred-forty-four persons who had died on the grounds of the convent was Valérie Moreau. The few photographs that had been taken of her while she lived in the convent were destroyed in the bombings. So, also, were her personal records destroyed, including documents that verified her excellent grades as a student in the convent school and later in the nursing school that stood next to the convent hospital. At this hospital, the Sisters of Saint Joseph worked diligently to save war-wounded lives and to conceal within the hidden chambers of the hospital postal workers, farmers, school teachers, and railroad clerks who, after the Vichy troops discovered them working for the Resistance, had been shot and left to die on the rim of deserted roads or in the gutters of crowded streets. The nuns also worked to nurse and to hide hard-bitten, wounded maquisards who had made swift and circuitous journeys from the mountains and equally courageous Jews who were also wounded and on the run from the Nazis.

Like the brave nuns who had influenced her character, Valérie Moreau was a young woman worth knowing. So Marc told himself, after he heard from the maquisards the words that Sister Antoinette had spoken to them.

That none of Pierre Moreau's associates had ever met Valérie would work in favor of whatever young woman impersonated her. The influential associates who had glimpsed the few photographs of her that Pierre Moreau brought forth on the rare occasions when he wanted to suggest his fatherly interest in his daughter would recall the blonde imagery of a carefully nurtured ten-year-old child standing with other girls within a cloistered garden that flourished in the southwest corner of the convent grounds. They might also recall the image of a studious fourteen-year-old adolescent standing with her father in that same garden a few years later. More lately, Moreau's associates would have beheld in cursory appraisal the imagery of a genteel twenty-one-year-old woman whose beauty was concealed in part by the suffusion of sunlight that veiled rather than revealed the specific character of her features. Once more, she was standing within the late-spring efflorescence of the garden, and her father and Sister Antoinette were standing next to her. But all those photographs had been destroyed in the bombing of the convent and in the looting of Pierre Moreau's homes in Paris, Italy, and Belgium after he had been assassinated.

Marc felt certain that, having studied the intricate outlines of this brave woman's life, Simone could continue to be Valérie Moreau. Like Valérie, she was a tall, blonde beauty with multilingual proficiencies and with careful training as a nurse. She was scientific as well as artistic, and her perceptions were anchored to a realistic world view. In addition, Simone possessed skills that Valérie was only in the last months of her life beginning to master. She was an experienced wireless operator, a ferry pilot, and a Resistance agent who had killed her enemies with a V-42 Stiletto, with a Fairbairn-Sykes fighting knife, and with a MAS-38 submachine gun. With precise rehearsal and razor-sharp instincts, she would continue to immerse herself in the role of Valérie quite naturally. The conflation of their personas would impart its own plausibility. Valérie, gone to death and to a nearly anonymous heroism, would be for Simone more than a doppelgänger, a ghostly double or wraith hovering about the idiosyncrasies of her own identity. She would be a ghost made visible and sent to replace the human being known to her loved ones and to her friends as well as to her enemies as Simone Bergman Roussillon.

The continued melding of their identities held, of course, perils that could not be altogether anticipated or completely prevented. There were all manner of perils that, like minefields, she would have to avoid. An extemporaneous and careless word or a failure to recall a place or an occasion that Valérie would have known might arouse the enemy's suspicion. Danger might also arrive in the unexpected appearance of one of the few persons who had in recent years met Valérie at a public theater with her father or at the hospital where she had served as a meticulous and empathetic nurse. That she could make of her union with the imagery of Valérie a convincing twinship was all to the good. But only as a wily meeting of their authentic identities could Simone continue to be Valérie.

With these thoughts in mind, Marc made his way to the Royal Air Force Station at Ringway, which was located eight miles south of Manchester. From this station, about thirty-five miles from the home of his parents in Derbyshire, Simone was negotiating wily meetings of a different order. As a flight officer within No. 14 Ferry Pilot Pool of the Air Transport Auxiliary, she flew Bristol Beaufighters, Avro Lancasters, De Havilland DH98 Mosquitos, and Handley Page HP57 Halifaxes in combat conditions. Because hers was essentially a non-combat assignment, she was allowed only occasionally to bomb enemy targets. Should a Nazi pilot detect her aircraft, she would have to elude his pursuit of her by quickly guiding her four-engine heavy bomber into the clouds or across a higher altitude so that it could be safely delivered to the combat pilot and his team of war-hardened men who were waiting for it at an Allied air base.

His own understated authority and honed-sharp confidence would, Marc believed, carry him far in this new, private mission that brought him once again into the presence of the only woman he would ever love. But his quiet authority and intimate association with her might not be enough to win him success in his mission. He might not be able to draw Simone away from her important work as a pilot and as a Resistance agent who, while disguised as a brunette starlet working in French films or as a titian-haired cosmopolitan German widow or as any other fictive woman and after being carefully briefed by her commanding officers, would drive a plot that ensnared whole cadres of field-grade Nazi officers or that killed a general attached to the German High Command.

There was, he had to admit, every probability that her allegiance to the Women's Auxiliary Air Force and her romantic involvement with Hans Mueller would compel Simone to turn down the assignment that targeted Mueller as a Nazi agent.

Still, he refused to hesitate before so uncertain a prospect. In ways that he could not yet anticipate, he would find the words that persuaded Simone to join him as he tested the loyalty of Hans Mueller. That manipulative language and cunning subtexts would shape his new meeting with her made him momentarily uneasy and even melancholic. More than a few times, he had promised himself that there would be no more lies or disguises in their relationship. Nor would he import into the ambiguous intricacies of their relationship new deceptions or dangerous ruses of any kind. This promise of a renovated honesty between them had quickened his belief that they could once again make things work for themselves. But his breaking this promise now could not be helped. The strategies of war had no use for nostalgia or for the regret that inspires a new way to see. He needed to trap a spy. He needed to convince himself and others that Hans Mueller was guilty. To yoke his plan to calculated plausibility, he needed, as well, a woman who had already gained Mueller's trust. There was always the chance that, if Mueller *were* guilty, he might inadvertently reveal the words that proved he was a Nazi.

Simone was the best agent for the assignment. Convinced of her precise and cool-headed skills and of her value as an accomplice in the killing of Mueller, he was ready to activate whatever device or stratagem it took to bring her into his plan.

Chapter Six

Other Wily Meetings

Marc began by telling Simone that she could make Valérie live again. By continuing to impersonate her, she would carry forward the mission that Valérie had already initiated for herself before she died. That Valérie had spurned the protectiveness of the convent to enter the maelstrom that was the war-torn world revealed much about her character. Anchored to a Spartan realism, she had joined the Resistance and, with the formidable nuns who had cared for and educated her, she had already begun her battle against the Nazis.

"For a few more weeks or months or for as long as it takes, you can *be* Valérie," he told Simone. "In her name, you can do all the things that she would have done, had she lived. You can keep her name alive and bring honor to it."

Simone studied him carefully. Then, without consenting to this dangerous plan that with wily aptitudes he had devised for her, she challenged him with a question which reflected her own wiliness.

"Why are you doing this?"

They were riding away from the east hangar of Royal Air Force Station Ringway. Within its dome-like space—all steel-ribbed solidity, rolled steel sections, and light steel lattice girders—she had been working with her maintenance crew to fit with photo reconnaissance cameras the Avro 683 Lancaster that she would be ferrying to Cornwall. There, she would deliver the heavy bomber to No. 341 Squadron RAF. He knew this group of fighter pilots well. They represented the Free French hunter squadron Alsace, and he and his father had often flown with them. In league with the British, the squadron would be making sweeps over Nazi-controlled Brittany. Until recently, he believed that he would be joining them. Perhaps one day soon he would be flying with them again. For now, though, his fate was drawing him into a different battle.

He was not alone in confronting new and complicated battles. Even now, while with harnessed intensities he was urging Simone to enter this different peril, he was aware of the preparation (as surreptitious as it was methodical) for new large-scaled battles and for adversaries both lethal and unexpected. Here, along the seven acres that compassed the heft and span and resilience of RAF Ringway, ferry pilots were ascending the skies as they flew Blenheims, Beaufighters, and Lancasters from these camouflaged airstrips to the squadrons who were based hundreds of miles away. Here, too, within aircraft hangars that also wore subtle disguises and that were carefully dispersed across all seven acres of Ringway in order to minimize losses in the event of aerial attacks, maintenance units were positioning armament and radios in factory-delivered Gloster Meteors and Vickers Wellingtons. Inside distant hangars within northerly fields, flying instructors were guiding women as well as men to a reliable mastery of heavy bombers. Within busy aeronautical shops that stretched across the furtive terrain of the southwest fields, ground engineers were revving aircraft engines as they searched for defects or tested newly completed repairs.

Outside these shops, along winding roads that shot forward into surprising turns and unforgiving curves, auto technicians were training cadets for service as motor transport drivers. In the faraway distance that bordered a forest of elm, oak and spruce trees and toward which he (at the wheel) and Simone (as his reluctant passenger) were riding briskly in a borrowed Willys MB air force jeep, secret agent recruits (both men and women) were taking parachute training jumps from a tethered barrage balloon seven hundred feet up in the air. Each of the recruits was suspended in a box-like cage with a central trap door. At the word of command from the instructor who had accompanied them in their caged ascension, these novice paratroopers would leap into the listing surround of space. Fast descending, they skillfully kept their legs together to prevent breaks and, just before reaching the ground, rolled their bodies over to soften the impact of their landing.

As he drove across the wide span of Ringway, he saw all of these things. Even now, they were hurrying past him, animated and elliptical in his scanning glance. All around him were speed and impetus and momentum. There was activity bellowing its strident powers—a cacophony of roaring aircraft leaving and arriving and of carpenters' whirring drills connecting sheets of corrugated steel, beams of horizontal timber, and slabs of concrete that would become barracks and office buildings. There was the sometime roiling wind whose autumn warmth nearly tempered its lashing aptitudes. There was the pale glow of the sun enveloping the landscape with a ghostly membrane. And, always ahead of Simone and him, there were the emphatic scarlet oaks, golden elms, and blue-gray cypresses at the north edge of the forest that, wind-tossed and dominant, rose as with savage wings and waited to receive them.

Before his implicated senses, the day was disguising its accuracies, offering to his incisive awareness an imagery of half-truths and deceptions. With the skill of commandos disguising their presence or of a double agent imposing upon a scene a *trompe l'oeil* or trick of the eye that confused an enemy, the RAF staff had made of Ringway a fabricated reality. They had transformed the look of the airfield into a countrified illusion that was meant to fool the Nazi bomber pilots who were strafing aircraft factories and RAF airfields. Here, hangars and repair workshops and Nissen huts wore covers of artificial bushes and tree branches that, from an aerial perspective, appeared to be what those buildings were not—the clustered greenery of the forest. Adjacent fields of silvery miscanthus grass, of cotton lavender shrubs, and of Himalayan yellow poppies—breeze-tossed and vivid—quickened the rural intimations of the land.

When they reached the edge of the forest, he and Simone left the jeep and stood facing each other by a massive elm, its gold-red leaves and outstretched branches a swaying canopy in the quickened wind.

He was the first to speak, echoing the confident words he had used to override the tension of their meeting.

"You are the only one I can trust," he said. "You will get everything right. Together, we can trap this double agent and kill him."

Even in a military tan shirt and gray-green flier's overalls, Simone looked lovely. But no longer was she the soft and vulnerable girl that he had first met in Switzerland when she was fifteen. Now, nine years later, with her blonde hair pulled back to form a neat coil at the nape of her neck, beauty still attended her. But the ongoing turmoil of the war years and the abrasive experiences of their marriage had dimmed her radiance. Today, her blue eyes were observing him without the fervor or the trust that in their early years together she had always brought to her regard of him. The special light had gone out of her eyes, and a smile no longer influenced her unadorned face. Nor did she make any effort to rouse his sensual interest. Her manner now was matter-of-fact, while she drew her words from the hardened part of herself.

"Your plan won't work," she said. "You are targeting an innocent man."

"How can you be certain of that?"

She paused. She was measuring the cost of telling him what he did not want to hear.

"I know Hans better than you do. I love him."

Anger flicked its sparks inside him. But he held himself steady.

"That is not important. What is important is that you use my plan to find out more about him."

"I already know everything that I need to know about him."

"You may not know as much as you think you do. You may be leaguing yourself with a man who is a Nazi. My plan will put him to the test. If you become part of that plan, you will know for certain who Hans Mueller really is."

"I've told you that your plan won't work."

"My plan *will* work," Marc insisted. "You can make it work. With Mueller, you have not stopped being Valérie Moreau. Now you can go on telling him that, unlike some of the British and the French, you truly believe he is no longer a Nazi. Tell him that you understand what it means to be distrusted by the British and the French, even though you are fighting alongside them. You can remind Mueller that the British and the French have not really forgiven you for being Pierre Moreau's daughter. They distrust you, too. You can convince your Hans Mueller that you want to avenge your father's wrongdoing. Tell Mueller that you want to kill as many Nazis as you can. Remind him that you have the necessary skills to be a double agent. Killing Nazis has become your stock in trade. But conquering the Nazis won't be any good unless Hans is right there beside you. Tell him that you want to be with him as much as possible. Tell him all of that. You can make him believe anything you say. Then you will be around him often enough to find out his every move."

"This is madness," Simone said. "Let it go."

Marc pushed further.

"We can put an end to Mueller and save thousands of lives."

Once again Simone protested.

"You aren't even certain that Hans Mueller is working against us. You have no proof that he is a double agent."

"I think that he is," Marc said. "But you are the only one who can find out for us. You have won Mueller's trust by becoming Valérie Moreau. You can find out everything that we need to know about him."

Simone studied him quietly before she spoke the blunt words that told him even more firmly how it was with her.

"The war has changed you in ways that I had not imagined. You used to think on a realistic level. You never allowed wild schemes to confuse you."

"This is no wild scheme," he said. "If Han Mueller is a mole, if he is the double agent who is feeding information to the Nazis so that they can win the war, my plan will find him out. But you have to be a part of the plan. You have to be there with me."

"Get someone else to work with you," Simone said. "I want no part of your plan. What I do as a ferry pilot and sometimes as an agent for MI5 may help to win the war. I believe in that work. I do not believe in your plan."

"You don't believe in *me*. You don't want to work with me. That's how it is with you."

"You are only part of it. I don't believe in your plan, either."

Now Marc met her bluntness with the sting of angry words.

"Think, woman. Think. We have a chance to push the Nazis

back. We have a chance to kill the traitors in our midst. I'm not asking you to love me again. Just work with me. That's all you have to do."

His anger, which was a momentary flare of his bitter sorrow, gave her pause. He saw that she recognized the sorrow and the bitterness. They belonged to an anguish not unlike her own. But still she resisted him. Still she refused to work with him. Telling him so, her voice became to his ears—and all in the same moment—a muted crying out, a taut denial of his petition, and a weary lament.

"I can't," she said. "I can't set a trap for an innocent man."

She was remembering what he had done to Gerhard Hauptmann, the German who had stolen her love from him. Gerhard was a ghost now who never left her.

Quickly, Simone turned away from him and hurried back to the jeep. For a few moments, he stood alone there, at the edge of an army of tall scarlet oaks and golden elms that, wind-whipped and restless, made the forest a dark and menacing thing. He watched her while, tight-lipped and sullen, she climbed into the jeep. In that instant, she appeared to his eyes to be a stranger, a woman whom he knew only slightly even though they had often been in each other's company. By the time he returned to his place behind the wheel, she had recovered herself. Once more she was matter-of-fact and self-possessed. As he drove her back to the hangar where she had been working with her crew, she spoke of many things. Her words seemed more extemporaneous and natural than his as they shared their thoughts about the new Hawker Tempest that each of them had recently tested, the Webley & Scott 9mm semi-automatic handgun that they favored, and the risks of flying in daylight.

Only when he was alone again, driving the thirty-five miles to his parents' home in Derbyshire, did he allow himself to recall all the words that Simone and he had spoken and to imagine the ones that their pride or their remorse or their uncertainty had kept them from speaking. But the words that echoed in his mind most of all were the ones he had not meant to say. Over and over, he heard himself telling Simone that he was not asking her to love him again. But those were disingenuous words. They were words that did not tell Simone how it was with him. He had told her those words to keep her from turning away from the wily plan that he had devised. That plan might destroy her trust of Mueller. It might help him to catch a spy, if Mueller were guilty, or to find a way to kill him, even if he appeared to be innocent. It might also bring Simone and him together as the lovers and the married couple they once had been.

Though his meeting with her had not gone well, he was

determined nonetheless to draw Simone into his plan.

Drawing his wife into his plan would not be easy, even though that plan involved their pursuit of a man who had been a Nazi and who might now be a double agent. As wily as he was adept, Marc resolved to enlist the assistance of his parents. With their strong-minded and realistic appraisal of even the most conflicted situations, Henri and Marianne would evaluate his plan as if it were a blueprint for intricate sabotage or a chart devising the path to a necessary assassination. If they believed that his distrust of Hans Mueller was plausible, his parents would urge Simone to help him carry forward this plan to test Hans's loyalty. His parents had already become part of the team pursuing the suspected traitor.

It pleased him to know that his parents were among the most formidable enemies of the Nazis and of their Vichy counterparts. On numerous occasions, he had worked with both his father and his mother to help the Allies win the war. As pilots in the Free French Air Force, he and his father, the world-famous violinist Henri Roussillon, had often flown in the same combat missions. Accurate and murderous, they had shot down more than a hundred enemy aircraft, and they had bombed more than sixty German munitions factories and airfields.

On the ground, they were just as lethal while they carried

forward their assignments for the French Resistance. They did the things that they were trained to do. Without hesitation or scruple or the recrimination that falters before the retrospective inward glance that might show them their crimes, they tortured and maimed the French traitors who were collaborators in the service of the Nazis. Usually, they broke the legs and the arms of their opponents to obtain the information they needed to know about the Germans who had overtaken France. On some rain-drenched mornings or inside sun-blanched afternoons or within the obscurities of random midnights, they gouged out an eye of each hardened traitor they had captured. They held their drowning faces in toilets, and they cut through the bare flesh of their backs with heavy whips or with sharp razors. Then, after long days and nights of torture yielded them the necessary truth, they shot their captives through the heart. Or, if they preferred to save their bullets for the encounters with the Milice and with the Germans they were always anticipating, they strangled the traitors they had caught.

His country had trained even women to kill. Marianne, his mother, had the unforgiving heart of a killer. She also had a sharpshooter's eye that enabled her always to hit the target. She, too, had tortured and maimed her enemies. She had killed them with dagger, rifle, pistol, and the hangman's knot. Her quick-witted ability to disguise herself, her precise use of a stiletto as well as a grenade, and her swift slitting of a throat or the gouging of an eye made her a valuable member of their group.

Once again, from the darker recesses of his awareness and with new and harsh intensities, bitter thoughts rose up to haunt Marc. Grim-faced and unflinching, he scanned the brute imagery of himself and of his parents. The war had made them savages. It had activated their primitive instincts and their capacities for inflicting pain and death upon their enemies. In their willingness to torture and to kill, they were not unlike Fabien and Gaston. Like them, they were brutal and unsentimental. Like them, they were cunning, resourceful and well-trained.

But, unlike Fabien and Gaston, they had not been savages before the war. Unlike them, they had never been traitors. Though they carried within themselves a tattered honor, it was honor nonetheless. What had been disfigured or destroyed was their idealized imagery of themselves. Now each of them was a chipped self-mastery. Each of them was, in subtle ways, a dislocated personhood. Each of them, in spite of well-honed self-control and tough-minded resilience, was a fractured humanity. No longer were they guiltless or irreproachable or uncompromised. They had killed and would go on killing until the enemy killed them or until the war ended. Yet, if they survived the war, their country would readily accept them. It was, after all, their country that had changed the rules and had given them permission to kill.

Marc had become as hardened as his parents. They, too, had trained themselves rigorously to forget the killings. If, on occasion, a blood-stained and unforgiving apparition flared out of their memory, rushing forward without warning to haunt them, they confronted it as he did. Stoic as well as cynical, they accepted the harsh truth of the memory—all of its violent recoil and all of its soul-plundering implications. Then, casual-seeming and austere, they pushed the memory away.

Although Simone had worked effectively with both of his parents, she had more often joined his mother in their assignments as ferry pilots and as secret agents who were members of Britain's Special Operations Executive (SOE) network. As SOE agents, they had not trained together. But the brace and bulwark of their proficiencies derived from identical schooling. In Scotland, within the rugged wilds of Arisaig and Meoble that were accessible only on foot over a mountain track, they had trekked with other men and women across some of the country's roughest terrain in bad weather. They had waded through cold rushing streams and crept through thorny undergrowth to hide from other groups of trainees that had been sent out in patrols to hunt for them. More than a few times, they had dived from cliffs into churning waters and had swum a mile to the safe harbor of a distant village or an obscure inlet. On this desolate western coast of Inverness, they learned as well how to assemble, dismantle and fire various types of pistols, rifles and sub-machine guns including Sten and Bren guns, which were the weapons most often dropped from Allied planes to resisters. At Arisaig and Meoble, they also trained to be ordinary-looking couriers and expert radio operators. It was in those locations that they learned how, with a hat pin or a Fairbairn-Sykes knife or a V42 stiletto or a poison pill, to kill silently.

For the next phase of their training, they left the fierce conditions of the highland behind them and journeyed to England. At Beaulieu, while being yoked nonetheless to a rigorous and intense concentration, they enjoyed the rewards of a patrician estate in the New Forest that lent its vast landscape and its sequestered accommodations to the ongoing war effort. There, in a countryside setting which often solaced them and where their instructors compelled them to master new levels of intrigue, they were enrolled in a graduate course in survival that imagined them caught in an occupied country. They learned well how to use their false papers and how to conceal documents from the French Fascists and the Nazis who might be inspecting them. Again and again, they underwent interrogation sessions that simulated the grim reality of being captured, questioned, and tortured by their enemies. They learned how to lay an explosive charge on a railway track, how to use explosives to destroy crucial bridges, and how to steal a police car and bring it back. All this while, they were learning how to immerse themselves in the fictive life of the person named on their identity cards and ration books, so that, when they were questioned, they could without hesitation and with natural understatement provide the names of family members, the names of the schools that they and their relatives attended, birth dates and anniversaries, job history, and the names of streets in the town or city where they lived.

This time Simone would have to continue to be a person who had actually existed. In such an assignment, Marc knew, there was a greater danger that Hans Mueller would discover who she really was. But he believed that Simone would be willing to go on accepting the risk if he and his parents convinced her that she was essential to the success of his plan for finding out whether Hans Mueller was a traitor. With this thought in mind, he drove his jeep even more swiftly to Derbyshire.

He was surprised when his parents defended Hans.

"Everything that MI5 has found out about Hans points to his innocence," his father said. "The MI5 people are still investigating him, just to make their certainty even more certain. Let them decide who Hans Mueller really is. You can stay in it. You can go on investigating Mueller. But keep in mind that you carry a great deal of baggage with you. You have personal reasons for wanting to find Mueller guilty. That does not make you the best man for this job."

"What you are doing is wrong," his mother said. "You are contriving accusations against Hans. You want to win back Simone, and Hans is in your way. But your killing Hans is not the answer. Nor should you use this week, here in Derbyshire, to persuade Simone that Hans is a traitor. She is convinced that he is innocent. If he *is* a Nazi spy, she will find him out. Use this week, instead, to test your relationship with Simone."

"I thought that the two of you would be in this with me all the way," Marc said. "I was sure that you would see Hans as I do."

"We see him as he is," his father said. "We pay attention to the facts. So far, Hans Mueller is in the clear. Don't worry, though. MI5 is still watching him, and your mother and I are keeping a careful eye on him. You will be wise to forget about killing Mueller. You want to kill him, even if you find that he is not guilty. You are not thinking straight. You are forgetting that, if you kill Mueller without cause, you will be no better than a thug—a vicious murderer."

His father's blunt remarks did not please Marc.

Sensing his suppressed anger and his disappointment, his

mother hurried to explain the plan that might reunite him with Simone.

"I'll invite Simone to the party that your father and I are giving next week," his mother said. "I think that she will come, because there will be new guests here who believe that she is Valérie Moreau and because she needs to get away from her troubles."

Marc wondered.

"She may not want to come if she knows that I am going to be here."

They were sitting in his father's study, sharing an after-dinner brandy while his parents reviewed his plan to trap and kill Hans Mueller. There would be, Marc knew, a moment when his father would offer them his thoughts about Simone and about the manner in which they should approach her. But now he preferred to hear what his wife had to say, tough-minded and experienced as she was, and to judge as well the troubled words of their son.

"You are right to believe that Simone is wary of being near you," his mother said, "but not because she hates you. On the contrary, Simone has not yet decided whether she can ever hate you or whether she can completely sever the bond that still exists between you. What makes her uneasy is the thought that she still loves you, though she is trying not to. She is testing herself by living at her barracks most of the time, without you. But she hasn't given you up completely. There are days when, in spite of herself, she misses you very much. Those are the days when she wonders whether she can revive what she had with you before Gerhard and before Hans. She asks herself whether the two of you together can go past Gerhard."

His mother's words brought him no comfort. He, of course, saw the truth in her words as well as the liabilities. He might win back Simone's love. Quite possibly, though, she might decide to go forward without him. The ambiguities within Simone's attitude toward him might have left him always uneasy. But he had learned to suppress the uneasiness, pushing its melancholic residues way back into the deepest recesses of his mind. All his thoughts about Simone saw her as the prize he had won and lost. He intended to claim her as his own once again. In spite of his parents' defense of Hans's innocence, he would not let go of his conviction that Hans was guilty or of his plan to destroy him. That his scheme to trap and kill Hans might bring Simone back to him was all to the good. He was well aware, as though he were re-living a dark memory, that once again he would be killing a man to whom Simone had given her love, if Hans Mueller turned out to be the traitor. Not even his certainty that Hans's death would condemn Simone to bitter days and months of grief would put him off his proper course.

He was certain of something more. Simone had to take part in his plan for killing Hans. That was the only way she could exonerate herself for loving a Nazi spy. That was the only way he could forgive her for loving a man other than himself. Her feelings about the killing should not be the most important issue. Nor should he reveal to her his true motive for the killing. He was plotting to kill his rival and win back Simone. He would not permit himself to lose sight of that goal. The hardened part of his nature, which he drew upon during his bombing missions and for his MI5 assignments, was going to keep him anchored to realistic priorities. His first priority was to hunt down his rival and kill him.

As if he were reading his thoughts, his father spoke up now, his words nearly brusque and his manner as hardened as his own.

"Don't make a move against Hans Mueller without cause," he said. "Give Simone a chance to prove that Hans is innocent or guilty. Mueller is the reason why we are asking her to join our team. She already knows him well. If she finds that he is a secret Nazi, she will not back away from the truth. She will know what to do. That is why we want her with us. She is the best woman for the job."

For an instant, Marc grew very still. Here, within a room that had always kept the dangerous world at bay while he was visiting it, he no longer felt solaced or safe. All the images in the room that to his mind were once a promise of the balance and proportion he could discover in the larger world if he surmounted its dangers appeared today to be emblems of disguise. The burnish of cedar paneling, the plush of a Beauvais carpet, the symmetry of ample chairs and a desk of cherry wood, and the gilt-edged sheen of book-shelves with special editions—all these images belonged to a contrived reality. Nor was it this room alone that seemed unreal, a willful artifice that confused the senses and left the onlooker even more vulnerable to the day's betrayals. The profuse and radiant colors of the gardens that he could glimpse from the panoramic window behind his father's desk seemed in this instant even less real. Seated as he was, on a richly upholstered chair just beyond his father's desk, he viewed the landscape outside that window as camouflage that hid rampant danger. The greenery out there was an illusion that offered a merely tenuous haven to the war-weary and the lost. It was a will-o'-the-wisp that flashed its benign imagery as a trick to thwart naïve believers. On this autumn afternoon, the green, undulant hills that rose all around his parents' home away from Paris, here in the East Midlands, did not excite his senses. Nor did the frisky Tobianos that were cantering inside a paddock, there in the southerly distance far beyond the panoramic window, ease his spirit. The world was a savage place, without safe harbors or dependable sanctuaries. He would not let down his guard. Nor would he accept his parents' defense of Hans or their warning that his killing Hans Mueller would destroy any possibility of saving his marriage. He was determined to listen to his own counsel and to activate the plan that he was devising.

Now, in a spate of matter-of-fact words yoked to his suppressed anger, Marc told his father—and his mother, too—how it was with him.

"Simone *is* the best woman for the job," he said. "But there is another important reason why I want her to work with me. I need to find out who she really is. I do not really know her anymore. We have become strangers to one another. I need to find out whether she can ever be in love with me again. I have to figure out what I am going to do with my life if she cannot love me."

With penetrating eyes, his parents carefully observed him. He had surprised them. Rarely had he opened himself to them about his troubled marriage. Nor had they intruded upon his need to keep his relationship with Simone a private matter. He was aware that Simone, tormented by the guilt of her infidelity, had sometimes confided in his mother. But seldom to his father and his mother had he ever revealed any information about the wayward trajectory that his life with Simone had taken.

Whatever they knew, his parents had, for the most part, discovered with their own eyes or through Simone's ambiguous confessions. The dark narrative that his marriage to Simone had spun dismayed his parents without shocking them. They knew the world well, having reveled in earlier times within its synthetic glamour and having fought during these darker years on its war-torn fields and inside its embattled skies. In this uneasy moment, Marc recalled that their own marriage had been troubled, shaken as it was by his father's infidelity and his mother's reluctance to forgive.

Perhaps this memory of the discontented phase of her marriage pushed his mother to break the spell of silence that was now overtaking them. With her clipped inflections and her penetrating insight, she chose words that were meant to keep him on his proper course.

"Your father is right," she said. "Don't bring your personal feelings about Hans Mueller into our plan. Give Simone a chance to find out more about Hans. Keep remembering that, once we set the plan in motion, she will no longer be Simone. She will be Valérie Moreau."

His father said more.

"Remember that, if Hans does turn out to be a Nazi, Simone will be keeping company with a very dangerous man. She is putting her life on the line for us. In this mission, she is not the wife who belongs to your troubled marriage. She is the agent that you have to save if MI5 and your mother and I have wrongly believed in Mueller."

Marc threw out quick words to tell his parents exactly where he stood.

"I'll do everything that I can to save her," he said, his voice holding firm its curt intensity. "I'll always do everything. Only if I am killed will she be on her own. But, no matter what happens, I'll be thinking of her as my Simone. She will always be my Simone."

For an instant, his parents glanced at each other warily. Then, right after his father had signaled her with their private language of eyes, his mother told him what he needed to know.

"Don't be too sure that Simone belongs to you," she said. "Keep in mind what I have just told you. She is trying to work her way into a different life that may not include you."

Once again Marc protested.

"She will never be able to do it," he said. "I know Simone well. She will never be able to live happily without me."

"I think that you are right," his father said. "But she has to find that out on her own, and you have to step back while she is doing it."

"I can do that," Marc said, grim-faced and tough-minded. "Whether she is being Simone Roussillon or Valérie Moreau,

I'll be keeping an eye on her."

His mother saw in his words the traces of menace. That she recognized his muted anger did not surprise him. But her next remark gave him pause. Clearly, she wanted him to come face to face with the darker possibilities of his wife's once more immersing herself inside the identity of Valérie Moreau .

"Will you be willing to step back if Simone goes on sleeping with Hans Mueller?"

His words turned blunt and rancorous.

"If she really loves me, she won't sleep with him."

In this moment, while the force of these words cast a pall upon all that they had been saying, his father pushed him further. He, too, wanted him to face up to the way things might change for Simone, once they set their plan in motion.

"Simone may not have a choice," his father said. "Sleeping with Mueller may be the only way that she can get the information we need."

His mother did not like the scenario into which they were moving.

"Are you certain that you want Simone involved in this plan?" she asked. "We can call in another woman to work with us."

For an instant, he pondered the complications of working with a stranger. Then, he stood firm with the decision he had made days earlier.

"I want Simone to work with us," he said. "I can't say that I know everything about her. But I know most of the important things. I also know that she is not a secret Nazi."

These new words eased the tension without dispelling it.

"Her not being a Nazi is, of course, the essential thing," his father said.

"But remember what happened with Gerhard Hauptmann," his mother warned him. "Don't make Hans Mueller another Gerhard."

"I'll remember," he answered her, while in his mind's eye the violent imagery of Gerhard's death flared up from his past. "Maybe Simone had better remember, too."

Chapter Seven

The Ghost Lovers

Just how effectively his mother's plan to draw Simone back to him was working, Marc learned when, a few days afterward, she conferred with him in the privacy of his family's home in Derbyshire.

During that first week in October, his mother had sent Simone a formal invitation to the party that she and his father were hosting. The invitation, which was printed on gilt-edged paper that was scented with lavender, promised a glamorous setting and carefree activities. If she accepted the invitation, Simone would join fourteen guests who were driving in from London, as well as eight others who lived in the area, for one of the extraordinary weeks that his parents occasionally hosted. The war and their frequent absence from Derbyshire had reduced the house staff. Currently, Mrs. Dowling served as the primary housekeeper and as an accomplished chef. The eight other persons who had remained on the staff were prepared to make the week a successful one. Only ten guests would be there at any one time. Many of them would stay two or three days and then return to their war-driven obligations. The holiday spirit that Henri and Marianne Roussillon invoked was, everyone knew, the Roussillons' way of subverting for a few temporary days the bleak atmosphere of the war. A famous playwright and an equally renowned poet would be there. Among the other guests there would be an ambassador in the service of King George; two MI5 agents with their wives; RAF and Free French Air Force bomber pilots—a few of them with their latest girlfriends; and the owner of a diamond mine in South Africa who was contributing large sums of money to the British war effort.

At first, not even the promise of days and evenings that offered festive amenities persuaded Simone to accept the invitation that his mother had sent to her. But, at RAF Ringway, when—after a busy morning and on separate assignments—they had been preparing to ferry an Avro Lancaster and a Hawker Hurricane to Fighter Command squadrons in Glasgow and Normandy, his mother urged Simone once more to come to the party that was going to quicken the autumn week and that would surely dispel the wearying gloom that pervaded everyone's life. At that moment, while they took a few minutes away from a lunch break with their maintenance crews, they were conferring privately within a corner of the hangar where they had been working. With their crews, they had been fitting with reconnaissance cameras the heavy bombers that they would be piloting.

Polite yet firm, Simone once again declined the invitation.

"If I came to your party, I would have to be Valérie Moreau," Simone told his mother. "But some of the guests know me as Simone Roussillon. One of them might be a double agent. I had better not come. The risk is too great."

With cool-headed assurance, his mother brushed aside her hesitation.

"Henri and I have known our guests for a long time. We have screened them carefully. They understand the importance of your maintaining your disguise as Valérie Moreau. They are willing to collaborate with the scenario that requires you to be someone who no longer exists. In fact, your being this Valérie—this ghost made visible—intrigues them. Before the war, they would have found pleasure in the success that you have thus far achieved with your disguise. But war has hardened them. It has made them more discerning. They find no pleasure in the danger that you have taken upon yourself. Believe me when I tell you that Henri's and my guests will do everything they can to help you elude the danger."

Still Simone hesitated. Still she resisted the invitation. Now his mother chose the words that, she believed, would draw

Simone to the party.

"You will meet so many interesting people," she said. "Some of them are already your friends. Two of them are very special men for you. One of them is Marc. You know who the other man is."

Hearing these words, Simone grew very still. But her skill at concealing her emotions could not dispel the tension that was rising within her. As though she were challenging his mother to speak the name that she expected to hear, she held her in a steadfast gaze.

His mother hurried forward to say the name, all the while allowing herself to be impressed by her daughter-in-law's tough-minded silence.

"Henri and I have invited Hans Mueller for the entire week," she said. "We want to see you with this man who has become very special to you. We want to see you with him and with Marc in the same room."

His mother noticed how carefully Simone modulated the civil tones of her response. But her civility could not altogether dismiss her unease.

"I do not care to have my personal relations put on display," she said. "I am surprised that you and Henri imagine that I would."

Maintaining her own poise, his mother began reasoning with

Simone.

"Henri and I are doing this for *you*," she said. "You need to be in the company of Marc and Hans at the same time. When they are together with you in any of the lighthearted occasions that our holiday week will offer you, you will have a better chance to find out what you really feel for each of them."

"I know what I feel," Simone said. "I am in love with Hans. Whatever love I felt for Marc is finished. He needs to move on, just as I do."

"Marc still loves you," his mother insisted. "In spite of everything that has gone wrong for the both of you, he believes that you love him."

"He is mistaken."

"Are you certain of that? Has the Gerhard episode destroyed all of the love that you and Marc shared for eight years?"

"I can never forgive Marc or myself for what we did to Gerhard."

"A moment ago, you said that you needed to move on. You are right to say so. You do need to move away from your past. But you do not have to move away from each other. Give yourself another chance with Marc. Give *him* a chance."

An anguished frown scattered the careful effects of Simone's self-control.

"I can't," she cried out. "I can't. I can never love Marc in the same way. Maybe I can't love him in any way that is important to either of us."

His mother pushed further.

"I don't believe that you are as certain of your feelings as you pretend to be. You are not admitting what you truly feel."

"You do not understand me, Marianne. I do not know whether you ever will. How, when you are outside it, can you comprehend the hell that I have been living through? In every one of these wretched days and weeks and months after Gerhard, I have been trying not to feel anything for Marc. That is the truth. That is what has happened to me."

Simone's words gave his mother pause. Yet, without compromising her belief that her son's marriage to Simone was not over, his mother soon found the words that urged Simone to test her feelings.

"Use this week to let Marc know how it is with you," she said. "Prove to him—and to yourself—that you love Hans Mueller completely and that you are finished with loving Marc."

"I can't do that," Simone said. "Nothing will come of it except angry and bitter scenes. I'd rather leave things the way they are. I know who Marc is. I know how dangerous he can be. Though I do not know everything about Hans, I trust him. I am not afraid to take a leap in the dark with the Hans that I do not know completely."

These words did not please his mother. Her tone became brittle, and her determination even more steely. Now she threw out a different challenge to her daughter-in-law.

"It is essential that you come to Derbyshire," she said. "You may not be ready to prove that your love for Hans is greater than whatever remains of your love for Marc. All that is less important than the other test you need to make. You need to prove to yourself and to all of us in the Resistance that Hans is not a double agent."

Whether it was this challenge that intrigued Simone or whether it was her ambivalent feelings for *him*, the husband whom she had loved for so long and from whom she was now estranged, or whether it was the perversity of spending a week with him and his rival, his mother did not know. Nor did Marc know, when a day or so later his mother told him about this conversation with Simone. But, in that moment when his mother urged her to prove that Hans Mueller was not a spy for the Nazis, Simone accepted the challenge.

"All right," she conceded, her determination as steely as his mother's. "I'll come to Derbyshire. I'll be there for Hans and only Hans. I'll show you that he is the one man I love. I'll show you that he is not a Nazi."

During his first days in Derbyshire, Marc was rarely alone with Simone or with Hans Mueller. Willful and intrepid, he kept emotionally detached from the gregarious scenes unfolding around him, even while with disarming vitality he participated in all of them. He went out of his way to befriend the new, young people that his parents had invited to share the joy of being untethered from the burdens of the war. They were pilots and nurses, as well as artists and musicians and journalists. They perceived Simone as Hans did. She was the glamorous Valérie Moreau, an agent for the Resistance who was bravely fighting the Nazis. These new guests understood that he was Marc Roussillon. But they were unaware that he was married to Simone. Among them was an especially pretty girl named Deirdre Sullivan. She had left her parents' home in Galway to serve as a nurse in the 28th Station Hospital in nearby Sudbury. With her and with all the other new people, he entered the lively occasions that these festival-seeming days were offering them. He simulated an easy camaraderie, and he brought to every group activity a natural skill that anchored its proficiencies to a hardy regimen and to a healthy disposition.

That week, the weather was their friend, providing them warm, sunny days; cobalt-blue skies; and soft breezes. On these days, they canoed on the lake behind his parents' Georgian home. They swam in the heated pool within the west wing of the main house. They rode cantering Tobianos and Sorraias across the wide span of the property. They played tennis and lacrosse, and they cycled along the autumn-colored Monsal Trail in the Derbyshire Peak District.

The evenings favored them, as well. The autumn moon shone vibrantly, the stars gleamed, and the white traceries of clouds appeared docile and luminous. During one evening, the music room within the west wing became a home for a concert. To invoke the happier days before the war, his father and his mother, who had withdrawn from their successful careers as classical musicians when the war began, agreed to perform. His father pleased his audience with a moving rendition of Mozart's *Fifth Violin Concerto*. His mother impressed everyone with her sensitive playing of Chopin's *First Piano Concerto*.

On other nights, he and all the other guests danced in the ballroom of his family's home. It was a large and splendid room, replete with a barrel-vaulted and coffered ceiling, gold-leaf paneling, full-length French doors, and silk damask draperies. For a few evenings within this extraordinary week, his mother and an interior designer transformed the room into a posh nightclub. In such a setting and with the bluesy sounds of a popular orchestra enhancing the atmosphere, many of the guests ate Cordon Bleu cuisine prepared in Mrs. Dowling's immaculate kitchen, drank champagne drawn from his parents' well-stocked cellars, and danced away the evening. He danced only with Deirdre Sullivan, because he wanted everyone there to imagine that they were beginning a romance. He also wanted to diminish the significance of even the most casual attention that he might show occasionally to Simone. That he might rouse her jealousy because he was so often in the company of Deirdre pleased him.

With her titian hair, oval face and fair complexion and with her full-bodied femininity, Deirdre was a rare, young beauty. Her being drawn to him might have consoled him, if he were not the prisoner of his past and of his obsessive love for Simone. Deirdre carried herself with a quiet confidence that banked its powers within an inherent strength and a mastery of the grim experiences to which the war had exposed her. Shadowed by her own mystery, she was reluctant to speak of those experiences. In their earlier meetings, he had to prod her to tell him about the things that she was doing for the war. He witnessed, while face to face with her in the telling, the radiance of her eyes and her face dimming almost imperceptibly. He sensed the rigorous discipline that kept her words matter-of-fact and unsentimental. He recognized, from his own experience, the self-protective will that drove her responses whenever she confronted or recollected the days and nights of her hospital duties. She had fought her battles away from combat zones. But they were grim battles, nonetheless. She had nursed the wartorn bodies of men who had lost their eyes and limbs and part of their faces. She had watched their wretched faces grimace with anguish. She had heard their cries of despair. She had reached out to all of them—the wounded pilots, the demolition specialists, and the infantrymen. She had tried, after the surgeons' scalpels had worked their repairs, to nurture their gaunt frames and to revive their tattered dreams. The war had shattered her innocent perceptions. It had stolen her girlhood expectations and her romanticized view of the world. Teaching her its hardened realism, the war had made her a strong, young woman. She had learned how to do battle with the horror. She had learned how to rescue herself from the despair that sometimes consumed other nurses and how to guard the life-sustaining hope that, in spite of the war, lived within her.

So, in their first meetings, Deirdre told him, with the elliptical brevity that makes terseness a vivid emphasis. In all the occasions that they shared during this extraordinary week, he noticed her quiet strength and her genteel manner. Although the war had taken her innocence from her, she had kept intact the conviction that, inside the maelstrom that was the war, she would go on nurturing the wounded whom the war had left whole and intact and rescuing the disfigured who had lost limbs and believed they were lost. Perhaps, her desire to help others and her willingness to focus on their needs influenced the healthy glow that gave to her beauty an ethereal quality. Perhaps, this concern for others far more than for herself was saving her from being drained or from becoming altogether haunted by the ruined and dying men that she served in the hospital. Even in this brief week of knowing her, Marc formed a deep admiration for her. Deirdre was steadfast. She was sensitive and strong and open. She was authentic. So many times during this week, he wanted to leave his ghosts behind him. He wanted to tell Deirdre how it was with him. He wanted her to dispel the gloom that was hovering secretly inside him. But, if he were to reach out to her, he would have to leave Simone behind. He could not turn away from Simone. He could not cut her out of his life without cutting away his only chance for real happiness. To cut Simone away from his life was to leave himself a maimed and tormented man.

He did not tell Deirdre about the past that haunted him. Instead, at one of the glamorous dances that his parents had arranged, she told him about her own ghosts. On that evening, their friends were dancing all around them or dining at nearby tables when Deirdre allowed him to lead her onto the dance floor. He felt the soft delicacy of her hands as he gently clasped them, and he knew the shapely contour of her back as he pressed his right hand upon it. He noticed her blue eyes, her perfect nose, and her gleaming smile. In the distance, standing together on a stage with the proficient band, a tall blond man and a petite brunette were singing a ballad about the true love that lasts. Their poignant voices and the blue notes of the band kept floating across the crowded room and mingling with the excited voices of the guests.

He danced with Deirdre in silence, consenting to their nearness with a pleasure that surprised him. So moved was he by this unexpected moment with her that he refrained from speaking any words that might break the spell. He felt deeply about her, and the truth of the feelings that he had been suppressing now awed and confused him. Still he accepted the spell. Over and over he gave himself to the whirl and sway of this dance with her. She, with graceful rhythms and with her soft blue eyes sometimes looking up at him to meet his pensive gaze of her, collaborated with him completely. Then, as the two singers were ending their song about newly discovered love, he noticed the tears that were welling in those blue eyes of hers that had influenced his belief that she could possibly save him. Now she spoke the words that broke the spell and hurried them into the darker reality that was their own and that they had so briefly eluded.

"I wish that it could be this way with us always," she said, her voice a melancholic whisper. "But I'm not ready for this.

I'm not prepared. I was not expecting you."

He recognized the anguished tremor within the soft textures of her voice. The feminine timbres could not diminish the emotional charge of her words. Lost inside a wilderness of remorse and despair, he began in this instant to understand that Deirdre was fighting her way through her own wilderness.

"Do you want to talk about it?" he asked her.

"Yes," she murmured.

"Let's go out to the terrace," he said. "We'll find a private spot there."

"I would like that," she said, while she continued to accept the clasp of his hand and the intensity of his brown-eyed gaze. "I would like that very much."

With masculine and courtly poise, he led her away from the dance floor. The jazz-laden sounds of a different melody were filling the room now, as the musicians began playing a new set of ballads. The petite brunette, with glamorous sensuality, was singing this time about loneliness and about the lover who had left her. While he held Deirdre close to him, he made his way smoothly through the crowded room. A montage of images swirled around him. As Deirdre and he were leaving the dance floor, couples young and older were swaying to the slower, more intimate rhythms of the music. His mother, still youthful and tonight especially fashionable, was dancing with a British ambassador who had come to express the prime minister's gratitude for the large sums of money that his parents had contributed to the war effort. His father, sophisticated and dapper, was partnering a beautiful French film star who had, during that morning, visited the wounded pilots and soldiers in the 28th Station Hospital. Leaving the dancers behind Deirdre and him, he hurried with her past the ornately decorated tables beyond the dance space, where other guests were enjoying their dinners. In the far distance, to the left of the dining area, some of the guests were drinking bourbon, vodka, and whiskey at the bar. Farther than that even, in the southwest corner of the room, Simone and Hans were emerging from his mother's rose garden. As he guided Deirdre toward the terrace, Simone and Hans were only a flash or flare of imagery upon his keen-eyed awareness. Dressed in a form-fitting blue gown, Simone looked radiant. Hans Mueller, dashing in a tuxedo, was kissing her as they returned to the party that, Marc imagined, they had abandoned so that in the midst of the garden they might enjoy each other's company in private. But only for a moment did he glance at the flare and flash of their suddenly being *there,* clinging amorously together on the threshold of the room. Maintaining a steady pace, he and Deirdre arrived at the opened door to the terrace, leaving behind them the large, elegant room with its quick and colorful textures that were people and music, wine and food, laughing words and intimate voices.

The night air was mild, and the moonlit sky was a glowing canopy. In the distance, the lake glowed, as well, and the hills glimmered. A raven, taking flight above the lake, called out a shrill cry, and the forest of tall trees accepted the familiar sheen of the moon. In earlier years, on a night such as this one when Simone loved him as much as he loved her, he would have gratified his need of her with passionate kisses. But tonight, he did not kiss Deirdre. She was, after all, not Simone. Yet her warmhearted beauty drew him, nonetheless, into its spell. She was a soul mate. She was lonely. She was as troubled as he was.

For a few minutes, neither of them spoke. Instead, with pensive attention, they went on studying the moonlit sky, the glowing lake, and the glimmering hills and forest. Then, to displace the silence that had come between them as if it were watching them, he offered her a cigarette. With the genteel manner that defined who she was, she refused, even as she consented to his smoking one of his South American brands. Only after that did she begin to tell him how it was with her, threading her way to the telling by admitting at first her reluctance to do so.

"I really should not be doing this," she said. "I am ruining your evening."

"I want to help you, if I can. I regard it as a privilege."

Reassured, she began to speak quickly, as if her brisk pace might hurry her past the melancholy that was closing in on her.

"My husband was killed in a bombing mission over Germany two months ago."

"I'm sorry."

"You may have known him. His name was Conor Sullivan. He was stationed at the air base in North Killingholme."

Marc paused, connecting for the first time Conor Sullivan with Deirdre. Many Sullivans were serving in the RAF. He had not imagined that Deirdre had been married to Conor.

"I met him a few times," he explained after a moment's reflection. "But, even before I met him, I had heard of him. Everyone had heard about him. He could handle an Avro Lancaster better than anyone else. Conor Sullivan was one of the great pilots."

His mind's eye saw Conor now. The memory was vivid and nearly palpable. Conor had been unusually tall, standing with confident and muscular ease at six foot four inches. He had curly black hair, mischievous blue eyes, and a friendly smile. He had been a team player, never courting the glory that frequently came to him or undercutting the excellence of other pilots in his squadron. Marc was not surprised that Conor had won the love of this beautiful Irish girl who was grieving over her loss of him.

"Conor and I grew up together in Galway," Deirdre said. "We had always been friends. But, while we were at the university there, we fell in love. I think that we had always felt deeply about each other. We had always been in love. But we did not want to give in to it right away. We wanted to be certain."

"I understand," Marc said.

She glanced up at him, still reluctant to draw him into her grieving.

He wanted to encourage her to talk about the man who had died only a few months ago and who still lived on, a permanent influence upon her existence.

"Tell me more about it," he said. "I'd like to hear about you and Conor."

"When the war brought us into England, we decided to marry. We knew that we might not have much time together. We understood that the war might soon kill one or both of us. But it was important that, even if the war gave us only a little while together, we belonged to one another officially."

"For how long were you married?"

"Eight months. We did have those eight months. I am grateful for every one of them. During that time, I was assigned as a nurse in a hospital not far from Conor's air base. We rented an apartment in the area, and we spent as much time together as we could."

Deirdre paused, the recollection of her days with Conor once more an uneasy memory.

He waited. While he waited, he tried to imagine the unbearable sorrow she was suffering. He pitied her. He wished that he could rescue her. To lose the person whom you loved most of all was to lose everything. It was a kind of death. It was your own death, an anguished dying that clung to you even while you remained alive.

Deirdre found words now that pushed her forward.

"After Conor died, I came here to Derbyshire, because I was needed and because I wanted to get away from North Killingholme. I know that you will think that I am a bit mad. But I kept seeing Conor there. I saw him as clearly as I see you. One time, on a rainy afternoon two weeks after he died, I saw him sailing his favorite yawl on a summer lake. Only days after that, I saw him in a sun-glanced corner of our parlor. He looked up from a book that he was reading and smiled at me. At night sometimes, I saw him lying in our bed, waiting for me. He looked as handsome then as he had on our wedding night. I was certain he was really there. But, when I reached out to him, the image that I had seen of him disappeared."

"You are going through a hard time. Just keep bearing up. Keep going forward. If you have to look back, remember the happiness that you gave him."

Tears welled in her blue eyes, and her face—gone pale now—struggled against this new evidence of sorrow.

"We had so little time together."

"I know."

Blunt, matter-of-fact inflections gave to her words a new, bitter emphasis.

"Conor is gone. He was killed in battle. Nothing can change that."

"No."

Her lovely face tightened itself against a further show of grief. Yet her new words revealed her weary awareness of the way things were for her.

"I'll never see him again."

"Don't think about that."

Her voice sounded hard now and determined.

"I have to think about it," she said. "I have to keep telling myself that Conor is not coming back to me. Then, one day I may not see him on the lake or in my parlor or my bedroom, as though he were actually there. One day I may be ready to begin my life without him."

"You are a strong girl," Marc said. "You have already begun a life without Conor."

"But I haven't given him up. He is still in my life. I am not ready to let him go."

"No," Marc said. "You are not ready."

Sorrow touched his voice, because he could not rescue her. Nor could she become his rescuer.

In these furtive days in Derbyshire, while he maintained an easy camaraderie with all the guests, he never relinquished his ambivalent regard of Simone and Hans. As discreet as he was devious, he swam with them in the heated pool. Always partnered with Deirdre, he also played tennis and lacrosse with Simone and Hans. With them as his and Deirdre's competitors, he fired his Remington skeet gun in a southwest meadow that stood, breeze-touched and sequestered, opposite a forest of swaying larches. He cycled with them across the long road that made a winding trail into a sun-misted clearing in the forest. He shared lighthearted conversations with them at the glamorous dances that his parents were hosting. In every moment that he was in their company, he played his wily game. Affable and apparently carefree, Hans accepted him as a new friend. Rarely alone together, they managed, nonetheless, to speak of many things. Each of them had kayaked in Finland. Each had parachuted from a B-17 Flying Fortress. They had piloted Bristol Beaufighters and Avro Lancasters, and they had blown up strategic bridges, rail lines, and canals in the Nazi sections of

France and in German-controlled Norway. They had also bombed Berlin, Hamburg, Munich, Cologne, and Bremen.

On the surface, at least, Hans appeared to be authentic. He was a brave man who knew when to take risks. He was an intrepid fighter who had saved many of his comrades. Even against his conscious will, Marc found himself respecting Hans Mueller without liking him.

One memorable time, during another of his parents' lavish dinner-dances, he was alone with Hans. On that evening, Deirdre had spilled champagne on her gown, and Simone had hurried away with her to help her change in the room within the west wing where, as a guest for that week, Deirdre was staying. It was at this time that he and Hans left the dance to enjoy a cigarette in his mother's garden. They took their places on a comfortable bench not far from delicate topiaries of a doe and her fawn. For a few minutes, they sat together without uttering a word. To a casual observer, they might have appeared as two rugged men who, weary of the dance, had come into the garden to enjoy a cigarette even as they breathed the crisp air and savored the variety of muted colors that, in their scanning glances, wore the fleet emphases of a montage or the imagery within a kaleidoscope.

Before Marc's contemplative eyes, the moonlit night was changing the colors of flowers and ferns and of trees and shrubs, disguising in subtle ways the reality of their forms. A soft wind with tactile energies animated these forms, and the intermittent light kept translating them into eerie and watchful presences. Or so Marc allowed himself to muse, for that moment regarding the imagery around him as an ambiguous play upon his senses. Only after that did he turn to observe Hans Mueller, who was sitting beside him. Contentment worked its bright traces upon his handsome face, redefining the intricacies of his poise and of his pensive manner. The sight of him roused Marc's anger. Certain that Simone was involved with Hans's contentment, he wondered all over again whether he had lost her forever.

He withdrew further into the stillness that had overtaken him. It was Hans who, moments later, was the first to speak.

"This week has been a wonderful gift," he said, inhaling the rum-scented fragrance of his cigarette. "It is a rare holiday that your parents have made possible for all of us here. The party atmosphere permits me to enjoy the luxury without feeling guilty."

"In a time of war," Marc answered him, "everybody feels guilty. That is one of the penalties. That is the permanent anguish."

He meant to sound matter-of-fact. He meant, by subverting Hans's easy cordiality, to disdain this German's belief that, by entering the fabricated peacetime of this holiday period, he might escape the war even for a week. He meant, first of all, to unsettle Hans by representing with brisk words a hardened realism that allows no escape. But his words sounded more blunt than brisk. They anchored themselves not to the steadying realism that finds its strength and its freedom in confronting every moment of bleakness. His words clung, instead, to the wary sullenness that made him his own prisoner. Was there any wonder that he should be sullen? He had expected Hans Mueller to be handsome. He had imagined that his solid masculinity might, in Simone's eyes, appear charismatic. But, even though Simone had mentioned it, he had not anticipated Hans's uncanny resemblance to Gerhard Hauptmann. He understood at once why Simone was drawn to him. Hans was exactly as Simone had described him. Gerhard, in this bodily form of Hans Mueller, had come back to her. Hans was Gerhard's ghost made visible.

Hans noticed his sullenness and his wariness. For a moment, he studied him with keen-eyed interest. Marc, returning his penetrating gaze, allowed himself to appear even more sullen. In this suddenly complicated hour, he did not care to express a casual friendliness to this German whom he distrusted. Hans took no offense. He remained well-disposed toward him and continued to regard him as a brotherly compatriot.

"It isn't just the war that is bothering you," he said, as he tried to decipher a reason for the unhappiness. "It is something else."

"Maybe," Marc answered, terse and understated.

Hans probed further.

"Woman trouble?"

"Could be."

"That is trouble worth having."

"Do you think so?"

"Absolutely."

"You are a romantic German."

Hans ignored the irony.

"You love her completely," he said. "But you are not certain that she feels the same way about you."

"Yes."

"Well, don't give up. Believe in your love. Believe that your love can win her."

If he had met Hans before the war and if this dubious German were not involved with Simone, he might have appreciated his generous spirit. But now, while the war was raging and because Hans was his rival for Simone's love, he lingered on the edge of antipathy.

"I wish it were as easy as that."

Hans pondered his remark. Then, as though he were

revealing a melancholy that he had carefully suppressed, he began to tell him who he really was.

"Before the war, I might have said that woman trouble was the *only* trouble worth worrying about. But not now. Not the way things are in the world."

"Then you are not a romantic."

"I take romance as I find it. Love comes. Love goes. If it stays, you are one of the lucky ones."

"Maybe I'm unlucky."

"Don't let it get you down. Don't worry about it. Tell yourself that there are more important things."

Having told him so, Hans became very quiet. A frown creased his brow, and the cigarette dangling from a corner of his mouth made him appear a bit jaded. He looked like so many other war-hardened men. He had made the journey into hell, and at every single moment, whether he was inside combat or away from it, he was fighting his way through. The light of the moon cast its rays upon his blond features now and gave to his being here in the garden a spectral emphasis. In this instant, Marc saw in him the brooding image of Gerhard. But he was not Gerhard Hauptmann. He was Hans Mueller, and he had fallen in love with Simone.

The thought stirred Marc's anger anew. The anger might have flared out of him, while he spewed accusatory words that challenged Hans Mueller to prove that he was not an agent working in secret for the Nazis. But Hans turned to him now, drawing him to the anguish that he was trying to conceal even from himself.

"There *are* more important things than woman trouble," he began, echoing the words that coiled themselves around his brooding thoughts. "I know some of them. I know them well."

Marc remained very still. He waited to hear the new words that might reveal who Hans really was.

"Have you ever had a best friend?" Hans asked him. "Has there ever been in your life a friend that you regarded as your alter ego or as a spiritual twin, in spite of his not sharing the same blood line?"

"Yes," Marc said, thinking of his friendship with Jean-Claude Jourdan, the brotherly cohort whom, two years earlier, he and Simone had rescued from the Nazis. "I still have that friend. We think alike. We have played on the same teams. We have trained together in flight school and as agents for the Resistance. We have helped one another to resolve our troubles and to do battle against our enemies. One day, when he has recovered from his war wounds, he may join me in other battles."

"You are very lucky to have such a friend," Hans said.

"And you…do you have the same kind of friend?"

"I did, once. But the war killed him."

"I'm sorry."

"Perhaps, you wouldn't be sorry if you knew that he was a German who was fighting for the Nazis."

"I am sorry that you lost a friend."

"If there were no war, you would have liked him. Everybody did. His name was Henrik Brühl. We first met as civil engineering students in Heidelberg University. Henrik was the top student in our class. He and I made so many plans for redesigning the industrial areas of Berlin, Mannheim, and Stuttgart. When the war came, Henrik and I tried to join the RAF or the French Resistance. We wanted no part of Hitler and his Nazi nightmare. But neither the British nor the French trusted us. I come from a military family that had fought against France and Great Britain in several wars. Henrik's father and his grandfather, too, were bankers who were driven by their materialism. They always leagued themselves with the political forces that were winning the people's approval. So there was no way out of Germany for us. We had to join the Nazis or be executed. If we had refused to fight, even our parents would have been shot. Henrik and I believed that we would not survive the war. But, at least, we could die honorably, and we could protect our family name. We did the only thing that we could do. We trained together as officer candidates in the

Junkerschule and later as pilot recruits in the Luftwaffe.

"We did our share of killing. We bombed many Allied cities, including London, Antwerp, Oslo, and Amsterdam. The Nazi regime regarded us favorably. Our lives as pilots were grim. But they also brought us good food, warm lodgings, and pretty women. There came a day, however, when all those rewards were not enough. From the beginning, Henrik and I knew that we were fighting for the wrong side. We believed that the Allies would make a quick job of the war and defeat the Nazis. But that did not happen. What did happen was our increased awareness of all the innocent lives that Hitler was destroying and all the freedoms that he had stolen even from the men and women who were fighting his war. We hated what the Nazis were doing to the Jews and to all the other people that had made Hitler their enemy."

Hans inhaled his cigarette and then lowered his head. He looked beaten, but only for an instant. Quickly, he looked up and rallied whatever interior forces impelled him to go on.

"Henrik and I found it hard to live with ourselves. The war had made us savages. It had stolen our humanity. But the war was stealing more than that from us. By continuing to fight for Hitler even when we perceived him to be the monster that he was, we were losing our souls. We were losing the very selves that we had been working to create. It was this feeling of having lost our best selves that compelled Henrik and me to leave the Nazis behind us and to make a pact with the Allies. About this plan, Henrik was even more enthusiastic than I. But he made the mistake to tell his parents about his plan. They were shocked. They were disappointed. They wept, and they pleaded. If he left the German Air Force, they would be executed, and their family name would be reviled. By that time, my parents had been killed in the bombings, and my two sisters had fled with my aunt and my uncle to South America. There would be no reprisals against my family. I had no one to lose. So Henrik's parents reminded him. But, if he betrayed the Nazis and joined the Allies, they would lose their lives and their fortune.

"I remember how difficult it was for Henrik to stay behind. You must understand, of course, how difficult it was for me to leave Germany. I was leaving the country that I knew well to enter a territory that regarded me as an enemy who had abandoned his post. When I made contact with a double agent who was working for the British, I did not know for certain what my future held. The British or the French might draw information from me and use me for a bit of espionage. Then, they might choose to kill me because I had been a Nazi. Possibly, it was the uncertainty of what might happen to him, as well as his need to obey his parents, that convinced Henrik that he should not leave Germany.

"My being here with the Allies has not been easy. But I am still alive, and my friend Henrik is dead."

"Was he killed in a bombing mission?"

"No. The RAF did shoot down his plane during a bombing mission over London. But he survived the crash. The British captured him and brought him to a hospital where surgeons repaired his damaged spleen, his dislocated shoulder, and his broken arm. Only after he was well did MI5 agents take him away from the hospital. They brought him to a cottage inside a forest within Hampshire, where they interrogated and tortured him."

Again, Hans paused. He was finding it even more difficult to talk about Henrik. But, Marc was convinced, he needed to tell Henrik's story. Now he hurried forward.

"The MI5 agents tortured Henrik for days and days. My RAF squadron commander told me about it afterwards. At first, they forced him to run in circles while he was carrying heavy logs. If the logs fell away from him, two big-boned guards would kick him until he fell out of consciousness. Later, they bound his naked body in chains. Then, as though they were making a tourniquet, they pressed the chains deep into his flesh. They smiled when they heard his cries of pain and when they saw the blood spurting out of him. On some mornings, they burned his arms and his legs with lighted cigarettes, with the fire of wooden matches, and with hot candle wax. At night, they often hung him from roof beams and beat his body with barbed wire sticks. They tortured him in all the ways that might have broken even the toughest men. But Henrik never broke. Never did he give them information about the locations of German airfields or about the new bombers that, it was rumored, Nazi pilots would soon be flying. Nor did he tell them anything about his commanding officers or about the more lethal types of bombs that were being dropped on Allied cities. It took MI5 two weeks to decide that Henrik Brühl would tell them nothing, no matter in what ways they tortured him. So they brought in one of their new agents to kill Henrik.

"They were testing this agent. He had been a Nazi before he joined MI5. He had also been a friend of Henrik Brühl. If he were really on the side of the Allies, he would not hesitate to kill this friend who had remained a Nazi. So the new agent, who had left Germany to fight for the British, did what he was told. With a Colt Pocket pistol, he shot Henrik through the head."

Hans stopped talking. He froze, as if he could no longer find the right words to complete his remarks.

Marc probed further. He was guessing what had happened, even as he pushed Hans deeper into the truth of his telling.

"You were that agent. You killed your best friend."

A pallor covered Hans's face. He sat very still, as though he were waiting for his next breath. When he answered him, his voice was low and far away.

"Yes."

Once more, Hans looked at him directly. He wanted him to understand who he was. In spite of everything that had happened to Henrik and to him, he was the same Hans Mueller who had always been Henrik's loyal friend. Holding Marc in this steady gaze, he found all the words that would summon the memory of what finally happened between them.

"Every day since then," he began, "I remember the October morning that two MI5 agents brought me to the cottage where they had been torturing Henrik. It was a day without sun. Storm clouds hung low in the sky, and a raw wind had overtaken the trees in the forest, flailing their branches and ripping away their red and gold leaves. When I first saw what MI5 had done to Henrik, I could not breathe. After the MI5 commander and I entered the hidden room behind a wall where they had held Henrik prisoner, the men who had been torturing Henrik untied him from the chair where they had bound him. They forced him to stand up and to salute the commander and me. The face that I saw did not at first recall my memory of Henrik. His blue eyes were nearly closed with crusts of blood. His bleeding nose was broken, and some of his front teeth were missing. His neck was filled with welts that the beatings from a heavy whip had left there. His left arm dangled helplessly, and a bone jutted from the place where the arm had been fractured. His right hand was crushed, and his body swayed uneasily, as though he were about to fall.

"I think that he knew what was going to happen to him. He knew that an MI5 agent would kill him. He was prepared to die. But he did not imagine that I would be his executioner. At first, he did not recognize me. Possibly, the beatings had robbed him of his keen awareness of things. More probably, he had shut himself off from everything that was happening to him. It was not his familiar self who was being tortured. It was some other man whom he had been called to represent as bravely as he could. I believe that mind-set helped him to endure fourteen days of torture without breaking."

Again, Hans halted in his telling. Again, he inhaled his cigarette and then hurried to speak the words that he needed to speak.

"As I said, Henrik did not recognize me. Not at first. But a few minutes after we had entered the room, my commanding officer directed his blunt words at me.

"'You know why you are here, Mueller. Get on with it.'"

"'Yes, sir,'" I said.

"Henrik heard my name and, right afterwards, my voice. He stared at me, not really believing that it was I who was going to kill him.

"'Not you, Hans,'" he cried out. "'Don't let it be you. Let someone else do it.'"

"The three MI5 agents, grim-faced and hardened, were quietly watching me. Each of them had in his hand a semi-automatic revolver. They were ready to shoot me, if I did not kill Henrik.

"Just before I fired my pistol, Henrik was still frowning and still crying out the words that have never left me: 'No! No! Not you!'

"I shot him in the heart and shot him there again. His body lurched and swayed and tottered before it fell to the floor."

When Hans finished telling his story, Marc stood very still. He wanted to go on studying him very carefully. But, his cigarette dangling from a corner of his mouth, Hans turned away from him and walked a few feet onto the marble path that meandered through the garden. With his right hand, he began rubbing his eyes. Instantly, Marc understood that he was weeping.

Marc did not move. Nor did he speak. Only when Hans turned back to him did he find the matter-of-fact words that might persuade this ambiguous German to tell him even more.

"You did what you had to do," Marc heard himself saying. "There was no other way, if you wanted to go on living."

Hans observed him quietly. Then, still bound by anguish, he answered him with husky timbres that suggested how weary he was and how self-hating.

"Yes, I go on living," he said. "I go on killing. I do whatever the war requires."

"We all do that. There is no other way."

"I should not be burdening you with this. I have never told anyone else about it. But this week here in Derbyshire, when for the first time in years I have been happy, I began thinking about the Henrik Brühl that I knew before the war and about the successful careers each of us had been planning. When we were university students, we often spoke of what the future held for us. After we established ourselves with large corporations, we might eventually form our own company. In those days, we made many plans. We even made a wager that, if I married a beautiful woman first of all, Henrik would have to pay for our expensive honeymoon. He would win the reward if he was the first to marry."

Hans paused once again. He inhaled his cigarette, as he reflected upon the past that was burdening him. Then, joining him once again on the marble bench that stood a short distance from the entrance to the garden, he shared other thoughts with him.

"It is ironic. I joined the British so that I could save my soul.

But I have not saved my soul. When I killed my best friend, I lost my soul forever."

"It can't be helped."

"No. It can't be helped."

Marc continued to study Hans. That the German was suffering, there was no doubt. In this moment, he allowed himself to pity this man who had lost his homeland, his parents and sisters, and his brotherly friend. He might have consented to the empathy that Hans's story had stirred within him. He might have admitted that they shared a bond because of the ways that the war had changed things for each of them. But only for an instant did pity touch his regard of Hans. In the next moment, Simone and Deirdre joined them in the garden.

On this evening, both women looked especially beautiful. Deirdre was a blend of dazzling and wholesome in an emerald-green silk-crepe gown. Simone, in white lace and tulle, was subtly alluring. Upon entering the garden, both women noticed Hans's forlorn expression. They noticed, too, the tension that hovered within him, the usually stoic Marc Roussillon.

Deirdre was the first to nudge away the gloom that had cast its spell over them. She was carrying a tray of champagne and scotch, and she was in a merry mood as she offered Hans and him the scotch and gave Simone a glass of champagne. Then, with her glass of champagne in hand, she spoke the bracing words that renewed Hans's and his awareness of the party atmosphere that they had left behind them when they entered the garden.

"Both of you look so somber," she said, maintaining still the lightness of heart that on this evening made her so appealing. "We have come here to cheer you."

She drew nearer to him and clasped his left hand. Her eyes gleamed, and her carefree air enhanced this newfound happiness that she was feeling. Though, Marc imagined, her happiness would be temporary, having been inspired by the champagne that she had already imbibed, there was honesty in her expression of this temporary elation.

"I want to see you smile tonight," she said. "You are most handsome when you smile."

"I'll do my best," he said, summoning the quick flash of a smile.

He wanted to please Deirdre. He wanted to conceal from her eyes the unhappiness that was consuming him. But in this very moment, while with a scanning glance he saw his estranged wife with Hans, Simone's manner roused anew his unhappiness and ignited his anger.

Lacking Deirdre's honesty, Simone pretended to be merry. She was not pleased to be in his company. Nor, he imagined, did she care to witness Deirdre's lighthearted exchanges with him. Yet Hans believed in Simone's show of exhilaration. Perhaps, Marc told himself, the sight of Hans's unconditional affection for her goaded his anger most of all.

Simone, too, expressed a mutual pleasure in being with Hans.

"May I remind you," she gently asked him, "that you do not have to carry the entire burden of the world on your shoulders?"

Hans beamed.

"You may," he said. "Let us drink a toast to that."

"I would like that very much," she said. "I have a tremendous need to celebrate our happiness."

Now she kissed him, her lips softly caressing his lips.

"I like the way you celebrate," Hans said.

Then he returned the kiss, his lips pressing more urgently the lips that had already quickened his senses.

Only for a moment did Marc permit himself to watch them. His anger was rising, and his hatred of Hans Mueller was once more a dark and festering anguish. To conceal his feelings, he began dancing with Deirdre along the marble walkway. From the ballroom, the sensual rhythms of music were filling the air and finding their way into the garden. A woman with a smoky voice was singing romantic lyrics, and the band was playing the melody that made the singer's words even more poignant. As he held her close to him while they smoothly danced, Deirdre was telling him that he was being wonderful to her and that she would never forget this week with him. Not far from them, Hans and Simone had also begun to dance. He heard her light laughter and the playful sounds of Hans's voice that were bonded with the intimacy that was growing between them.

"Hans must die," he told himself while, with apparently compatible ease, he went on dancing with Deirdre. "I have to kill him very soon, or I shall lose Simone forever."

On the next day of their holiday week, when with rigorous self-command he struggled to suppress his hatred of Hans and his apprehension that Simone could no longer love *him*, the husband who was willing to die for her and to kill because of her, he joined them as well as his parents and their guests on the brief excursions which had so often called him back to the acceptable persona he had cultivated through all the years before the war. With Simone, Hans, and the others, he joined squadrons of canoeists on the becalmed lake behind his parents' Georgian house. That he shared his canoe not with Simone, but with Deirdre Sullivan, the good-natured and pretty nurse from the 28th Station Hospital, might have intensified the anger that he kept always harnessed to the subtleties of his wiliness. But his awareness that he was living through the intricacies of scenes that he had already experienced compelled him, on this day while he was with Deirdre, to utter carefree words with understated inflections and occasional, makeshift laughter. Though the October afternoon was warm and bright, he felt a chill overtaking his body. He felt as if the part of him that had died during the two years just past had waited here for him, Spirit-chained to a place that had once brought him solace. His ghost (he told himself) was sitting beside him, here in the canoe that he navigated with smooth and efficient oars across the sheen of the sun-dappled lake.

In the distance, there at the edge of the autumn-tinted forest that stood apart from the lake, he saw—as if they were after-images or mirages from excursions through which he had already traveled—Chilean willow trees, Scotch elms, and blueberry ash trees bringing flares of passionate colors to the day's muted tensions. Much closer than that, inside the more proximate distance that was only a canoe ahead of his own, he saw Hans with Simone. They were laughing, carefree and exhilarant. Their blond features glowed, and their agile bodies that leaned into the oars became, in casual nearness to each other, a special intimacy.

The words they spoke to each other rose and floated on the autumn-languorous air.

"We'll have days and days like this," Hans was telling Simone. "This is only the beginning."

"I want more than that," she answered him through the light cadences of her laughter. "I want whole years with you."

"We'll have them. That is a promise," Hans said. "After the war, we are going to spend the rest of our lives together."

Hearing the words, Marc bowed his head. He needed to conceal his angry dismay from Deirdre and from the partying guests who were smoothly rowing within the busy surround of other canoes. The splash of water against their oars; the hearty laughter of these other guests; and sweet-natured Deirdre, sitting opposite him while with melodic intonations she began singing an Irish love ballad—all these sounds and images stirred his sorrow even as they excited the placid waters of the lake. When he looked up to offer Deirdre a simulated smile that, without any words, might convince her that he enjoyed the gift of song that she meant for him alone, he heard once again the laughter of Hans and Simone. After offering Deirdre a fleeting smile, he looked once more at *them*, at his estranged wife and at the man with whom she wanted to spend the rest of her life.

Happiness kept caressing their sensual laughter. It displaced the gentle inflections of Deirdre's song, and it roused his dark memory of the year when Simone fell in love with Gerhard. The sight of them together—this enigmatic Hans Mueller and radiant Simone, the woman that he, Marc Roussillon, would always claim as his own—intensified his melancholic awareness that this bleak cycle in his life had condemned him to re-live the episode in which he sought to murder his rival. On some days, his better conscience told him that Fate had set a test for him. He must resist his urge to kill Hans. Only if he proved beyond a doubt that Hans was betraying the Resistance did he have the right to kill him. Only then would society regard the killing as justified. Hans's relationship with Simone should have no part in determining whether he was innocent or guilty of treason. If Hans proved to be innocent, then he would go on living. Simone might very well take a permanent place beside him. If that happened, if Simone did, at the last, turn away from him—the husband whom she had promised to love always—he would have to find the power within himself to endure the loneliness that would be his to bear. So he told himself while Deirdre, rowing in unison with his steady motion, sang her ballad. The other partying canoeists still glided smoothly across the water, their jovial voices melding with their camaraderie. And, all this while, Hans and Simone went on murmuring and laughing with the intimate pleasure that only two lovers can experience.

This excursion on the lake brought *him* no pleasure. His past coiled him in its chains and coiled as tightly the tenuous present that almost never granted him a reprieve from the new, murderous thoughts that kept disarranging his solace.

Yet, try as he did to suppress his desire to kill Hans even if he were innocent of treason, his memory of shooting and maiming Gerhard Hauptmann haunted him. On the first days of his return to Derbyshire, when he was struggling against his impulse to kill even an innocent Hans, the images of his shooting and slashing Gerhard rose like apparitions before him. Sometimes, in these flashbacks, he saw himself slashing and shooting Hans, the German whose blond muscularity made him Gerhard's alter ego. The images, as palpable as they were violent, haunted not only his sleep, but also those waking moments when the rage that was burning through his soul hovered there like a secret ally if, by chance, he caught sight of Hans and Simone together.

Tough-minded and pitiless, he willed himself by the mid-point of his stay in Derbyshire to resist these familiar apparitions—these ghostly memories that had the power to destroy him. Sometimes with many of the other guests and often at the side of Deirdre, he compelled himself to enter with casual poise and natural affability the life-loving activities to which his parents had invited everyone. The nearly serene occasions dispelled his violent ghosts. But the occasions summoned, nonetheless, the favorable apparitions that belonged to the years of happiness that were now, for most of the time, lost to him. Once again, as he kept living out scenes from his past, he cycled along the painterly Monsal Trail in the Derbyshire Peak District. With light-hearted affability (or its credible appearance), he stood at the top of Monsal Head and peered out upon a bronzed greenery of hills beyond hills, cloud-laden intricacies of mountains, and the sun-spotted corridors of space that were wheeling freely around and above and below him. His sister Nicole's absence made the experience of being there different, without dispelling the hold of the past upon him. Now sixteen years old, Nicole lived most often inside the safety of her school in Switzerland and sometimes, in disguise, on the cusp of danger in Belgium, Denmark, and Berlin as a courier for the Resistance. But, as in days past, his parents were there with him. So, also, were gregarious friends who brought a witty spark to the afternoon. Simone was there, too, her beauty suffused with the glow of the warm sun upon her. Her palpable immediacy, however, effaced his recollected image of her. On this day, she appeared as someone new, someone other than the woman who belonged to his past. In that spent time, she was cycling next to him. Now, Hans Mueller was her partner.

His calm acceptance of the moment pleased him. It brought him tentative proof that he could endure, for a few more days at least, the anguish of living apart from Simone. At the same time, he continued to tell himself that, by the end of these few days or in a week or two at most, if he followed the rules invoked by permissible scenarios, he would expose Hans as a double agent and reclaim Simone as the woman who belonged to him alone.

On other days when he yoked his energies to equally permissible scenarios, he—with his parents and their guests and with Simone, Hans, and Deirdre—would hike briskly through the diverse trails that drew them away from their secluded home into the picturesque villages and towns that served them as friendly neighbors. Once again the past sprang up before him, drawing him into episodes that he had already experienced. Though the present, with its revised implications, altered the episodes, the past and its vivid references cast a ghostly spell over everything.

On the fourth day of his visit here in Derbyshire, he and all the others climbed the Derwent Edge, which is the Millstone grit escarpment that lies above the Upper Derwent Valley within the Peak District National Park. As he had done in previous years, the rugged, white-haired guide accompanying the sixteen persons who made up the Roussillon party explained that glaciers in the last ice age had scraped away most of the grit-stone that had originally covered the Peak District. Raw Nature, as dominant here as it was formidable, had—through centuries of wind, rain, and frost—formed odd-shaped crags or tors. The crag that once again drew Marc's attention more than any of the others did was called The Coach and Horses, because the grit-stone that formed it resembled a coach and horses on the horizon. Though he admired its shape, he was especially impressed that the stone had weathered a long wilderness of centuries.

During these years of war, the imagery called out a message that, he believed, was meant for him alone. It reminded him of his own resilience, as willful and time-trapped as that was. In a world torn apart by uncertainty and violence, his capacity to overcome brute adversaries and wrenching betrayals was a life-saving weapon. This stark message that he took from the stones eased his senses more profoundly than even the colorful beauty of the earth that surrounded him.

He did not, of course, ignore that beauty. Once again, while he cycled across much of the moorland around Derwent Edge, he saw the Eurasian golden plover and the red grouse, as well as the quicksilver individuality of the ring ouzel and the mountain hare. Species of plants as vivid as they were rare included common cotton grass, mountain strawberry, and crowberry. In the days before the war, when his happiness was authentic, his sighting these extraordinary specimens had quickened his scientific curiosity and his satisfaction. But in this bleak year, when Simone was punishing him for Gerhard's death by giving her love to Hans Mueller, he could summon only a tepid enjoyment that he harnessed to a disguise of his unease whenever he was in the company of the wife who had always been his obsession and this other German whom he was waiting to kill.

Chapter Eight

Hunter

On the afternoon after his parents' lavish party, Marc decided that, during the following morning, he would kill Hans when they were hunting for deer in the forest across the lake. He planned to kill him only a day before Hans was scheduled to leave for an MI5 assignment that would bring him, in disguise, to Paris. Marc knew the forest well, having cycled and hunted there in many happier seasons. When they had trekked along the clearing that hurried into the darker recesses of the forest, he intended to shoot Hans with a Winchester Model 94 Carbine rifle. He would bury Hans's body inside a deep grave that he had already dug during a furtive trip to a nearly hidden ravine within the forest.

All of the friends who had visited his parents' home during that week had returned on the previous day to their wartime obligations. Even Simone had been called to a new assignment. The Women's Auxiliary Ferrying Squadron was sending her to an RAF air base in Cornwall. She would be ferrying Spitfires to the pilots who were going to bomb German air bases in Berlin, Dresden, and Munich. The senior Roussillons had left for an excursion into Hampshire. During these last few days of their leave-time from the war, they wanted to inspect the changes that an architect and an interior designer had made to their large country house there. For the duration of the war, their Hampshire house would be used as a convalescent home for wounded infantrymen and pilots.

That Hans had decided to remain in Derbyshire without her did not unsettle Simone. When she left Derbyshire on the previous morning, she had imagined that Hans would enjoy another day or two of swimming in the heated pool, boating on the lake, and cycling into the village. She was unaware that Marc had invited Hans to go deer hunting.

Simone was pleased that Hans had favorably impressed his hosts. They appeared to respect and to like him. She was, Marc saw, not surprised by their fair treatment. From his parents, she anticipated no less than a judicious detachment from the unhappy problems that had destroyed his marriage to Simone. They knew the world well. They were aware of the imperfect natures and the self-willed complications that drove the conduct of most individuals. They knew *him*, the son who had often made them proud and who had fallen from grace because he had destroyed the life of Gerhard Hauptmann, the German with whom his wife had fallen in love. In his love for Simone, Gerhard had remained untainted by a hardened consent to adultery. He had not known that Simone was married and that she loved her husband as much as she loved him—the new and mysterious partner that continually excited her.

Nor did this latest German in her life, this Hans Mueller, know who Simone really was. He did not know that she was married to the same Marc Roussillon whom he had befriended and who regarded him with carefully suppressed hatred.

To conceal his hatred from Hans and from Simone, Marc had pretended to be Deirdre's affectionate suitor. Without the hesitation that yokes itself to disbelief, Hans had quickly accepted Deirdre and him as the amorous couple they appeared to be. By the close of this carefree week here in Derbyshire, Simone had also perceived Deirdre as the lifeline that was reviving his spirit. Deirdre was the new partner who would accompany him on a happier path. Even his parents started to believe in his show of affection for Deirdre. They wanted what was best for him. With his happiness in mind, they had arranged this festive week that had passed so swiftly. They hoped that the merriment might dispel his angry sorrow and clarify his relationship with Simone. They preferred, of course, that the week might bring Simone back to him. At the same time, his parents understood that he needed to free himself from the ghosts of the past that had enclosed him inside their prison. If Simone no longer loved him, if she chose instead to make a new life with Hans Mueller, then he—their brave and conflicted son, their brooding Marc, who had loved Simone intensely and who would go on loving her forever—also must become new. He must make the leap. He must elude the death-in-life to which his anger and his despair were condemning him.

"It is hard to become someone new," he told his father. "It is hard to go on living without the only woman who has ever brought me happiness."

In that brief meeting, when they were alone in his father's study, Henri Roussillon had looked upon him with penetrating eyes. The troubled gaze was both knowing and dismayed. He did not need any words to understand what his father was feeling. The gaze told him everything. His father was looking upon the son who was not going to escape the fate that was pursuing him. For days afterward, his father's eyes haunted him. They left him even more dislocated from the untarnished self that he had once been. They called forth earlier episodes in his life, when he was striving to please his father and when he believed that he could make his life both worthwhile and extraordinary.

On the morning of the deer hunt, when he expected to kill

Hans Mueller, Marc awoke from an uneasy sleep. The October sun at dawn was a pale gold flame on the horizon that flared its light into the French doors of his bedroom. He opened one of the doors and, while his tall, muscular frame dominated the threshold to a second-floor balcony, he breathed the crisp air and peered into the home fields. He saw fields of late-blooming flowers and orchards of apples ready to be harvested. He watched the breeze-rippled lake and the slow-moving yawl that held two rugged young men from nearby Sudbury who were patrolling the area, in search of intruders and of any other disturbing signs. Farther than that, he recognized multi-colored hills and wandering streams and the turf-laden road along which deer hunters sometimes drove their trucks and skillful riders cantered on their horses as they made their way into the forest. At this moment, the road was empty, and the forest loomed in the distance, a dawn-shadowed presence that beckoned him into its tangled wildness.

In this dawn that was only now rousing the new day, the image of the forest stirred his memory of other mornings when he had gone deer hunting with his father. Those, too, had been uneasy mornings that had bound him to their unforgiving obligations. On those earlier mornings, he had gone hunting so that he could please his father. As an overly sensitive youth, he had disdained any experience that required him to kill a living creature. He had no interest in hunting deer or foxes or rabbits. Nor did he enjoy fishing. But his father, whom he loved so much and whose acceptance he craved, persuaded him to alter his perspective. Hunting was a good way, his father told him, to find out a little more about the unformed person he was and the fully-grown man he was becoming. So, even against his natural inclinations, he joined his father in several hunting trips. Gradually, he came to tolerate and then even to enjoy hunting. The elusiveness of its rewards and the stern nature of its accuracies satisfied his need to test his rugged capacities. Hunting red stag in Patagonia wakened the wildness in his own nature and offered to his spirit a fiercer joy of life.

One time he found himself there during an October recess from school, when as a Spartan youth of sixteen he consented to rigorous disciplines. Many of them were self-imposed and all of them yoked to his need to please the strong-willed father who in his eyes yet appeared to be heroic and original. In that tremendous time (and, so, not like any other except those times that for his swift, exciting life had once been the most prodigious) he hunted within the Roussillons' vast landholding in the foothills of the southern Andes in Argentina. There, open space kept fanning out toward ever-vanishing horizons and emphases of groves and hills and mountains declared themselves formidable and stately. In that pulsating reality of two hundred thousand acres of grasslands, scrub-brush, and forests and of white-water rivers and sun-gleaming lakes, he and his father as agreeable hosts joined a company of other fathers and sons. Each of them was a skillful hunter who, on temporary leave from London's Bond Street pursuits and Swiss banking districts or from some of Europe's best private schools, had come to Henri Roussillon's magnificent *estancia* to kill the powerful red stag.

It was wonderful to witness, as if they were appropriating sky-dome cumulus altitudes or whole territories of the turquoise sky, the gold and orange elegance of giant poplars and acacias, the blue-green ascensions of eucalypti, and at the edge of Lake Nahual Huapi the surprise and sweeping grace of enormous white willows. There, in the valleys along the streams, they saw as well guanaco and geese and Montezuma quail. Within an enclosure of twenty thousand acres, they—still in scanning motion—saw superior breeding stags imported from New Zealand and wild boars from the Himalayas and from the Rocky Mountains the massive solidity of bison.

Morning upon morning of confident horseback rides through the long, rugged hunt for red stag, they passed by whole societies of amber-gold rustling poplars. They passed as well into the farther reaches of the Roussillons' magnificent ranch toward denser brush and hidden swamps and tangled copses of trees. They hurried by head-high grass, swaying and preeminent, and steep and treacherous mountainsides. On their supple stallions they forded turbulent streams, approaching those waters always at a steady pace and with a sturdy impulsion. Then, the jump into the water achieved, they sat up to control the horse while bringing it to trot. On a later day, they heard their horses' hooves clatter against the round rocks in other riverbeds. Clouds of dust rose upon their meeting dry land once more, like murky vapors overtaking the receding distance. Sometimes they noticed the flash of sparks in the darkness as shod hooves struck stones in the trail while with their hardy Argentine guides they were riding homeward in the star-filled evening to the ample lodge by the tranquil lake.

After the wonder of all these things, they saw in early afternoon of the eighth day—there, halfway up the western slope of a long valley sweeping through the area where they were hunting—a most impressive red stag. Its high massive beams reached up and out and back in, with eight long points on its left side and seven on the right and seven again in the crown that belonged to itself identified, as if sovereign and prevailing.

With his two guides, he dismounted limberly to lie hidden on the valley floor in scrub brush and to snake along on his belly through thorn-brush and mud and over rocks with knife-sharp edges. In that *now* gone past him and yet remaining in the precise rightness of its moment, he as a finely trained young hunter was once more testing himself in so punishing a crawl. His rough camouflage garb turned wet and was smeared with mud and torn by rocks. In that *now*, which was for him a supreme and memorable moment, he felt privileged to see the monumental stag rising out of its bed and ambling away. Two hundred meters in the distance it stopped, turned broadside, and was instantly translated in his eyes as a perfect target.

In that specific *now* and so, in the vivid rightness of its moment—he moved the Winchester Model 94 rifle into position and, in his scope, found the more-than-ordinary stag. Thereafter, with spontaneous acuity, he interpreted the essential intricacies of the shot (the distance...and the crosswind of ten miles per hour which, at that range, would move the bullet about four inches...and the thirty degree angle of elevation). In that *now* and in the irrevocable rhythms of its moment, with spontaneous yet practiced acuity he brought the intersection of the crosshairs of his gun sight to rest low and slightly forward on his chest cavity. Taking a deep breath and releasing half of it, he began his trigger squeeze until the rifle roared and the moist clubbing sound of a bullet striking a big-bodied animal hurried back to convince him. As if at the same time, he saw the stag drop suddenly and with precipitate-seeming energy tumble chaotically down the slope for about a hundred yards, to come at last to rest in a tangle of brush.

How calmly he had then approached the dead stag, the austerities of his detachment quietly guiding him to an acceptance of the scene unfolded before him. Juan Carlos and Antonio, as hunting cohorts, were there beside him to leap and shout and jubilantly pound his back. Having been there to assist him in his pursuit, they were the ones to touch the stag during the first minutes after its death. Efficiently, they dragged and then lifted its stilled magnificence into the waiting truck which would carry it to the *estancia's* butchery. Afterward they would carry the frozen head to a renowned taxidermist in Buenos Aires. Because they were there, Juan Carlos and Antonio, to handle the body in its death, he—Henri Roussillon's proficient son appearing as hardened as they—found on that day that he could accept the violent end of a splendid, living creature.

But he had not always responded so.

"You're thinking, I can tell, that there's an unfairness about all of it," his father had remarked one earlier time three years gone, while alluding to the complicated matter of hunting.

As a boy of thirteen, he had traveled with his father to the Pinyon-juniper forests of Montana to track in that autumn season the elusive whitetail buck. Being a canny father, he had by instinct and by observation learned how to read well the subtle dismay or quiet awe or sheer exhilaration of this strong-minded youth...this venture-loving son and only heir. Now he noticed how, with casual-seeming unease, his son had approached the perfectly formed trophy buck (a body torn now and irretrievably collapsed) that with keen-eyed marksmanship he had just killed.

"You're thinking just that," his father had said in deference to his innocent remorse, and patiently so.

Without compromising the brawny assurance that was his fatherly self, his understated words prefaced the remark by which he meant to temper his son's guarded disdain for brutalities that, during the novitiate he was in his early hunting years fulfilling, seemed too self-serving, too surreptitious and calculated to be regarded as necessary or fair. And so, in language direct and with even timbre modulated, he called forth fatherly words to dissuade his son from the brooding silence that he was, because of youthful compunction, choosing as his guardian power.

"And you're thinking so because you're too intense about all of it. But you need experience it only as the thing it is and not more than that: a first-rate sport to challenge your stamina and your skill."

He was at that moment rolling a fine Patagonian tobacco, cowboy-style, within the thinnest strip of paper. His big, proprietary hands in synchronous movements brought the cigarette to the right corner of his lips and, at the spark of a match, ignited its rum-scented pungency.

"Think of it, if you must, as a way to connect to your ancestors—all those men who hunted because for them there was no other possibility for survival. Think of it that way and find out if you're as tough as they were."

His father, he knew, was offering him a language of coolheaded detachment to remind him of the appropriate distance he must maintain between his feelings and whatever experience was unfolding about him. For he saw that his son, stalwart though he was in his young mastery of life's rapid processes, was nonetheless stymied that time by the analysis that too scrupulously probes the meaning of a deed. And so he had brought himself to speak husky, dispassionate words meant as a useful protocol by which to govern properly the obligations of the masculine senses.

Aware of the effort his father was making on his behalf, he found his way back to a levelheaded briskness that wears as its armature a stoic acceptance of all things irretrievable.

"Don't worry about me, sir," he said, his precise inflections dismissing the silence that like a well-trained sentry had hovered long about him. "I'm fine. Really I am. I've done the thing I came here to do."

His father, noticing the tense complexities of his son's clipped speech, was all the while (so he was to tell him months later) favorably impressed by his military bearing and by the tautened accuracy of his self-control, a discipline imparted rigorously by the private academy that, as a Roussillon of promise, he dutifully attended in the Swiss Alps. Even in that early time he was an athletic and quick-witted youth. Already he was on the path preparing him to be a leader in corporate enterprises or in government or in the even more creative world of architecture.

All through his early adolescence, he had imparted the rigor of that discipline by whatever codes of manly conduct his father had helped him to discover. But in spite of his brave show, his father knew, perhaps intuitively or because of the vague unease that stayed as a subdued influence upon his son's too-rigid posture, that words—his own and his son's as well— were not enough to dispel what he had understood at the start was his son's deep-seated grief for the slaying of a splendid creature whose life had pulsed benignly only a moment before his bullet felled it. And since his fatherly words could neither annul nor solace that grief, he now withdrew to the privacies of his own stillness. He wondered as he watched him whether his son could, on his own, thread his way unbaffled through this moment that for him was as lacerating as bitterness or remorse or early despair.

He and his father were there alone, briefly, before the fire at the evening campsite in the Montana hills. Their two guides and their other hunting companions busied themselves with tasks they two had already completed, preparing for the long journey homeward which was to begin early the following day. It was then that the mellow light of the moon, married in that moment to the saffron flame of the campfire before them, revealed to his inquiring eyes, as if revising or redefining the imagery that was his father, a tentative sensitivity. There was in his modulated response a stir of heartfelt empathy for him, the essential son who, as he himself had once long ago, was measuring his authentic responses, all the pulsing currents of their honesty and logic, against the precise forms and obligations that his gender required of manly behavior.

Luminous night revealed his father's muscular physique intact, finely honed and at forty-three italic still. That night, ambivalent tendrils of light with fleet apprehension scanned his rugged features and found in them the nearly imperceptible scar buried across the left side of his face. It was a fading emblem of the grievous war wound he had sustained in a bombing mission against the Germans in the First World War. The radiance of that same light noticed his curly black hair and thick, dapper mustache and subtle, charismatic influence. His was a casual emphasis of individuality that still maintained its own laws and privileges. No sooner had all these vital things impressed themselves upon his senses, than with muted attentiveness he saw his father fling his cigarette into the fire abruptly and rise, a willful and prevailing ascension as he tarried before the warm glow of the fire to stay as if or go. Perhaps he meant to gather the necessary words that would with him hurry away from his son's brooding dismay, which was even now casting its uneasy spell upon him.

But his father did not go.

Instead, he returned to his place by the fire, sitting there, calm and reliable, with his pensive son whose heart had not yet acquired a sufficient indifference toward the world's ordinary depredations. As if quite naturally, he took up once more the quiet counsel which might release his son from the very burden of remorse that he himself, once long ago while being initiated into the ways of the world, had for a time known well. He offered new words, informal still and drawing on the strong bond between them, that would, he imagined, help his son to keep in mind what other men expected of him. A time would come when on his own he would have learned to cultivate in full the tough-minded perception of things that by his experience he was now beginning to shape.

"You're doing fine," he told him, praising his skill of

hunting while holding a fatherly hand firmly on his shoulder. "Give yourself time to adjust to it, and you'll see it's all right."

He had recognized at once, enclosed though he was within the surprise of his grieving, that his father with understated matter-of-factness was guiding him toward a way out of his wilderness. But it was only years afterward, that he came to regard that moment by a campfire in the rugged hills of Montana as the emblem and nuance of his father's love for him. It was then, while learning of his father's life as an agent for the Resistance and as a pilot for the Free French Air Force, that he understood with new clarity how difficult it must have been for his father to approach his son's boyhood innocence. For, even then, Henri Roussillon had journeyed so far away from his own innocence. His aversion to the reticent or soft-spoken, as pronounced as it was contemptuous, surely rose out of his belief that the world was a fierce place, its abundant beauty not withstanding, and that only a tough cynicism or ingrained stoic discipline could effectively confront its formidable powers.

Within this new dawn many years later, when here in Derbyshire he and his parents' guests had enjoyed a brief recess from the war, his memory of those hunting days with his father had invoked scenes that, in his mind's eye, were still vivid and palpable. Yet these remembered scenes, which had unfolded into a swift montage inside his melancholic seeing, belonged to a time that was now lost to him. The image that defined his boyhood self was an apparition that his brooding tension had summoned. That knowing adolescent had come here with frowning gaze to watch him, the adult counterpart who had become a stranger. His younger self, intuitive and prescient, had come to remind him of the long-ago time when he had disdained the killing of every living creature. On this autumn morning, this idealistic youth who lived, usually secluded and often forgotten, inside his memory, was his stern pursuer, warning him against his murderous instincts.

So he told himself, aware of the consequences that might fall upon him after he killed Hans.

"When you kill Hans Mueller," the apparition whispered to him, "you will also be killing yourself. You will be a dead man. You did not fire the shot that killed Gerhard Hauptmann. To save you, Simone did that. But this time is different. This time you will fire the shot. You will kill Hans. After that, you will have to carry a body of death upon your back for all the time that remains to you."

Marc resisted the message. War-hardened and vengeful, he became even more determined to kill his rival. He hurried past whatever hesitation the furtive-seeming dawn and the recollection of his innocent past had wrought upon him.

Focusing on the things that he would need to do if he were to carry out the murder, he shaved and showered and dressed in the hunting clothes that would allow him brisk and stealthy movement when he was inside the forest. He wore a plaid flannel shirt beneath his green tweed jacket. He wore, as well, medium-brown corduroy trousers and dark brown riding boots. When he entered the breakfast room on the first floor of the southwest wing, Mrs. Dowling, the motherly housekeeper who had been in his parents' employ for a decade and more, greeted him with a courteous smile and with cordial words. He knew her well, and he was aware that his appearance impressed her.

"You are ready for hunting, Mr. Roussillon," she said. "And you have a bright, sunny day for it. You and Mr. Mueller should have a grand time."

Hans was sitting at the table. He had been sipping coffee while he waited for him to arrive. It was Hans who first responded to Mrs. Dowling's words.

"That is exactly what we intend to do," he said. "We are going to have a great hunting day."

He willed himself to join Hans in a smile.

"Yes, Mrs. Dowling," he said. "We'll make a fine day of it."

She had cooked a substantial breakfast that included scrambled eggs, sausages, and buckwheat cakes. He had no appetite for any of it, but he ate moderate portions that would satisfy Mrs. Dowling's need to please him. Hans ate heartily, possibly because he was happily anticipating the day's venturing and because he was savoring his last day of leisure before returning to the war. His athletic muscularity and his blond handsomeness, together with his warmhearted manner, had won Mrs. Dowling's approval within hours after she first met him.

In the hour that they were expected to return from the deer hunt, Mrs. Dowling would not be at the house to see that he had come back without Hans Mueller. On Mondays, she always drove into the village to buy whatever groceries and other supplies that the Roussillon land did not provide. After that, she would spend an hour visiting her sister, who lived in the village. She would not drive back to his parents' home until mid-afternoon.

Neither would her husband, who managed his parents' Derbyshire estate, nor the villagers who were harvesting the northeast fields and the apple orchards in the southwest corner of the land, be working in the vicinity of the main house. None of them would be able to report that he had returned from the deer hunt without Hans Mueller. They would accept as plausible the news that Hans had made a brief return to the house and then hurried on to his air base in Tempsford for a new bombing mission. During this time, he would bring the slain deer to the village butcher who, for a nominal fee, was going to disembowel and clean the carcass and then, as a gift from the Roussillons, disperse the meat to the villagers and to Mrs. Dowling's kitchen. Friendly and easy-going, he planned to share anecdotes with the butcher about the crops that were being harvested in the Roussillons' fields. He would mention his cycling trip into Derwent Edge, his careful tune-up of his Bentley, his skeet shooting in the southeast meadows of his parents' home, and his boating there on the autumn lake.

With these thoughts in mind on the morning of the deer hunt, Marc stayed clearheaded and self-possessed. During breakfast, he spoke affably of many things. He mentioned the hunting he had done in Patagonia with his father. He spoke of the hunting that he had done here in Derbyshire. He also declared his preference for Winchester rifles. He listened attentively when Hans recalled hunting years earlier in the Black Forest of Germany with two of his boyhood friends. The morning was progressing smoothly. His casual air suggested that he was as happy as Hans and that he was enjoying this last free day before he, too, returned to the war.

The next hour pushed his plan into action. His farm truck brought them swiftly into the clearing inside the forest. The Winchester rifle with which he planned to kill Hans lay in the bed of the truck, alongside Hans's Remington Model 550A rifle. Two basset hounds sat patiently near the guns. They were fine hunting dogs, though to an inexperienced eye they might appear too docile to be effective. As a youth, he had admired their distinctive appearance. They had large, droopy eyes; loose, hanging skin around their faces and necks; big pendant ears; and short, stubby legs. These Derbyshire hounds had black, white, and tan coats and an uncannily accurate sense of smell. He planned to shoot Hans when the hounds were running ahead of them, flushing out a red deer stag from a thicket of trees, perhaps, or a female deer from behind the russet hills that had concealed her. He did not care to have the large eyes of the hounds witness his murder of Hans.

While he drove toward the clearing, he and Hans spoke of riding in a hot air balloon in Paris, of testing a De Havilland DH.98 Mosquito in London, and of snowboarding in Lausanne. Their congenial exchange might have forged a bond between them, if he had really meant to make Hans his friend. He held that thought only for a moment, before pushing it away to concentrate on Hans's casual remarks and on his own understated responses. At the same time, because he needed to harness tightly his murderous thoughts and to displace the anger that might compel him to shoot Hans right here inside the truck with the Colt snub-nosed revolver that he was carrying inside the pocket of his jacket, he directed his attention to the landscape around him. He noticed the autumn colors of the day flourishing within his seeing. Sun-dried fields were turning ochre, and seedpods were opening. Village workers whom his parents had hired for the harvesting were cutting cornstalks and gathering pumpkins from twisted vines. A field of magenta loosestrife was fading, but the sheen of goldenrod still lingered. As his truck approached the forest, he noticed the flaming red of massive maple trees and the dark green of tall pines. A row of these sun-touched trees was throwing fan-like shadows forward across meadow grasses. Above them, inside the azure sky, a flock of birds was hurrying past the white puffery of clouds. But the sight of all this beauty, which had always before eased his senses, could not subdue his anger or allay his apprehension.

His need to kill Hans goaded the fury that he warily suppressed.

When they entered the clearing, he parked the truck within a shady alcove. Then, with the hounds running ahead of them, he and Hans trekked into the deeper regions of the forest. An eerie quiet pervaded the scene, as though the forest and all its living forms were carefully watching them. No breeze shook the leaves of the trees. A barred owl, perched high upon the branch of a maple tree, paused in its search for rodents. Its speckled brown plumage, orange-yellow bill, and streaked belly were flares of color in the silence. Even the tawny fox that scampered before their witness into an adjacent alcove of rust-colored brush left no echoing sound behind him. Neither did he nor Hans leave a sign of their passage. Experienced hunters, enveloped in this moment within a shaft of shimmering sunlight, they moved along the turf-laden path like rifle-bearing spirits or phantoms that could be seen, though they had no physical existence. They had to trek for another twenty minutes or so before the hounds, taught long ago to recognize the scent of deer, became restless. Then, Hans and he concealed themselves behind the large trunks of maples, while the hounds hurried toward the scent. For five minutes or more, he stood very still. He could not see Hans, hidden as he was behind the trunk of a distant tree. Had he seen him, perhaps he would have shot him then.

Now the hounds began barking. They had flushed out their quarry. He and Hans left their places behind the trunks of the maples and hurried forward about two hundred yards away. The barking hounds drew them to the green-gold mound where a female deer and her doe were standing. Quickly, because there was no time to lie prone within the tall grass or, with the help of a steel ladder-stand, to climb a tree where, in the crook of its branches, he could balance himself, he assumed the firing position while standing. He started high and then, while lowering his rifle and finding the intersection of the cross hairs and the mother deer's image in his gun sight, he was about to press his finger against the trigger when Hans called out the words that stopped him.

"Don't shoot," Hans said. "They are too beautiful to kill."

He turned to face Hans, whose steady gaze held him in its muted authority and whose blunt words anchored their command to friendly and matter-of-fact persuasion.

Hearing Hans's voice, the deer and her doe darted away.

"You have a soft heart," Marc said. "At this rate, we may never bring meat back to the village."

"Let them live," Hans said. "Let them live because they are beautiful and because we will never have to remember that we killed them."

Marc stared at him without speaking. The recoil of these words, inspired by Hans's love of beauty and by the stirrings of his conscience, unsettled him. They put him in mind of the long years of punishment that would be his to bear, after he murdered Hans. This rugged German, this sensitive Hans Mueller who had won Simone's love, was better than he was, though he carried the honorable name of Roussillon. Hans spared the lives of the mother deer and her doe. But he himself would have shot them. Long ago, even before the war, he had lost that sensitivity. His need to emulate his father and his ongoing obsession with Simone had tainted his character. In different ways, he loved both of them. Yet he really understood neither of them. Perhaps, his father's hardened nature would also have disdained the killing of the doe and its mother. Perhaps, Simone's ambiguous obsession with him would have resisted the killing of a rival, if he had ever been drawn to another woman. The truth of these suppositions quickened his self-hatred. Yet only for an instant did he allow the thought to stymie his will. He wanted to kill Hans, even if the killing meant that he would lose Simone forever. Yet he could not bring himself to shoot him as they stood together, face to face. Instead, as he found the words that reminded him of the reason why they had come here, he drew Hans toward the trap that he was setting for him.

"Let's find a stag," he said. "You can move ahead of me by a few hundred yards. I may have a better chance of meeting up with a stag that runs away from you after you shoot it. Or I may see one that you did not see, hiding in a dark gully or within a cluster of trees."

"Fair enough," Hans said. He grinned, obviously pleased that they had spared the lives of the mother deer and her doe. "Your plan sounds like good team work."

Hans hurried forward, the hounds running ahead of him.

After a few minutes, Marc followed him. He imagined that Hans would soon be approaching the ravine where, two days earlier, he had dug an open grave. In pursuit of his quarry, he maintained a stealthy pace that brought him nearer and nearer to the moment when he would kill him. At first, he did not see Hans. Only the sun-misted road, the overgrown brush, and the corridor of tall trees were in his seeing. Silence hovered once more around him. He wondered whether Hans, sighting a deer that darted onto an adjacent clearing, had left the path on which they had begun their hunting. He wondered, also, whether Hans had recognized him, after all, as the enemy that he really was. Hans might be taking cover in some shadowy alcove, waiting to shoot him, the French adversary who was in pursuit of him. These dark thoughts did not deter his nearly silent passage along the road. Perhaps, Hans *was* going to shoot him. Perhaps he, Marc Roussillon, was the one who would die. But there lived within his calculation of this possible scenario a thought that kept him moving toward the place in the road that Hans should have reached. Though wounded and dying, he might still have a chance to fire the bullet that would kill Hans.

Now, right after he heard the barking hounds, he caught sight of Hans. There, three hundred yards away, he saw him. The German was standing tall and dominant as he held a steady position and fired his Remington at a big-antlered stag, its red-brown coat and its strong body gleaming in the sun. The stag had paused on a mound and was peering at the hills beyond him. The stag lurched and slumped and then, as if with stunned recognition, looked back in the direction where Hans was standing. Hans fired again, and the stag, lifted by the impact of this second bullet, appeared to rise up before its massive body rolled down the mound, the left side of its heart blown away and one of its legs dangling.

Hans moved briskly forward, prepared to claim his prize.

Furtive and unnoticed, Marc followed him. Then, as he approached him, he raised his Winchester and found Hans's image inside the cross hairs of his gun sight. His finger was about to press against the trigger when a powerful hand took hold of his arm and forced it to his side.

Astonished, he turned to find that his father had taken hold of him.

"What are you doing here?" he asked, his angry voice a raspy whisper.

"I've come here to protect you from yourself," his father said. "I've come to save your life."

His father had hurried there, driving in his Willys jeep. He had returned from Hampshire earlier than expected.

To his father's remark, he made no reply. Instead, he

accompanied him to the foot of the mound, where Hans was examining the fallen stag.

"You have done well," his father told Hans as he observed the splendid body of the stag. "Our neighbors will be pleased."

Hans beamed. He was, Marc could see, unaware of how close he had come to being killed.

"Their children will eat meat for many weeks," he said.

"Yes," Marc answered him. "You have done a good thing."

For the next few minutes, his father never left his side. When they were away from Hans's hearing, his father urged him to hand over his weapons.

"I am protecting you," he said, echoing his earlier remark. "You have to let me help you."

For one wild moment, he believed that he would hurry away from his father and quickly kill Hans and himself. But the idea flared only for an instant. Something, some vague instinct of preservation or his awareness of how much his father meant to him, held him back. After that, without uttering even one word, he placed into his father's hands both the Winchester rifle and the Colt revolver that he had carried into the forest. As if he were trapped inside a reluctant dream, he watched his father's movements. Adept and quick, his father concealed the snub-nosed pistol within the pocket of his tweed jacket. Then he took hold of the rifle and emptied it of its cartridge. Only after that did his father look at him with a grave face.

"Hans has fooled you, too, I see," he told his father. "You are too eager to believe that he is one of us. But, I tell you, he is our enemy."

"Can you prove that? Do you have evidence that he is still a Nazi?"

Marc fell silent.

"You still don't get it," his father said. "You still don't understand."

Surly and self-defensive now, Marc threw out other incisive words.

"You should stay out of this. That is what I understand."

Still his father's gaze held him within its intricate layers of pity, affection, and judgment.

Once again, Marc fell silent.

Only after the next uncertain moment did new words intensify his unease.

"Before you do battle with your enemy," his father warned him, "be certain that you have conquered yourself."

After that, neither of them spoke. Leaving the silence that was between them and returning to his jeep, his father placed the Winchester across the rear seat and rode away.

Marc went back to the truck. Brisk and efficient, he drove to the clearing that was a few yards from the mound, where Hans stood waiting by the dead stag. There, the two of them lifted the body of the stag into the bed of the truck. They covered it with a canvas cloth, so that the hounds that were lying next to it would not howl or become restless. Then, they brought it to the village butcher who was going to clean and disembowel it and cut its body into sections. On the following day, under the watchful eyes of Mrs. Dowling and her husband, the reliable manager of the Roussillon property, most of the meat would be carefully portioned out to the needy families in the village. All the while that he was driving toward the village, Marc said very little to Hans. Instead, he listened in silence while Hans reminisced about his earlier hunting days in France and in Germany. Marc imagined that later, when he conferred with his father privately, he would not find any new words that might dispel the anger and the shame he felt because his father had peered into the murderous heart of his son. He, that self-conflicted son, was lost to his father. He was lost to Simone. He was lost to himself. The burden of that knowledge left him brooding and wary.

But he would not let go of his plan to kill Hans. Once again, he determined to wait for a favorable time. But this time he would act swiftly.

Later that day, he did not care to hear the new words that, with incisive firmness, his father and his mother spoke to him. They knew the wild anger that was in him. All through the earlier years when he was defining his individuality, they had witnessed the ways that he showed his love of others and the ways that he acted upon his hatred. In those earlier years and during these war years, they were often dismayed by his obsessions and disappointed by the rage and despair that overtook him whenever he felt betrayed by the day's unexpected complications or by a friend's ambivalent actions. There was a ruthless streak in him that his war-hardened parents did not disdain. But his lack of self-control and his murderous impulses disturbed them. The courage that he showed in battle and his love of his homeland validated the extraordinary aspects of his character. Yet there was in him an inordinate desire to punish or to destroy anyone that he perceived as his adversary. His need to punish Simone and to maim Gerhard had destroyed his marriage. That need had defeated the driving purpose of his plan. He had, at least temporarily, lost Simone's love. Whether he would ever regain her love, his parents could not say. But killing another rival was not the answer. So his parents told him once again in the privacy of a somber discussion that occurred when they were walking with him along the green banks of the lake. They were aware that he had not abandoned his plan to kill

Hans. They were trying to call him back to his better self. They wanted to prevent the tragedy that would take Hans's life and wreck his own.

He was not surprised when they joined him as he was walking alone by the lake. The autumn sky, with its blue-opal radiance, was tinting the waters of the lake. In wind-blown blue cotton shirts and trousers, each with rolled-up cuffs, he and his father were walking side by side. His mother, in a rose-colored blouse and gray slacks, stayed a few paces behind them. The afternoon was unusually warm. In spite of the ochre fields, the harvested orchards, and the scarlet blaze of the garden, the day was disguising itself as summer. As he walked with his parents along the smooth bank of the lake, he observed in the sun-misted distance the familiar white cliffs rising out of the waters as if they were the remains of a ghostly world that had otherwise disappeared. Nearer than that, a flock of black-headed gulls was hurrying across luminous clouds. Tall larch trees were swaying in unison at the southwest edge of the woods, and a yawl that belonged to his father was hastening across the shifting colors of the quickened lake. Hans was piloting the yawl, and three farm youths from the village were enjoying the ride.

"There is the real Hans," his father said, as they observed the yawl leaving the spray and spume of water behind it. "Your mother and I believe in him."

"I have to do things my way," he said. "I do not share your trust in Hans. I believe that he is a double agent and that he is helping the Nazis win the war."

"You have no proof," his father said. "You have no valid reason to kill him. In fact, there is strong evidence that Hans Mueller is exactly the man he says he is. He is a German who has been fighting bravely for our side."

Marc bristled. A flash of anger gave a bitter edge to his words.

"He does not fool me," he said. "I'm on to the game that he is playing."

His father halted his quick pace and turned to face him directly.

"You want to kill Hans because Simone loves him," his father said.

Now his mother was by his side, reminding him of the consequences that the murder would bring upon him.

"If you kill Hans," his mother warned him, "you will lose Simone forever."

"You will destroy yourself," his father said. "Whatever part of your soul the war has not already destroyed will be lost to you forever."

"You will be killing an ally," his mother reminded him

once more. "You will be taking the life of an innocent man."

"Hans is no innocent," he said, his voice an angry rebuttal of all that his parents were telling him. "He is a German."

His parents looked at him with probing eyes. They were, he imagined, fathoming the depths of his hatred and the intricacies of his murderous inclinations. They were looking at him as though he had set himself on fire and was beyond their rescue. But they said nothing more to him. The three of them continued their walk along the banks of the lake in silence.

Chapter Nine

Hunted

The next morning, after his parents and Hans had left Derbyshire for new flight assignments and only a few hours before he would report to his air base in Lincolnshire, an MI5 agent paid Marc a visit. Marc had been expecting him. A message on his wireless transceiver had advised him of the visit. The agent's name was Clive Harrison. He was a tall, burly man in his fifties. His gray hair, cragged features, and large, callused hands gave him the look of a laborer. His cold eyes, aquiline nose, and clenched jaw made him even more forbidding. But Marc had met his type before. Harrison belonged to the group of men who have contempt for any sign of weakness in other men. Even during times of peace, these men are often sadists and bullies. In war, they have no aversion to torturing and mutilating their victims. They have unforgiving dispositions and a killer's instincts.

From the moment that they met, Harrison cast his cold eyes upon him. He was taking his measure. He was determining the accuracy of the reports that his superiors had transmitted to him about the Frenchman named Marc Roussillon. The reports, Marc guessed, must have told Harrison about his RAF bombing missions and about his assignments for the Resistance. The favorable reports would have won him this agent's respect. But Harrison would have refused to be impressed. He had his own challenge to set before Marc Roussillon. This challenge would test his wits and the fiercest layers of his courage. It might cost him his life. So Harrison was to tell him during this private meeting that was taking place in the library.

"You rich folks know how to live in a grand style, even in wartime," he said. "Maybe that makes you better fighters. You have a lot to lose if you don't kill your enemies."

Harrison was observing the meticulous appointments of the room: the butternut paneling, the sun-tinted French doors, the Louis IV needlepoint sofas and chairs, the bookshelves with special editions, and the Renoir, Caillebotte, and Corbet canvases adorning the walls. When he first entered the house, he had cast the same cold eyes upon the rotunda, with its marble floor and Corinthian pilasters, its vast arches and large chandelier, and its decorative plasterwork and iron balustrades. Here now, in the library, a sneer touched his lips and vague resentment made his gaze more piercing.

"Everyone has a lot to lose," Marc answered him,

"whether they are rich or poor."

Harrison refused to let go of it.

"The rich always have more to lose," he insisted.

Marc did not bother to answer him immediately. Instead, he poured another round of scotch. Then, lifting his glass, he offered Harrison these casual words.

"Here's to the winners," he said, "whether they are rich or poor."

"Oh, I don't mind the rich," Harrison said," as long as they are good fighters. Take you, for instance. I hear that you are a very good fighter and that you hate all Germans. That raises you in my estimation and in the estimation of all the other MI5 agents. That is why we are sending you on this new assignment."

"What assignment is that?"

"We are sending you into Paris, because you loathe Germans and know how to kill them and because you know the Parc Monceau area well."

Harrison swallowed the scotch quickly and then held his glass forward, so that Marc could fill it again.

"Did you know that the Germans killed all my family?"

"No, I did not know. I am sorry."

Harrison grimaced. With his rumpled manner and his gravelly voice, he appeared even more somber and worn down.

But there were no tears in his eyes. He was not asking for pity. He was simply stating the facts and struggling to decipher their finality.

"They bombed the suburban areas outside London and killed my wife, our two daughters, and their four children. They killed all of them."

Marc changed the subject, reminding Harrison of the reason why the two of them were meeting here in the privacy of his parents' Derbyshire home.

"Why is the Parc Monceau important?"

The question called Harrison back to the moment that was enfolding them inside its complicated patterns.

"Our wireless people have intercepted the recent correspondence of the German High Command. Some of their top generals and a few important Vichy officials will be meeting in one of the mansions in the park that the Germans have seized for their own uses. MI5 wants those Nazi generals and the Vichy officials assassinated. Aerial bombing of the building during the daytime hours when they will be meeting is out of the question. With your demolition training and your knowledge of the area, you are the MI5 man most likely to succeed in this mission."

"Will I be working alone?"

"No. Another agent will be assisting you."

"Who is he?" Marc asked. "Is he someone that I know?"

"You do know him…a little."

He noticed that Harrison was not ready to reveal the identity of the man. So he hurried to describe the sort of man that he wanted as his partner in this mission.

"To get the job done, I need to work with someone who has been on my team before. He has to know what he is doing. He has to know how to handle explosives."

"You will be working with a well-trained assistant. When we have sent him on similar assignments, he has always come through for us."

"Tell me his name, and I'll tell you whether he is the right man."

With his beady eyes and with a wily manner, Harrison stared at him while retreating to the privacies of his morose disposition. He took a moment to pour another scotch and to swallow it slowly. He enjoyed making him wait for the name of the man who would be working with him. But, at the same time, Harrison seemed pleased that he had demanded, rather than petitioned, the name of the man. When he did speak, he was brisk and matter-of-fact.

"You met him just a few days ago. His name is Hans Mueller."

Hearing the name, Marc stayed in control. The protest

that the name drew from him was understated.

"You are making a mistake. You are asking me to work with a man who may be a Nazi."

Harrison was enjoying himself again. The scotch had relaxed him, and he had recovered his hard-edged detachment. He was eager to correct a junior agent's misperceptions.

"Hans Mueller is no Nazi, though he is a German. The agency has checked him out thoroughly. For a time, we did wonder whether he was a mole whom the Nazis had planted in our midst. So we kept a close watch on him. We have tested his loyalty at every turn. All of our people have concluded that Hans Mueller is the genuine article. He is a true ally. We rank him among our best fighters. Within the year since he joined us, he has risked almost certain death every time that we sent him, in disguise, back to Germany. While he was there, he darkened his hair, wore eyeglasses, and lost thirty pounds. At first, he was a clerk in a railroad station who gained access to the schedules of the trains that would be carrying army battalions to distant battlefields. Then, in the early hours before dawn, he used his demolition training well. He placed gelignite or amatol or plastic explosive beneath the rail and a fog signal detonator on top. When the trains passed across the rail, they blew up, killing or maiming the German infantrymen and a cadre of field-grade officers who were on their way to do battle with our allies.

"Later, he used the same strategy when, imitating a public works engineer, he bombed bridges, canals, and aircraft factories in Berlin, Stuttgart, and Munich. Once, he was daring enough to impersonate a general's aide-de-camp and stole important war plans right under the noses of the High Command. Shortly after that, he pretended to be a sadistic doctor whom the High Command had sent to administer lethal injections to three MI5 agents that two Nazi officers had captured. That time, he shot the Nazis who, for more than a week, had been torturing the MI5 agents. Then, he managed to escape with those agents—each of them in convincing disguises—across the German border into Switzerland. This Hans Mueller is an exceptional man. He has come through for the RAF, as well. I do not need to remind you that he is a first-rate bomber pilot."

In spite of what Harrison was telling him, Marc remained adamant.

"Mueller is not the man that I want on my team."

"You have no say in the matter. MI5 wants Mueller. And the agency wants you. That is how this mission will proceed."

"Hans Mueller is my enemy."

"Of course, he is. Your wife is in love with him. But that is your problem, not MI5's. We want you to help us win the war. We are not interested in your marriage."

"Apparently, the agency knows all my secrets."

"I would never say that. You probably harbor secrets that MI5 will never discover. But we do know that you want to kill Hans Mueller."

"Then why are you involving him in this mission?"

"Maybe we are testing both of you. Maybe we are giving Hans Mueller another chance to prove that he is a steel-true ally. Maybe we are giving you a chance to find out who Mueller really is. We have no way of knowing what this mission will show us. Possibly, you will find an excuse to kill Mueller. He is, after all, a renegade German."

"Are you telling me that MI5 wants me to kill Hans Mueller?"

"I cannot speak for my colleagues in the agency. As for me, I hate all Germans. I shall not mind if you kill Mueller. But you had better find a good reason for doing so."

Four days later, only hours before he and Hans were going to begin the dangerous mission that would bring them into Paris, Marc was surprised by a visit from Simone. On this late October afternoon in 1944, she had found him sitting with two pilots from his squadron in a booth within a shadowy corner of the pub that stood half a mile away from his air base in Lincolnshire. When they saw her slipping into the space beside him, her pale blue chiffon dress and navy-blue jacket enhancing her poise, his friends—who had recently been assigned to the base—were unaware that Simone was his wife. But, instantly upon seeing her with him, they perceived Marc and Simone as a romantic couple. They respected Marc because of his skill as a pilot, his courage in battle, and his care of the men in his command. They were not surprised that a beautiful woman had sought out his company. Marc Roussillon stood high in their unsentimental and probing judgment of the men around them. His two pilot friends saw him as the confident and hardy man that he was. He was tall and dark-haired, and his big-boned physique and manly grace suggested that he was a well-trained athlete. They well understood that all their encounters with this twenty-four-year-old pilot had involved them in his quickened awareness and his subtle calculations. If they were to ask him to describe his scanning impression of the place where they were sitting with him and with Simone, Marc would have offered an accurate location of entrances and exits, of the eight persons seated nearest those exits, and of the man and woman who were dining at the booth next to theirs.

Except that their meeting was fraught with the surprise of Simone's being so suddenly there with them,

Marc's friends would have—even in this crowded pub—allowed themselves to admire more than an instant the poise and decorum of Simone. She was, besides being very young, one of the two or three loveliest women they had ever seen. Her blond beauty and delicate bones lent an ethereal expression to her manner. But her warm spirit and her confident inflections told them that she was very much a woman of this world. They enjoyed the sight of her. But, after they noticed the love that was in Marc's eyes as he sat next to her, they knew what to do. They excused themselves and walked over to the bar in a distant corner of the room.

"I have come here to tell you what is on my mind," Simone said, after she had changed her seat to the place opposite him. She wanted (Marc imagined) to look directly into his face as she spoke to him. She wanted him to look at her, as well, as if, by so looking, they could more precisely interpret the subtleties of their careful language and their enigmatic facial expressions.

Marc wanted to charm her. He felt that he must ingratiate himself with her. Realist though he was, he tried to convince himself that her coming to him in this way was a hopeful sign.

"I am always ready to hear what you have to say to

me," he told her.

"I have something important to tell you," she answered him. "But, first, let us spend a friendly hour together."

So, while he waited for her to speak the words that were meant for him alone, he enjoyed lunch with her. They shared a torte filled with zucchini, eggplant, and tomatoes, as well as a round of Glenmorangie scotch, pungent even with its caramel and vanilla textures. They spoke of lighthearted things, including their favorite Criollos, their kayaking trip to Finland years earlier, and their skiing in Gstaad. But, all the while, he sensed that she was waiting for the right moment to tell him the important words that she had saved for him.

In the distance, smoky vapors rose and coiled about the crowded bar and about the wider spaces of the pub. The images, the sounds, and the scents in this and the adjoining rooms became vivid and palpable even as they recalled his past visits here with Simone. The tangy fragrances of food—beef stew, cider apple chicken, trout braised in Riesling wine, and lemon sponge cakes—floated languorously into the vaporous atmosphere. French and British pilots in blue Air Force trousers and brown leather jackets were drinking whiskey, rum, and ale at the bar. Some of them were sitting at tables or in booths while eating lunch and making contact with old friends or new acquaintances. They were talking about the latest rugby matches or about hunting trips they had taken in South Africa or about the skiing they had enjoyed in the Swiss Alps before the war. Most of these men were partnered with pretty girls in colorful dresses who lived in the town and who liked the company of combat pilots. Caught within the cacophony of voices, Bing Crosby, Vera Lynn, Frank Sinatra, and Judy Garland were singing romantic ballads on jukebox recordings.

Marc clearly perceived all of this reality of people and fragrances and sounds. But the reality that was far more pressing belonged to Simone and to him as they sat together and as he wondered what she was going to say to him. After they finished their meal and after they drank a second round of scotch, she studied his face as if she were looking upon him for the first time. Her blue eyes held him in her gaze, and she permitted herself to clasp his folded hands. Only then did she tell him the words that were important for her to say and necessary for him to hear.

"This week has been good to me," she began. "MI5 has told me that, in a few days, I will no longer have to be Valérie Moreau. Hans is in the clear. They have tested his loyalty many times, and he has always come through for them. Now I can be myself once again, and I can tell Hans all about the person that I really am."

Marc became very still. Then, with a flick of his hand, he signaled a passing waiter to bring him another scotch. This casual gesture suppressed his anger, even as he cast a slur against Hans Muller's character.

"Why do you want to be with a Nazi?"

Simone ignored the slur. She hurried to remind him how it was with her.

"I love Hans. I do not care to live without him."

Now Marc was brusque.

"You love a ghost. You love a man who reminds you of Gerhard."

Clasping his hands once more, Simone tried to reason with him.

"Be happy for me. Be happy that I am making a new life for myself. You need to move on, too. Deirdre may be your answer. She may be the woman who can help you to make your life new. We are not the answer for each other."

"You are the only answer for me. You are the only woman I will ever love."

Simone pressed her hands upon his. Sorrow touched her voice and influenced her blue-eyed gaze.

"You are the one in love with a ghost. You love a woman who does not exist. I am no longer the girl who fell in love with you from the moment she met you eight years ago. I am not the woman who married you and loved you completely. I am not that Simone. Too much has gone wrong for us. We have lost so many of the wonderful things between us that made our being together not only happy, but also inevitable."

"We can get all of it back. You need to give us a chance."

"There are no more chances for us if we stay together. We'll be the prisoners of our past. We'll be the prisoners of each other."

"Don't say that. Don't make everything so final."

"We have to break free of each other. There is no other way to save ourselves."

His voice was sullen now.

"You must really hate me."

"Oh, no," she protested, her soft, melancholic inflections anchored to matter-of-fact appraisal and to the genuine feelings for him that still lived within her. "That is not true. I shall always love you, but not in the same way. I do not want to hurt you. Just try to understand that I cannot be your Simone anymore. I am someone different. I am learning how to save myself by not living with you. You have to do the same. You have to find a new lifeline."

"So that's it, then. It's over between us."

"Yes."

Remorse weighed down his next words.

"Hans Mueller is not the answer for you. He could never love you the way that I do."

"Maybe not," she said, reflecting upon the implications of his judgment. "But I do not need your kind of love anymore."

He resisted her words.

"I need you. One day, you will need me, too. I'll be waiting for you."

She pressed his hands once more. Then, rising from her seat, she spoke even more gently, before hurrying away.

"It is over between us. Try to understand why."

For a few minutes, he sat alone with his brooding thoughts. Then, his two pilot friends came back to the table and joined him in a round of scotch. He exchanged anecdotes with them about playing rugby during their school days, about hunting whales in the Azores, and about flying the latest Avro Lancaster. All the while that he and the lieutenants were conversing, he was telling himself that he had not lost Simone. Bereft and embittered, she would come back to him after he killed Hans in the Paris assignment that was already flaring its promise of danger and of betrayal.

Imperiled though it was by the risks that he and Hans were taking, the mission that brought them into France went reasonably well, at first. No enemy aircraft fired upon the Lockheed Hudson that was making a night flight to the Aix-en-Provence vineyards, where they would stay until morning in a safe house that belonged to an affluent and aged member of the Resistance. The pilot of the Lockheed Hudson, who was one of his comrades in the Free French Air Force, knew what to do. At one point, he flew as low as fifteen hundred feet, so that Hans and he could make a parachute jump over the night-darkened greenery of the vineyards that spanned four hundred acres. The drop was the nearest that he and Hans could make without drawing the Nazis to themselves. It also brought them to the fearless owner of the land. Like the pilot, he also knew what to do. He had secured for them the false identity and ration cards, the workmen's clothes, and the semi-automatic pistols they would need. He had obtained for them, as well, the government work permits that carried the official stamp and the signature of the French prime minister.

Despite the tension that hovered about their arrival at

the home of their Resistance benefactor, Hans and he spent a comfortable night there. Though they sometimes heard, rising out of the far distance, the booms and volleys of the night-bombings that were overtaking nearby villages that had harbored Jews and Resistance workers, they were not unduly disturbed. Their host and his wife gave them a delicious meal and very good wine. They also reviewed with them a detailed map of the Parc Monceau and an equally precise blueprint of the Second Empire building in the northwest section of the park. That building had been overtaken by some of the most formidable officers in the German High Command. It was the building that he and Hans, with work papers in hand and with accurate Belgian French inflections, would enter as skilled electricians. Ostensibly, they were there to improve the electric circuitry within the five rooms close to the suite of rooms where generals and field-grade officers would be conferring with important Nazi party members who were visiting from Berlin. Though the building had remained intact during a recent bombing of the city, other buildings around it had sustained considerable damage. But, as a sign that life in Germanized Paris was still flourishing, the High Command had kept the park open to the public.

At dawn, their Provençal hosts offered Hans and him a

quick breakfast and gave them the large and sturdy metal kits that contained the essential tools of an electrician's trade: lineman's pliers, side and cable cutters, crimping pliers and crescent wrenches, hack saws and hammers, and channel locks. Hidden in a secret compartment beneath the top level of each kit were thirty pounds of explosives that would, if they succeeded in their mission, blow up the building and kill the Paris-based German staff and the visitors from Berlin. Hans's and his Provençal hosts, who remained anonymous, also provided them with a Willys truck. Then, with Hans beside him in the passenger seat, Marc made the four-hundred-mile journey into Paris. Every time that they were stopped at a Nazi checkpoint, he and Hans kept their hands near their concealed Colt revolvers. They were prepared to shoot their way past the checkpoints. But, while they studied them carefully, none of the Nazi guards questioned their papers. So he maintained a speedy passage.

When they arrived at the elaborate mansion that the Germans were using for their military purposes and sometimes for their grand soirées, the well-groomed guards gave them no trouble. These two guards, young and muscular, perceived their work permits as authentic, and they allowed them easy access to both the interior and the exterior of the building. The junior and senior officers, who passed them by as they changed the wiring in the wide array of rooms and inside the paneling of the long corridors, either ignored them or nodded stiffly. The young, pretty French stenographers smiled at them, and one offered them coffee. Only a scar-faced colonel approached them as they began working in the rear of the building. Observing them when they first surveyed the rooms where they would alter the electric wiring, the colonel asked them a spate of questions about Belgium and about the streets and districts in which they had lived and worked. Without hesitation, both Hans and he, who had often visited Brussels, Antwerp, Bruges, and Liège, named specific streets and accurate locations. Their answering the colonel in perfect German as well as in fluent Belgian French appeared to satisfy the middle-aged officer. But, as the hours in which they worked passed by, he continued to watch them, nonetheless. Marc felt a grudging respect for such vigilance. At the same time, he found himself despising the tall, gaunt Nazi with the relentless, searching eyes; with a hawk-like nose that seemed to sniff and categorize every human scent within its vicinity; and with a vague sneer that twisted the right corner of his mouth. From the start, Marc anticipated that, of all the people in the building who were observing him and Hans with fleeting glance or with more studious concentration, this colonel was going to bring them trouble.

So proficient were he and Hans as they altered the wiring within the wall paneling of the various offices and of the wide corridors, that even this colonel appeared to accept them for the persons that they said they were: experienced electricians who had come there to help Germanized Paris and to replace the French electricians who, under the Compulsory Work Service Law recently invoked by the Vichy government, had been deported to Germany to work as forced laborers for the war effort there. At this time, as if he were signaling his reluctant and tentative acceptance of them, the colonel returned to his office at the end of the corridor where Hans and he were working. Within the next two hours, Marc and Hans completed their work inside the building. Then, careful to maintain a natural pace, they moved outside the building. They were not surprised by what they saw in the rear of the building. They had studied well the blueprint of the grounds that their Resistance contact had provided them. There, at the threshold of an asphalt-paved yard, they passed through an unguarded gate and approached a powerhouse in the north wing of the building. Attached to this boiler house were two huge power transformers.

As quick as they were adept, he and Hans placed thirty pounds of explosives unobtrusively beneath each transformer. They left a half-hour's delay on the explosive mixtures. The half-hour would give them time to return to their truck, drive away from the building, and—after passing beyond Place St-Augustin and just before entering the streets that would bring them back to Provence—listen for the explosions that would demolish the building and kill the Nazi officers and their Nazi staff. That the pretty stenographers would also die did not disturb Marc. He saw them as enemies. He saw them as French women who had betrayed their homeland and had unwisely chosen to assist the Nazis. So he whispered to Hans right after they completed the work of laying the explosives beneath the transformers and, upon closing their tool kits, were about to leave the yard behind the building.

Hearing his callous words, Hans frowned. He perceived the young stenographers in an altogether different way.

"I am not proud that we have planted the bombs that will kill those girls," he said. "It is hard enough that we are killing the young men who serve the High Command in that building. Not so long ago, I called them my brothers without having met them, because we are German and because we shared the same experience of life."

Marc did not have time to scoff at Hans's sensitivity or to doubt even more fiercely his allegiance to the Resistance. No sooner had Hans expressed his remorse in barely audible tones, than both of them noticed that the colonel with the rapid and questioning eyes was standing behind them. A brawny lieutenant had accompanied him there. His grey uniform was flawlessly pressed. His brown boots gleamed. Around his waist was a leather holster that carried a Luger. He kept his right hand near his pistol.

"I want to inspect your work," the colonel said. "I want to see whether you have done all that you were called here to do."

The lieutenant stood in his tracks. He was serving the colonel as a sentry.

Neither Marc nor Hans revealed any unease. Instead, Hans directed the colonel toward the transformers and, with confident assertiveness, began to explain the work that he and Marc had just completed. He was stalling for time. He was hoping that the colonel would not see the explosives that were concealed within the manicured bushes and the late-blooming roses which gave an autumn sheen to the space beneath the transformers.

At first, the colonel did not see the explosives.

"Your work is good," he said. "You Belgians are better trained than the French."

He did not smile. But he permitted himself to nod his head slightly as a sign of his approval. Even the lieutenant relaxed his posture and moved his hand away from his holster.

For an instant, Marc believed that he and Hans might pass through this inspection without any violence.

Just then, the early afternoon sun flashed new light upon the transformers, and the grass and the roses swayed in the brisker energies of the wind. The excited motion of the grass and the roses drew the colonel's notice. As he was turning away from the transformers, he stopped. With a more incisive gaze, he needed to validate what his eyes had already shown him. Moving closer to the transformers to study them more carefully, he parted the grass and the stems of roses. Then, he saw the explosives.

"What is this?" he asked. "What have you done?"

Aware of the colonel's tension, the lieutenant reached for his Luger.

At the same time, the colonel, still leaning toward the rose bushes, whirled around and began firing his MAB Model D pistol.

The bullets flew past Marc.

With no hesitation, Marc fired his Colt Pocket Hammer revolver and killed the colonel. The two bullets lifted the tall, gaunt body momentarily. They blew out the walls of his heart and the left side of his skull. The body, spraying the air with globs of blood and spewing brain cells and tissue, fell at the edge of the rose bushes.

The lieutenant fired more accurately than his colonel. His bullets grazed Hans's left shoulder and his right leg. In simultaneous action, Hans shot him through the forehead and watched the young body keel over.

Now Marc and Hans moved even more swiftly. They scooped up the Luger and the MAB pistols and placed them inside the pockets of their work jackets. Then, they dragged the bodies of the colonel and the lieutenant and concealed them behind the rose bushes. They took hold of their tool kits and, with a nearly casual pace, walked out of the yard and made their way into the main area of the park. They could not be certain, but in these uneasy moments they told themselves that nobody had heard the gunfire that they had exchanged with the colonel and the lieutenant. The sound of electric drills and the thud of hammers were still rising from the massive apartment building and the elegant Renaissance house that carpenters were repairing a few blocks away, on the Rue Rembrandt. Those sounds had muffled the noise of the shooting.

With Hans trailing behind him, Marc increased his pace as he headed toward the gate that would bring them onto the Rue Rembrandt. He and Hans had some distance to cover before they reached the Boulevard de Courcelles, where they had left their truck. Each of them looked nondescript. Each of them mingled effectively with the men and women who, on their lunch break from their work as office clerks or as skilled laborers, were entering the park to buy coffee and a sandwich at a concession stand and, while sitting on a park bench, to enjoy the autumn landscape that was flourishing around them. For these five minutes, everything went smoothly. Marc told himself that he had a chance to get out of the park alive. He would also seize the opportunity to kill Hans as they were leaving the park.

But then, without warning, the ground beneath him shook. The air rumbled and heaved with loud explosions. The bombs had gone off too early. Looking back, he saw the mansion that he and Hans had just left break apart. Windows were bursting, walls collapsed, the roof flew away, and flames were soaring higher and higher. He heard agonized screams merging with the explosions, and he witnessed a man on fire jumping out of a shattered third story window. The men, women, and children around him were already scurrying for cover toward forest paths that might bring them to safety or toward the gates through which they would find their way out of the park. Deliberately, he merged himself with them. Only once now did he look behind him. The flames that had overtaken the building were rising higher, and the rippling explosions still pierced the air. But Hans was no longer behind him. Where he had disappeared, Marc had no time to guess.

Exactly at that moment, two young Nazi officers, who must have rushed out of the exploding mansion that had served as the headquarters of the German High Command, were racing after him. As fast as his legs would carry him, he ran away from them and mingled with eight or ten university students who were running for the sheer pleasure of the exercise, perhaps, or for honing their proficiencies as athletes. With them, he swerved his direction onto a new path that brought him past the monument to Guy de Maupassant and past other Belle Epoque monuments that commemorated equally prominent French writers and musicians. He ran straight ahead, toward a moss-covered Corinthian colonnade that curved around the edge of a tiny lake with a floral island in the center. Then, while leaving the group of university runners, he turned left onto the Allée de la Comtesse de Ségur and ran the length of this solitary route until he arrived on the Avenue Vélasquez.

There, he paused and scanned what he had expected: a wide, tree-lined street filled with nineteenth-century, Neoclassical mansions. But, as soon as he had verified his location, he noticed at the north end of the bustling street two other Nazi sentries racing toward him.

Heading in the opposite direction, he increased his speed. Within minutes, he reached Avenue Van Dyck, re-entered the park, and turned left into the second small, winding path. There, merging once again with passers-by milling near him, he weaved his way around a mossy pyramid, antique tombs, a stone arcade, an obelisk, and a small Chinese pagoda. Veering into a different direction, he turned right onto the first path past the pyramid and walked back to a more secluded area of the park.

He concealed himself within the long, shadowy corridor of the forested area that was flanked by French elms and Norway maples. His breath was coming fast now, and pain was shooting through his left leg, which had been riddled with Nazi bullets only a few months earlier during a bombing mission over Munich. It was time to stop, not only to rest but also to determine whether he had outrun the men who were pursuing him. That it was just past noon was in his favor. The autumn sun kept welling up from the after-glow of morning and held him in its muted radiance. For a few minutes, he lingered behind the thick trunk of a towering elm, his right hand held firmly upon his Colt Vest Pocket pistol. He listened for the sound of footsteps running toward him. But only the excited chirping of forest birds and the breeze-tossed flutter of October-crisp leaves broke through the stillness.

For a few minutes more, he waited within the secrecies of this dark tree-lined path. Then, because he had not detected the sound of a human foot stepping on a fragment of a fallen branch or heard the rapid breathing of the killers pursuing him, he hurried to the Avenue Hoche and the threshold of light that was revealing the rose-tinted clouds of a blue sky, the tall buildings rising toward those clouds, and the few trolleys, automobiles, taxis, and Nazi jeeps and trucks that were filling the wide and newly-swept street. When he reached the long, wide street and while keeping his right hand upon his pistol that filled the inside pocket of his jacket, he hurried into the midst of the few men and women who were passing by him. The men, white-haired and grizzled or dark-haired and prematurely grim-faced, wore gray or brown windbreakers and rumpled overalls. They carried lunch pails and seemed beaten down by life. Nor did the two or three women whom he regarded with fleeting glance look much happier. Middle-aged and blowsy, they might be desk clerks in seedy hotels or waitresses in nondescript diners. The Nazi officers were not among them.

He paused at the edge of the sidewalk. Then, looking eastward, he observed in the distance, not more than two hundred yards from the place where he stood, the same two Nazi sentries who were hunting him down. Instantly, he hurried into the Rue de Courcelles entrance from which he and Hans had, during the dawn hours, walked into the park. With no one around to notice, he ran inside the convoluted florescence of the gardens. He slowed his pace now, walking with casual-seeming self-possession through the six acres that encompassed the colorful landscape. Two young men and even younger women, sauntering ahead of him, had already begun their visit to the gardens. They appeared to be newly-married couples whose brisk manner enhanced the excited words of approval which the scene drew from them. They wore stylish fabrics, and they spoke in the clipped fluencies of French and of German. From the fragments of their conversation which rode across the air, he learned that they had come to the park early so that they might witness the dawn rising over the gardens. They had stayed several hours, visiting the ornate mansions, pagodas, and arcades that had remained untouched by the recent aerial bombings and enjoying a delicious brunch in the one restaurant that, despite the war, was serving meals to the public.

Except for these four, he saw no one at this time.

He passed through the French garden, which swayed in delicate rhythms with the early afternoon breeze, the grace of its movements implicating rows and rows of late-blooming pink tulips and ellipses of boxwoods and daisies. A fountain sculpture of three dancing girls stirred a momentary tension and compelled him to finger the trigger of his concealed pistol when he detected a sudden movement on the bottom side of the fountain, where clusters of yellow, scarlet and orange nasturtiums were blooming. He was about to take out his pistol and begin firing it. But the reedy physique of a tow-headed young groundskeeper, with a spade in his left hand and a container of mulch in his right, rose from his crouching position and stepped back to survey his work.

Now the man noticed him and, after abruptly placing his spade and his pail on the ground where he had been working, he moved toward him with a lurching gait. Marc then guessed that the man's right leg had been deformed at birth or made crooked by an unforgiving civilian injury or by a war wound.

Marc paused, his hand gripping his concealed pistol.

Still the man moved toward him while his blue eyes

flashed with recognition, as though he had been waiting for him.

"I've been noticing that you really enjoy looking at the garden," he said. His voice was raspy. It was a voice that might have belonged to a much older man.

When he pushed his right hand into the pocket of his overalls, Marc started to bring his pistol out of his jacket. He paused once more as the man lifted out of his pocket a large black handkerchief and began wiping his mulch-stained hands.

"It feels good to know that someone appreciates my work," he said. "You look like a man who has cared for his own garden."

He offered him a friendly grin. Marc saw that there was no danger in him. He just wanted to pass the time of day as his way of breaking the solitariness of his work or of forgetting momentarily the screaming sirens and the billowing smoke that, in the faraway distance, were rising from the building that he and Hans had bombed. Years earlier, on any day during peacetime, they might have shared some talk about baseball or about the landscape design of the park. But today was different. He was in a hurry. He needed to elude the men who wanted to kill him.

So, even as he resumed his hastening pace, he saluted the good-natured gardener as he called out his own friendly words just before leaving him behind.

"You are right," he said. "I do like to garden."

He passed more quickly now through the Italian garden, glancing at the vivid imagery as if he were looking upon a montage. He was aware of a wisteria pergola arching over a walkway that wore medallions inscribed with the names of famous French statesmen; an expansive lawn surrounded by clipped hedges of yews; a twelve-foot-high jet fountain; and two impressive allées of pink and white crabapple trees hurried, temporary and kinetic, across his scanning glance. Years earlier, when, as university students, he and Simone visited this garden, the breeze-tossed stirring of the trees and the soft chirping of birds enhanced the peaceful atmosphere. But on this afternoon the distant explosions held the place in its violent thrall. Yet there was no sign of the Nazis here.

He walked even more rapidly, his young body agile and proficient as he made his way into the English garden. He barely noticed, in the center of a lush green lawn that seemed both vast and endless, the topiary of a boy playing his pipe to attract birds and a girl offering a bowl of water for them to drink. But he was fully aware of the perfumed scent of autumn magnolias and of Japanese lilac trees that bordered the main paths. He was conscious, also, of two aged men who were observing the English garden with the eyes of horticulturalists.

Both were tall and gaunt and looked professorial. They spoke about the topiary in the husky inflections of Swedish, a language that he knew more than a little. They were not the Nazis who were pursuing him.

Thus far, he had eluded the killers. But, at the same time, he had lost track of Hans Mueller.

He reached the middle of the park now, just north of Rue Murillo. It would be better, he thought, for him to return to the trafficked street and make his way quickly to his truck. Just then, as he was preparing to leave the park, he saw—in the sun-misted distance that kept fanning outward, undulant and profuse—the Nazi pursuers who wanted to kill him. There were three of them now. For an instant, he thought one of them was Hans Mueller. They were looking back in his direction, yet apparently not seeing him. Or perhaps, having seen him, they were making their lanky forms a visible snare to trap him. With a slower pace that seemed contrived, the Nazis walked into a more secluded area of the park known as the North Woods. A river lay at the bottom of a ravine there and flowed under massive stone arches before connecting southward to a pool that hurried by grassy banks and weeping willows into a rushing waterfall. The ninety acres that encompassed the North Woods made a tranquil spot that felt a world away from the surrounding city.

In this war-torn afternoon hour, a person might be swiftly murdered there, and his body—lying amidst the entangled greenery or beneath cascading streams—could remain undetected for days or even weeks. He kept wondering whether one of these men who were hunting him was Hans Mueller. In spite of the risk he would be taking, Marc hurried forward in pursuit of these men. He wanted to kill both men, and he hoped that one of the Nazis was Hans. If that were so, then in the same instant of the shooting, he could kill Hans and walk away guiltless. Moving with stealthy precision and always observing the main path that he had left, he kept himself concealed along the inside rim of six-foot flowering evergreen shrubs that he recognized as rose mallows and blue hydrangeas, red barberries, and yellow-gold junipers. He treaded softly within the dappled shadows cast by the cloud-like sprays of fringe trees and the spreading canopies of pink hawthorns. Always, he listened for the muffled footsteps that might belong to the killer stalking him. But only the scurrying of two playful squirrels and the crinkled hiss of the breeze-tossed leaves rose up to disarrange the stillness. There was no sign of the killers.

But, he told himself, the killers were in these woods, waiting for him to make the wrong move that would render him vulnerable.

Just then, about thirty feet ahead of him, as he reached the grassy banks and the rushing waterfall of the pool that gushed out of a boulder grotto on the park's southern shoreline, Marc saw a scar-faced, red-haired Nazi major darting beneath the weeping willows and skimming past the aquatic plants there. Concealed always by the shadowy woods and never losing sight of the major, he took out his Colt pistol and hurried after him. He was so intent upon keeping the image of this man in his sight, that he did not at once comprehend the different imagery that suddenly rushed toward him.

A young wild-eyed woman, wearing a wide-brimmed navy-blue hat and a navy-and-white woolen suit, was running onto the path where he stood. She was holding securely a Beretta M 1934 revolver, which she fired repeatedly at him. The shots were erratic and betrayed her rising panic.

He was thrown back by the impact of one of the bullets that grazed his left arm. But his astonishment at seeing this new enemy and the dull pain that with throbbing tentacles was clasping his wounded arm held him in their influences for no more than a few seconds. With smooth and militant swiftness, he fired back at her. The first bullet blew out her left brown eye and the second crashed through her forehead, lifting strands of her titian hair away from her neck. Blood spilled from her eyeless socket down upon her pale face and scattered out of the back of her head, spewing cells, tissue and bits of flesh onto the shoulders of her jacket. Her body dropped down hard upon the jagged edges of a giant boulder. A flurry of frightened blue-winged teals flew up to the branches of tulip trees, and a white-tailed deer leaped from the path into an enclosure of swaying heliotropes.

In the same instant and from the shadowy enclosure, the red-haired major ran toward him while firing a Luger P08 semiautomatic pistol. His scarred face was a mask of hatred, and his racing motion a blur of intensity upon his seeing.

"Bastard!" he shouted, the impetus of his gravelly voice riding on thick Germanic inflections. "Rotten bastard!"

Marc gave him no chance to shoot again.

Fast-moving and accurate, he fired a bullet into the man's heart.

The hard, lean body crumpled as if in slow motion. For a full minute, it remained on its knees, swaying forward and sideways. The eyes, glazed in death and sightless, were staring at him. With a vague contempt for this enemy, Marc peered at the eyes and afterwards at the hole in the man's chest. Although he was repelled by the imagery, he moved closer and kicked the left side of the body. He watched it fall away to its right side and come to rest by the rushing waters of the pool.

For a brief moment, he looked about him in the solitary space where he had confronted his would-be assassins. He stared at the petite body of the woman sprawled across the boulder and the long-limbed body of the man lying inert at the side of the pool. That he had killed them while sustaining a mere flesh wound pleased him. There would be others like them hunting him down in this park. They would be better trained, and they might be luckier. Having told himself so, he made his way to the Boulevard de Courcelles. Arriving there, while hearing the vernacular sounds of spirited voices and the cacophonous honking of cars, he saw new crowds of hastening people and the jagged swiftness of traffic. Then, with vigorous strides that would cover the long walk before him, he turned onto the path that would bring him to the Rue de Monceau and to his truck.

A crowd of terrified men, women, and children were running ahead of him and sometimes at the side of him. They had seen the German High Command's headquarters bursting apart. They had witnessed the mangled bodies being heaved from the wreckage. They had watched the French Nazi police troops spreading their powers like a net across the park and racing to kill the men who had bombed the building. Whether these onlookers, seeing his work clothes and his tool kit, accepted him for the ordinary electrician he was impersonating, Marc did not know. If they connected him to the explosions, they would have secretly cheered the sabotage that he had achieved. Most of them were French. Their feelings about the Nazis were secretly hostile or, at the least, ambivalent.

Now, when he reached the edge of the park and had only a few paces to tread before he hurried onto the main street, he was taken by surprise. There, on the wide path before him, in the midst of the people hurrying away from the park, stood Hans, disheveled and wounded. His workman's jacket and overalls were stained with blood, and he was limping. His blue eyes were wide with fury, and his face looked tense and grim.

The visitors who were fleeing the park stared at his formidable presence. Apprehensive, they cleared a path for him and hurried on their way out of the park.

For a moment, Hans swayed uncertainly. It was now that Marc noticed the bloodstain on the left side of his head. A bullet had grazed him. It had nearly killed him. The thought that Hans had come so close to dying, yet had not died, roused Marc's bitter hatred. Perhaps, he told himself, the next Nazi bullet *will* kill him.

Still the visitors kept milling around them. Still they stared at them, uncertain and apprehensive. Still they went scattering out of the park.

Marc waited for Hans to speak. In these few seconds, he was deciding whether they should run back into the park and weave their way toward the path that would bring them onto the Rue

Rembrandt.

Noticing his silence, Hans told him what had happened.

"The Nazis are on to us," he said, nearly out of breath because he had been running from his enemies. "I've killed three of them. But it's not enough. They are all around us."

Marc had no time to answer him. Two French Nazi policemen were running toward them from the Rue de Monceau. As they ran, they were firing their Lugers at them. The people around them were screaming and running away. A man fell down, wounded or dying. Just then, Marc felt the pain of a bullet entering his left arm. He flinched momentarily, even as he fired his Colt at the taller of the two policemen. He shot him in the heart and watched the lanky body fall away to the ground. The French Nazi's brown eyes were glazed with astonishment, and blood spewed out of his mouth and from his chest.

In the same instant, Hans shot the other policeman. The first bullet entered the policeman's forehead, and the second blew out his skull. The body keeled over and fell inside the gate through which they needed to pass if they wanted to leave the park.

Without hesitating, they ran onto the Rue de Monceau. Nobody on the street had witnessed the killings. Nobody there had heard the gunfire. The noise of the traffic and the sounds rising from the building that was still exploding had muffled the gunfire. Only the visitors to the park had witnessed the killings. But the drivers and the pedestrians crowding the Rue de Monceau would regard their running out of the park, terrified and screaming, as an inevitable consequence of the explosions that were still emanating from the park. When they saw Hans and him hurrying out of the park, dressed as they were in laborer's clothes and carrying the tool kits of electricians, these same drivers and pedestrians might imagine that the park administrator had commissioned them to complete some repair work to one or more of the buildings.

As he and Hans moved swiftly along the wide sidewalk, Marc saw his truck parked on a corner about three blocks away. They had outpaced the men and women who were hurrying behind them. But other men and women, coming toward them from the opposite direction, looked equally tense and even furtive. Their seeing Hans and him together did not deter him from his resolve. When he reached his truck, he would turn to Hans and shoot him. He would jump into his truck and make the journey back into Provence. Later, after the Lockheed Hudson had brought him into London from the same field where he had landed the previous night, he would tell MI5 that a Nazi had killed Hans Mueller.

After she was told that Hans had died, Simone would, he

imagined, close herself off from him and from all those persons who were her loyal friends. He would not immediately seek her out. But one day, after she became weary of her grieving, he would gently approach her. He would commiserate with her. He would ply her with recollections of their happier past. He would coax her into the vivid possibilities of the present. He would teach her to fall in love with him again.

As he hurried forward, only a few paces away from his truck now, all these thoughts quickened his need to kill Hans. His right hand was grasping the Colt in his jacket pocket. He was about to pull the revolver from his pocket, when—without any warning—a Nazi captain hurried from a Daimler-Benz that was parked in front of the truck and fired a bullet into his shoulder. The searing pain and the impact of the bullet threw him back. He lost his balance and had no time to bring his Colt out of his pocket. He was vaguely aware that Hans was firing upon another Nazi policeman who was running out of the crowd toward him and firing his Luger.

The pedestrians around him were screaming and running. At first, their milling presence saved him. Though the Nazi captain fired again, the people rushing by him threw him off his balance. The bullet missed Marc's heart, but it did rip through his left arm. Marc felt himself gritting his teeth as he compelled himself to draw his Colt from his pocket and fire it. But the

Nazi dodged the bullet and, closing in on him, was pointing his Luger at his head.

"I am going to die," Marc thought, struggling to raise his hand and fire his revolver. For that instant, there flashed before what only his eyes could see the beautiful face of Simone, the steady gaze of his mother, and the determined expression of his father, who seemed to be signaling him to keep on fighting. His head was reeling now, and his body, racked by the pain of his wounds, tottered as he raised his shaky hand and started to press his finger against the trigger of his revolver.

What happened next confused his senses even more intensely. The Nazi captain had pushed aside the milling people who were blocking his way. He, too, was pressing his finger against the trigger of his pistol. Though he fired it, the bullet shot past him. At least, Marc thought so, because no new pain wrenched his body. No blood spilled out of his mouth or from his forehead. Yet the body of the policeman fell back. Blood sprayed out of his eyes, his ears, his mouth, and his chest as his body collapsed with a dull thud upon the sidewalk.

Only now did Marc see Hans, with smoking gun in his hand, hurrying to grab hold of him, so that he would not fall. Without pausing in their flight from the park area, people glanced at him and at Hans. They saw Hans helping him into the truck. They saw Hans take his place behind the wheel. They may have heard

Hans say the few words that were meant to encourage him.

"We still have a chance. We can get out of here alive."

When, ten minutes later, they had reached the first of the roads that would bring them into Provence, Marc spoke the words he never imagined that, even with his grudging, raspy voice, he would say to Hans.

"You saved my life."

"So I did," Hans answered, with understated inflections. "Maybe, one day, you will do the same for me."

He still hated Hans. He still hated his rival. But he could not kill a man who had saved his life. The war and its complications had made a beast of him. But it had not stolen entirely his memory of what it meant to be good.

During the swift time before they reached the first checkpoint through which they must pass if they wanted to leave the city, he and Hans exchanged only a few words. At the wheel, Hans held himself with taut concentration. Seated next to him, Marc clenched his jaw. Like Hans, he was compelling himself to stay alert and to busy his mind with thoughts that intensified his consciousness. They needed to harness the reeling sensations which might overtake them. The pain of their wounds was burning through their awareness of things. In their quick passage to the first checkpoint, he focused upon the traffic around him: the sleek military limousines carrying Nazi commanders to distant meetings, the worn-down trolleys crowded with French and German civilians, the newly polished cabs accommodating black market racketeers and their ladies, factory trucks bringing canned foods to grocery stores, and the Bentley and Lamborghini driving moguls and matrons to elegant luncheons, as though there were no war. Around him, too, in the midst of the blare of traffic and the hum of pedestrian voices were the men and women who were crossing street after street or traversing sidewalks.

These kinetic images sharpened his senses. They melded with the private thoughts that deepened his concentration and put him in mind of the specific place to which his life had brought him. Those thoughts persuaded him to understand with clarified vision the Fate that had always been hunting him and that, with his full consent, had drawn him into a dark alliance.

Whether Hans had saved him for the living death that would be his to endure because Simone would no longer be a part of his life, Marc could not say. He was no longer certain about the trajectory of his life or about the man who he was. He had become a stranger to himself. He had left behind him, in the past that the war had thrown away, the life that had brought him happiness. He had lost that happiness. He had lost Simone. It was not the war alone, though, that had destroyed his happiness. The self-willed choices that he had made had betrayed him.

Driven by his obsession for Simone and by his jealousy of the first rival who had won Simone's new love, he had hunted down Gerhard Hauptmann. He had implicated Simone in the killing of Gerhard. From that moment, the love that he wanted to share with Simone was forever tarnished. Though the savage part of his nature could persuade him to suppress the memory of the Gerhard incident, Simone would not suppress it. She would not lie to herself. In death, Gerhard had taken revenge upon both of them. Together, they could no longer be happy. As long as they stayed together, they would always re-live the moment of his death. He would be a ghost visible to their senses alone and haunting them always.

They were coming to the first checkpoint now. By this time, while pausing at the side of the road at the start of their journey that would bring them to the waiting Lockheed Hudson in the fields of Provence, Hans had helped him to put on a clean work jacket. Hans had also wiped the bloodstains from his forehead and, with medical gauze, had stanched and covered the bleeding wounds on his arm and shoulder. Hans then cleaned the bloodstains from his own face and hands. When the sentries approached them, Marc took his cue from Hans and, with the easy inflections of Belgian French, acted confident and good-humored.

The sentries remembered them. Now, when one of the

sentries inspected their work permits, he merely glimpsed at the document. He trusted them.

"Will you be returning to Paris tomorrow?' he asked.

"No," Hans answered him, without hesitation and without even a hint of irony. "We have finished the job."

So they went on their way. They might reach Provence safely. They might board the Lockheed Hudson that would bring them back to London. If they did, they would go on fighting the Nazis. But no longer would he lie to himself. Hans had won Simone. He was the better man. Over and over, in the long and lonely years ahead of him, he—Marc Roussillon, the man whom Simone had once loved—needed to tell himself the truth of everything that had happened between Simone and him. Then, one day after he learned to negotiate with his bitter heart, he might begin his life again.